STANLEY AND THE WOMEN

Kingsley Amis was born in South London in 1922 and was educated at the City of London School and St John's College, Oxford. After the publication of *Lucky Jim* in 1954, Kingsley Amis wrote over twenty novels, including *The Alteration*, winner of the John W. Campbell Memorial Award, *The Old Devils*, winner of the Booker Prize in 1986, and *The Biographer's Moustache*, which was to be his last book. He also wrote on politics, education, language, films, television, restaurants and drink. Kingsley Amis was awarded the CBE in 1981 and received a knighthood in 1990. He died in October 1995.

ALSO BY KINGSLEY AMIS

Fiction

Lucky Jim
That Uncertain Feeling
I Like It Here
Take a Girl Like You
One Fat Englishman
The Anti-Death League
I Want It Now
The Green Man
Girl, 20
The Riverside Villas Murder
Ending Up
The Crime of the Century
The Alteration
Jake's Thing
Collected Short Stories
Russian Hide-and-Seek
The Old Devils
Difficulties with Girls
The Folks That Live on the Hill
The Russian Girl
Mr Barrett's Secret and Other Stories
You Can't Do Both
The Biographer's Moustache

Non-Fiction

New Maps of Hell: A Survey of Science Fiction
The Golden Age of Science Fiction (editor)
The James Bond Dossier
What Became of Jane Austen? And Other Questions
On Drink
Rudyard Kipling and his World
Harold's Years (editor)
Every Day Drinking
How's Your Glass?
The Amis Collection: Selected Non-Fiction 1954–1990
Memoirs

With Robert Conquest

Spectrum I, II, III, IV, V (editor)
The Egyptologists

Verse

A Case of Samples
A Look Round the Estate
Collected Poems 1944–79
The New Oxford Book of Light Verse (editor)
The Faber Popular Reciter (editor)
The Amis Anthology (editor)

Kingsley Amis

STANLEY AND THE WOMEN

𝒱

VINTAGE

Published by Vintage 2004

2 4 6 8 10 9 7 5 3 1

Copyright © Kingsley Amis 1984

First published in Great Britain in 1984 by
Hutchinson

Vintage
Random House, 20 Vauxhall Bridge Road,
London SW1V 2SA

Random House Australia (Pty) Limited
20 Alfred Street, Milsons Point, Sydney
New South Wales 2061, Australia

Random House New Zealand Limited
18 Poland Road, Glenfield,
Auckland 10, New Zealand

Random House (Pty) Limited
Endulini, 5A Jubilee Road, Parktown 2193,
South Africa

The Random House Group Limited Reg. No. 954009
www.randomhouse.co.uk

A CIP catalogue record for this book
is available from the British Library

ISBN 0 099 46104 8

Papers used by Random House are natural, recyclable
products made from wood grown in sustainable forests.
The manufacturing processes conform to the environ-
mental regulations of the country of origin

Printed and bound in Great Britain by
Bookmarque Ltd, Croydon, Surrey

To Hilly

CONTENTS

ONE

ONSET

It had been one of Susan's most successful evenings. After weeks of hot sun in the late June and July, the weather had turned cool and some of the people, especially the women, must have been quite glad of the candles round the dinner table. The room, which she had recently had redecorated, looked bright and cheerful. There was a comfortable, friendly atmosphere with everybody contributing something to the conversation. The first course, cold avocado soup with a sprinkling of red pepper on top, had been made by Mrs Shillibeer, the daily woman, under Susan's supervision, and it went down extremely well. So did the cold cooked salmon with cucumber, fresh mayonnaise and a sauce made out of chopped olives also by Mrs Shillibeer. They drank a rather good white Burgundy with that, four bottles between the eight persons there, and a small glass each of a sweet Rhône wine with the raspberries and cream. By the time Susan took them upstairs for coffee they were in excellent form.

The sitting room on the first floor had a low ceiling and a rather awkward shape, but she had done her best to turn it into an attractive place with carefully chosen lamps and bright rugs and cushions. The pictures were all personal in some way too, done by artists known to her or the gifts of friends. A long row of gramophone records, mostly orchestral, instrumental and chamber works, stood in a specially built wooden case, part of which housed the rather old-fashioned hi-fi. But naturally it was books that predominated – no science, no history, a bit of biography and some essays alongside a lot of plays, poetry, novels and short stories. Her own two books of collected pieces were among the essays somewhere, not in any particular place.

Quite a few of the books had come her way as review copies in the literary department of the *Sunday Chronicle*. Others she sold off in regular batches, an established perk that went some way towards making up her salary as assistant literary editor of the paper. Not far, though, especially considering how much of the literary editor's work she had to do besides her own. He was there that evening, old Robbie Leishman Jamieson, in fact she had very much set it up as his evening, with an American novelist also present and a new writer of science fiction or something of the kind, and their wives. Old Robbie was the centre of attraction on the pale-grey velvet settee with a shot of his favourite malt whisky in a cut-glass tumbler and Susan encouraging him to tell all his best Evelyn Waugh stories, especially the one about Noel Coward and the Papal Nuncio, which had to be explained to the American novelist's wife.

People used to say about Susan at this stage of her life that things were going not too badly for her after some rather rough times earlier on. Back at the beginning there had been a husband nobody seemed to know a great deal about, an unsuccessful painter or book-illustrator she married to spite her family, according to her, and started divorcing as soon as she found the family had been right about him all the time. Her main attachment after that had been to a considerably more successful left-wing playwright she lived with for six years but could not marry because he already had a wife, and as well as being left-wing was a Roman Catholic, not one of the sort that went in for divorce. That part lasted till the end of '78, when the fellow's wife developed a serious illness and he went back to her. On 12 February 1980 Susan began her second and present marriage and later that year moved into the substantial Victorian redbrick house up near the pond in Hampstead, once the property of a minor poet and antiquarian of those days.

She had passed her thirty-eighth birthday a fortnight before the party for Robbie Jamieson. At first glance she could have been quite that, a rather tall woman who walked and stood a bit off centre with her hands on her elbows very often, frowning, blinking rather above the normal rate and always pushing her upper lip down over her teeth and pressing the lower lip against it in a doubtful kind of way. In one of her grey cardigans or unsensational dark summer dresses she could have been mistaken for a librarian or even a secretary in a local-authority office, but only for a second and before she realized someone else was there. Close to and in conversation she showed up as younger, better shaped for a start and also much more definite in her appearance, with large clear brown eyes and a very distinctly outlined mouth, and glossy black hair that had a little grey in it but no more than was enough to show how black and how genuinely black the rest was. She looked clever, nervous, humorous, something like devoted or loyal when she gave a person her full attention, and gullible, and beautiful. It was true she lacked the withdrawn expression to be seen in most women considered beautiful, but there ought to have been a word for her combination of features, which was among other things completely distinctive, meaning less good versions of it somehow never seemed to show up, and the obvious word always had a lot to be said for it, quite enough in this case. Anyway, that was the conclusion I came to every time I thought about the matter. In fact I told her she had been looking beautiful that evening, when the guests had gone and I was helping her take the coffee things and the glasses out to the kitchen.

'That's good,' she said, kissing me. 'Even in my present state, you mean.'

'I don't know what you're talking about,' I said.

'What? Even attired in one of my old school nighties and without so much as having passed a comb through my hair.'

'I didn't say a word. Did I say anything at all?'

'You didn't have to, old boy. When I appeared as hostess you radiated courteous disapproval. Fairly courteous disapproval. For three seconds or so.'

'I very much doubt whether I radiated anything. You guessed I'd be feeling it, which isn't the same at all.'

'Well, you were, weren't you, so it's not so different. Not that I'm complaining, I promise you.'

I said, 'I don't think it's egotistical or funny or like a Jew or like a gangster of me to fancy the idea of my wife getting herself up in a bit of style. Which would indeed include a much more expensive dress than the one you're wearing. Nicer, too. Also something in the way of earrings or – '

'Of course it isn't funny, darling, it's sweet of you, but you know how hopeless I am, I'd still only pour soup over it. Here.' She pulled part of her skirt into the light. 'Actually this is probably mayonnaise. *Bugger.*'

I managed not to press the point. In spite of what she

had said just now Susan always kept her hair neatly trimmed and shaped, but with everything else I could think of her careless attitude to her appearance did seem pretty firm. It connected up somehow with her ideas about art and her position as a writer, an obviously important part of her life she had never wanted me to inquire into. I thought in one way it was rather a shame, not getting the most out of a complexion and colouring as good as hers, but I have always been a great believer in letting people decide things like that for themselves, and there was not much I could have done about this one in any case. So when she asked me in various ways if I thought the evening had been a success I not only said the right things but said them enthusiastically. I went on record as being quite sure the meal had been remarkably popular, old Robbie had had the time of his life, the Americans had gone down well enough with the others and had also been suitably entertained, and more in the same strain, not that she was in much real doubt in her own mind, of course. By this time we had finished in the kitchen and were back in the sitting room.

'Shall we have just one more last quick drink?' I said.

'Why not?' said Susan, screwing up her face.

I poured her a small brandy and myself a smallish Scotch and water. As I did so I realized I had put down a couple already that night.

'Good old Stanley,' she said in a very slightly dreamy way. 'Without whom none of it would have been possible.'

'What do you mean? You organized the whole thing.'

'That's exactly what I do mean.'

'It's true I was responsible for the wines, and there I feel I can claim some credit. The Beaumes-de-Venise in particular. Never been known to fail. Actually I think even old Robbie approved, don't you?'

'Darling, what I'm trying to say is, you let me have the entire evening exactly the way I wanted it even though it wasn't really your sort of evening. Just like you let me have my life the way I want it, as far as you can. Even though, well, parts of it aren't quite your sort of life, I suppose.'

We looked at each other and she smiled and half-shut her eyes in the way she sometimes did.

'You don't hear me complain,' I said. 'Shall I come and sit over there?'

'Let's go up.'

The words were not even out of her mouth when the buzzer from the street door went, a short burst but long enough.

'*Shit*,' said Susan with an annoyance I shared.

When I took the phone arrangement off the wall there was nobody at the other end, though not quite silence, more like a very loud seashell. I said Hallo several times and there was still nothing.

'Probably a drunk going home from a pub,' Susan said.

'Not this late I shouldn't think. Nobody left anything, did they? I'd better go and see.'

The outside door was at the far end of a short glassed-in passage over a dip in the ground. I opened it and looked around and saw nothing at all even when I stepped out, only street lighting and a few parked cars, in fact I was just about on the point of going back in when I heard somebody say something, a mumbled couple of words in a man's voice. I said Hallo again, still without getting any answer. Then after more silence the same person spoke again, tentatively.

'Dad?'

'Steve!'

There was no one else it could have been, though even now I had not really recognized the voice. I already knew that something was wrong, before I could think of any possible reasons. At the same time I felt the slight muzziness slip away from my head. I walked up the street a few yards and found my son alongside the next-door garage, or just stepping out from that corner. Nineteen he was that year, a tall lad, taller than me, also fairer, and of course less bald. He seemed to be wearing his usual assemblage of dark jacket and trousers and light-coloured open-necked shirt. I thought he was avoiding my eye, but it was hard to tell in the patchy light. Usually we hugged each other on greeting but not this time.

'Well, fancy seeing – '

'Okay if I come in for a bit?'

'Of course it's okay. It's great to see you, Steve-oh. What can I offer you? Drink? Bed? Food? Anything within reason.'

I turned away towards the house but he stayed where he was. 'Got some people in, have you?'

'No. We did have, but they've gone. There's just Susan and me. We were – '

'Have you got those colour photographs I took that year in Spain?'

'Hey, you're supposed to be in Spain now, aren't you, you and, er, you and Mandy? Why aren't you there? Didn't you go, or what?'

'Oh, yeah. See, I wanted to get my head together.'

'What?' That last bit bothered me for a moment, until

I put it down as another of the vague phrases he and his mates picked up out of nowhere, rode to death for a few weeks or months and suddenly forgot. 'But did you go? When did you get back?'

'Just now.'

'You mean today.'

'Just now. Victoria. I walked.'

'Not all the way here from Victoria, surely to God? It must be about . . .'

About six miles, I reckoned later, a couple of them noticeably uphill. Steve had no estimate or anything else to offer. He stood there on the pavement like somebody at the start of a long wait, not facing me quite head-on. His manner was not so much cold or off-hand as completely devoid of the friendly concentration on whoever he was talking to that he had always shown as long as I could remember. Suddenly I felt an absolute fool, a wash-out as a parent, nosey, pernickety, dull, only wanting to ask tiresome questions about taxis and buses, phoning, luggage and things like that. My head was full of some tougher questions about my son's state of mind, but they were going to have to keep likewise.

'Shall we go inside?' I said it very casually, as though the last thing on earth I wanted was to put pressure on anyone – I had no idea why.

'All right.'

We met Susan in the hall. 'I was just . . . Oh hallo Steve, it was you then, how super, darling,' she said. 'We thought you were meant to be away.' She seemed to notice nothing out of the ordinary, I was glad to see, not even when she went to hug him and he held back for a moment at first. She went on, 'Dad and I were just having a last drink upstairs. You did get to Spain in the end, did you?

Where was it, not that bloody place all the Brits go, what's it called, not Torremolinos? Well, that's a comfort, anyway. They tell me it's all frightfully cheap over there now.'

More of that kind of thing got us to our seats upstairs and Steve answered up, not in his old way but enough like it to make me begin to tell myself he was only tired, or had been feeling embarrassed about something he would let out to us as soon as he felt relaxed enough, not that he had ever been particularly easy either to tire or to embarrass. Then Susan turned to him in a way that could have meant nothing to anybody but that she was going to move nearer home, and I saw him shut himself in.

She said, 'Tell me, Steve, is Mandy still reading *The French Lieutenant's Woman*? I remember you saying she was never without it. Quite a read for anybody, of course.' She sounded and looked like a very expensive nurse, being very good with him, so good you would hardly have noticed. I suppose there was quite a lot for her to be good with him about, his accent, for instance, which was considerably worse than mine. I was very much aware of it when after a long uncomfortable silence he started to speak.

'Mandy and I don't have an amazing amount to say to each other, know what I mean? I mean we do talk all right, but we don't seem to communicate. So I thought, well, we're not getting anywhere, it doesn't really mean anything, it didn't really happen, so I thought I'd better try and get my head together, you know, try and get things sorted out, so I could decide what I was going to do. I mean you've got to do it for yourself, like sort out what you . . .'

He took some time over saying this because he put more

silences in. There was a sort of comic contrast between the importance Susan and I had been attaching to his account of himself before it came and what he had actually said, but I thought that as regards things like originality and clearness and compared with almost anything else from one of his generation his statement was not too bad. What had made it hard to listen to or sit through was nothing in the words themselves, not even in the way he delivered them, which was lackadaisical enough but no more so than would have been natural for somebody rather bored at having to explain himself or merely ready for bed after a long walk. No, he just left out completely all the small movements of face and body and inarticulate sounds that you get from people talking, all the familiar signs of an interest in being understood. I would never have thought that a negative change could be so noticeable, and certainly not that having noticed it I was going to take something like half a minute making up my mind exactly what it was. I did notice that he frowned once as he was speaking, but very briefly and not at anything in particular that I could see. Otherwise he was completely without expression, even when he said what he did about getting his head together and I had been so sure he would remember he had said it before, outside in the street, and would let me have some signal that he knew I was thinking it was funny or awful of him to say it again. That was the worst part.

Susan said, quite rightly, 'Do I gather you're not seeing Mandy at the moment?'

'Well, you know, not much going for it.'

'Is she staying behind in Spain for a bit?'

'Decide what I'm going to do.'

There was another silence. I was very relieved when he

got up, sprang to his feet in fact with no sign at all of being tired any more, but then in another second he had gone back to his lifeless, wrapped-up style. He muttered something about a drink of water.

'Of course,' I said, looking across to where we kept the tray with the bottles of Malvern and Perrier, but it had gone downstairs with the rest of the stuff. 'Sorry, there doesn't – '

'It's okay, I'll get it.'

'What's the matter with him?' asked Susan when he had gone out.

'He's exhausted. He walked all the way from Victoria, or so he said.'

As though we had both been dying for the chance we had moved instantly into what sounded like accusation on one side and excuse on the other. We kept it up while Susan went on about why no bus or taxi – I came back with queues at the station, why no phone-call – all his generation were like that, and why no luggage – well, nothing much to say there. Neither of us turned anywhere near fervent but it was odd just the same, especially since she had taken a lot of trouble over Steve and they seemed to like each other. Perhaps not so odd on second thoughts, merely a result of being a stepmother and a father and not one hundred per cent cool. I stepped out of the pattern when she mentioned his passport.

'No,' I said. 'I can't believe he's got it on him. Nor any cash either.'

'Well, you could . . .' She stopped. 'So he can't have come from Spain. Where has he been?'

'I don't know. I think I'll go and get a beer.'

'I don't blame you,' she said, meaning for wanting to keep an eye on Steve.

When I got to the foot of the stairs it was like being in a Channel steamer with the drumming and shuddering of the water-system in the walls and all about. In the kitchen the sound of the water itself as it hit the sink was more noticeable. There were pools of it, not very large or deep ones, on the floor and on the various work-surfaces near by. As I came in Steve was adding to them with what was bouncing off the glass in his hand. This he seemed keen to rinse as thoroughly as possible. Feeling ridiculously self-conscious I went past him not too quickly to the refrigerator and took out and opened a can of Carlsberg lager. He knew I was there, of course, but he took no notice of me, or perhaps he did, because he turned off the tap and turned it on again just long enough to fill the glass, which he drained and refilled the same way, all at top speed as though he had taken a bet, and without any signs of pleasure or of anything else. Obviously I had no way of knowing how many glasses he had drunk before I arrived.

By the time he was starting the fourth round of the process I had got a glass for myself, poured my beer and thrown the can away, so that from then on I was hanging about. I tried to force myself to stroll out of the room. Perhaps I ought to say something. I was sure I remembered reading somewhere that children could actually welcome discipline.

'Come and have a spot of Scotch,' I said, and tried to infiltrate lightness into the way I said it. 'All that water can't be the best – '

He looked at me for the first time. It was a glare that lasted less than a second. 'Jesus fucking Christ!' he shouted, so loudly that I jumped. After a weird moment of hesitation he hurled the half-full glass on to the floor and rushed out. Finally I heard the faint slam of the door of his old bedroom at the top of the house.

Susan found me brushing the pieces of glass into the dustpan. I tried to make what had happened sound more ordinary than it had been, but without getting anywhere much. She listened carefully and said in a reasonable tone that no one in fact wanted or needed so much water. I agreed with her.

'He's not normally given to throwing glasses on the floor, is he?' she asked. 'No, that's just it.' He had always been a quiet, easy-going sort of fellow, rather apt to walk out of situations when he felt cross or frustrated, but less so lately than as a boy, and never inclined to violence in any form.

'He doesn't seem to be . . . Something's upset him.'

'Something certainly has,' said Susan, nodding her head several times. She clearly thought there was more in the phrase than I had reckoned with. 'I bet you I know where that young man has just come from, and it's a long way from Spain. Unless of course *she* happens to have been there, which would explain a good deal, I suggest.'

The person referred to was my former wife and Steve's mother, Nowell by name, now married to somebody called Hutchinson. She had left me for him in 1974 and since then, or rather since the end of the legal hassle, we had not met more than a couple of times. Steve hardly ever mentioned her and I had stopped asking him about her. 'Oh, I don't know,' I said. 'I don't think he sees her much these days.'

'What about the time he appeared out of the blue after that cricket match and didn't speak the whole evening? And it turned out she was stoned in the Shepherd's Bush flat the entire time he was there. You remember.'

If other things had been different I would have enjoyed as usual her tone of voice for talking about Nowell, not a bit hostile, better than objective, sort of *interested*, putting the expression in like someone reading aloud in the family circle. 'Yes, but that was years ago.' I wondered if she would still be able to go on like that having met Nowell even for five minutes.

'And the school outing.' Susan glanced at me and went on in her usual way, though quieter. 'Tell me what you think is wrong.'

'I don't know what I think is wrong. He could have had a row with Mandy. They haven't been going together very long, but . . . '

'Three months? I expect that's quite a long time in their world, don't you?'

'Yeah.'

Having turned off lights and locked windows we got to our bedroom on the second floor. Steve's room was up a curving flight of stairs at the far end of this floor, and for a moment I tried to remember if the bed in it would be made up before telling myself that there were plenty of blankets within reach and that anyway he was not five years old any longer. I shut our door behind us. Susan came over and put her arms round me.

After a couple of minutes she said, 'You're upset too, aren't you? In a different way.'

'I suppose I am. I didn't think I was.'

'Have one of my sleepers. Quick and no hangover.'

The next morning things had settled back into proportion. The main event of last night had of course been the dashing and enjoyable dinner party. Steve would probably have slept off whatever had been bothering him and might be talked into staying on for a couple of days. He had always got up late and it came as no surprise that he was still out of sight when I cleared off my Blue Danube coffee and boiled egg in the kitchen and checked my stuff before leaving for the office. Susan appeared in a white terry robe just as I was on my way to the door. She had never been a great early riser either and had her hair hanging down loose round her face. There were faint brownish blotches on the fine skin near her eyes.

'I'm off this morning,' she said.

'I thought as much.'

'You haven't forgotten mummy's coming to lunch?'

'I had. Or else you forgot to tell me.'

'Perhaps I did. Anyway, can you come? Please? I know it's a nuisance but she does like to see you.'

Susan did it just right, appealing to me without putting the pressure on, making her mother out to be fond of her own way but in an amount I could probably put up with or not far off. In fact I was a long way from clear whether the old girl did like to see me in quite the usual sense of the words, but I was as ready as I ever was to see her any time, that is any time bar a Friday lunchtime, my preferred procedure being to take a sandwich at work midday and then beat the weekend rush-hour. Susan knew that perfectly well, and I was just going to remind her of it when I realized she had not tried to use my perhaps difficult son as an extra reason why I ought to be around. I thought that was excellent.

'All right then,' I said, 'I may be a bit late but if I am I'm still slated to attend.'

'Oh Stanley, you are gorgeous.'

She came round the table and began kissing me in a

very friendly way. In a moment I tried to put my hand in under the terry robe, but she prevented me.

'Later,' she said. 'I'm not awake yet.'

Susan knew I worried about being on time at work. The weather that morning was damp and blowy and I got a sufficient sample of it just walking the few yards to my garage door. Inside and soon afterwards outside was the Apfelsine FK 3. I could really have managed my surface travel perfectly well with taxis and the occasional hire, but I could hardly have justified keeping the Apfelsine if I had done that, and I was set on keeping it until something replaced it in its class. It was what used to be called a status symbol. I always thought it was much easier to understand than most symbols. I parked it at the other end in my personal space in the office park without turning a hair.

It happened by chance to be motorcars that I discussed in the way of business a couple of hours later. This was in a wine bar just off Fleet Street called La Botella that when I first went to it had been a sort of local for men from the nearby newspaper offices and law places, but for some years now had attracted drinkers mostly of no particular description. Spirits were sold there as well as wine.

As well as operating a stuffy rule about men wearing ties, the management at La Botella was hard on women, forcing them to sit down in the long narrow room at the side of the premises and then making it next to impossible for them to order drinks once they had done that. Lone women who were new to the place or had screwed their plans were always being stood or advanced drinks in the side room by decent chaps. When the man I was talking to there that morning had been called to the telephone, much to his disgust, and half a minute later Lindsey Lucas pitched up in search of a seat and a gin and tonic, I could hardly have turned her down even if we had been total strangers.

I had known her much longer than I had known Susan, though the two were exact contemporaries and old friends without ever having been close. In fact I had an affair with Lindsey after my first wife left me and had given her one or two a bit casually a couple of extra times between then and taking up with Susan. In those days a husband of Lindsey's had come and gone, perhaps still did. She was reddish-fair and well formed, medium-sized, with a good skin, very well-chosen glasses and a banked-down manner like a newscaster's. With this went a hard flat Northern Ireland accent which I liked as a noise without feeling it suited her especially well. For the past three years she had had a column on the women's page of one of the down-market dailies.

'You saw your ex was on the box the other night,' she said with very little delay. To someone else she might have sounded accusing but I could tell it was only those tight vowels.

'Yes I did see, I mean I saw she was going to be but I didn't see the play. Was it good? Was she good? Did you see it?'

'I did, the first half. One of those drama-documentaries about life in our hospitals today. She was the maverick matron who didn't really think they ought to be torturing the patients to death just yet. But get that – matron. Oh, it was called senior nursing officer or some such jargon but she was a matron. Fiery and vital and everything but a matron. Looking not too bad it must be said. What is she now, forty-four?'

'Just over. She's the same as me.'

'Looking quite good. A wee bit miscast in the role, maybe.'

Lindsey took a quick look at me from behind her glasses to see if I had fully appreciated this touch, then another, slower one. She knew well enough that chatting to an ex-husband about the wife who ran away from him was not altogether the straightforward business you might think it would be, even when there was no nonsense whatever about any lingering fondness, as in this case. He might thoroughly enjoy hearing of her misfortunes and love being reminded how terrible she was to have around, but the very next bit might throw doubt on his good sense or taste in ever having got involved with her in the first place. So Lindsey took her time.

'It wasn't a very big part,' she said, 'but I *think* I'm right in saying it was her first for . . . quite a while. And before it I can't remember anything since she was whoever it was in that version of *The Letter*, you know, the woman who shoots her boyfriend and then says he was trying to rape her when really he was trying to ditch her. We, uh, we thought she was just right for that, but it didn't go down very well, I believe. In fact that career of hers in television, which I remember you telling me she was so set on . . .'

So set on, I muttered under my breath and through my teeth, that you could almost say she left me to have a better crack at it – 'Yes, that's right.'

'I may have missed some things, but it doesn't seem to have come to very much. What about that husband of hers? – what's he called, Hutchinson is it?'

'Bert Hutchinson. What about him? Horrible bleeder. Wears suede shirts. And drinks like a fish, I hear.'

'Oh? Well, she should be used to that, Stanley. Perhaps

she likes her husbands to put it away. Not that I blame them.'

'No rudeness, please. He drinks like a fish, I just drink, right? Basic distinction. Anyway, he never turned out to produce or direct anything at all as far as I know. There was meant to be going to be a pricy series about Mr Gladstone, with Nowell as I imagine it would be Mrs Gladstone, but then it fell a victim to some axe or quota or whatever.'

'Oh my God,' said Lindsey, undoubtedly thinking of Nowell as Mrs Gladstone, though I had no real idea of why that should be so bad. 'I don't suppose you see much of her, do you?'

'No point. It was bad enough being married to her.'

'Have you seen their child?'

'No. I'd forgotten it existed until now.'

'You should. I can't imagine why Nowell ever agreed to have it. It's a girl. Naturally.'

'I don't know why you say that. Get invited there, do you?'

'Oh, somebody took me along. Are you doing anything for lunch? I don't think this fellow of mine's coming.'

'I wish I wasn't but I am. In fact it's starting to get tight already.'

'Come on, it's only – ' .

'I know, but I've got to get home.'

'To Hampstead? Do you go home to lunch every day now?'

'No, not every day,' I said, wishing I was queer and need never explain anything to anybody. 'Today, though. My mother-in-law's coming to lunch.'

I was scowling at Lindsey so fiercely that she just

grunted and took a good swallow of her drink, but she was not the sort to leave off when she wanted to go on. I caught sight of my bloke on his way back from the phone, and she saw at once that some interruption was a few seconds away. With an extra dose of the accent, or so I thought, she said, 'You certainly do marry some extraordinary people, Stanley,' obviously reckoning on any real comeback being ruled out. But the bloke, instead of keeping on his way towards us, veered aside in the direction of a pee, so there was no rush after all for the moment.

'Now I realize you haven't got much time for her,' I said, 'Susan that is, but I have. You don't think I know what I'm getting, do you? Well, I think I do, by and large. I like most of it, and the bits I don't like so well I can put up with quite easily, because there's nothing that says I've got to agree with her idea of what she's doing. So she'll pretend she's helping someone or being nice to them, and she really is too, but she's also showing off her genius and drawing attention to herself, which is what a lot of people do, and I'll go along with it. And that works out perfectly well, because she's not a thought-reader, you see. As I say, it's only a small part of the time. We've been married two and a half years now, and going together nearly four, so I reckon so far I'm probably going to be all right.'

'I hope so,' said Lindsey with a smile that looked okay, but making it sound as though she was rather hoping against hope. 'No, I'm not so much down on the old thing as perhaps you imagine. But according to me she's slightly mad, you know.'

I was far from sure how that sounded. 'What does that mean?' I said.

'Well I . . . she can't really believe that anything or anybody exists unless they concern her personally.'

'My God, all I can say is it's a good job we haven't got you in charge of committals to the nut-hatch or we'd all be in there.'

'Yeah, we all do most things but some of us do some of them more than others do. Of course I haven't seen her for years. She's probably grown up by now.'

'What's that bleeder *doing* in there?' I asked her, looking at my watch. 'Ah, how's . . . how's Barry?' I was pleased with myself for having come up with her husband's name just when required, but what I tried to get across to her was more that naturally in an ideal world there would most likely not be people called Barry. It seemed from her reply that this particular one was still around, at any rate not yet dead or required to keep his distance by court order. My bloke returned at last, closely followed by Lindsey's apologizing for his lateness. I settled things with mine in about five seconds, got her latest phone number off her, and left. By now I was medium late, so I grabbed a passing taxi.

My mother-in-law's lime-green Saab, with a fresh scrape on the rear door, was parked across the road from the pottery shop. In the quite recent past I had watched her have two minor accidents in it at walking pace, one with a stationary furniture van, the other with a simple brick wall, both in excellent conditions of visibility and road surface. At higher speeds she obviously took more care, or else was under some sort of special protection. I could let Susan see nearly all of what I felt about her mother's driving.

In the hall of my house Mrs Shillibeer was rubbing the stain off the floorboards in an area by the fireplace. At the first sound of this name I had imagined a chain-smoking old witch in a flowered overall and one of those turban affairs I had seen on the women who came to clean my parents' house in South London. In other words I had not expected a tall fat girl in her twenties whose usual get-up was a tee-shirt, jeans and pink brocade slippers. Under one of these at the moment there was a pad of wire wool with which she was doing her stain-removal in an upright position. In theory the person at work could have been someone different because her face was hidden by the paperback book she was reading called *The Myth of the Vaginal Orgasm*. Then when she heard the street door latch behind me she lowered the book far enough to see over the top of it.

'Hallo,' she said in a loud affected voice. 'Lady Daly,' she went on in the same voice and paused for quite a long time, 'hazz . . . arrived-uh.' She was given to making announcements of this sort. I could never tell whether she was being cheeky to me or so to speak joining up with me against whoever the announcement was about.

Lady Daly was naturally my mother-in-law. Her husband, fallen down dead before I ever came along, had been a Conservative MP for a safe Hertfordshire seat, given a knighthood for never having done anything. When I opened the sitting-room door she tried to shove back into its place on the shelves the book she had taken out and turn round and face me innocently at the same time, like Ingrid Bergman interrupted in a bit of amateur spying. They were not my books anyway.

'Morning, Stanley,' she got in quickly.

'Morning, lady. How are you today? Can I get you something? What about a spot of sherry?'

'Oh no. No. No thank you.' She gave me a peck on the

cheek, as near as someone without an actual beak could. 'But you have . . . have one.'

'I don't see why not,' I said, and started to make myself a small Scotch on the rocks. There were rocks on hand in the plastic pineapple instead of to be fetched from the kitchen because Susan had got Mrs Shillibeer to interrupt her other duties to put them there. Where was Susan? One of the troubles with getting on all right with people like your mother-in-law, or looking as if you did, or trying to, was that people like your wife took to leaving you alone with them to have a nice chat.

My mother-in-law managed to stop watching my operations at the drinks tray. 'Filthy traffic,' she said as one committed road-user to another.

'Wicked. Of course there's the weekend coming up.'

She turned on me indignantly. 'But it's barely Friday afternoon.'

'I know, but you know how it is.'

'I wonder some of them bother to go in to work at all. Well, a great many don't, as we see. They're *unemployed*.'

'Yes, I know.' I raised my glass. 'Cheers, lady.'

Mum was what I had called my first mother-in-law but this one had other ideas. I thought they were on the wrong lines. Lady Daly had to be a dodgy thing to be called in the first place and the nickname or whatever it was reminded you of that dodginess. Also I very much doubted whether she had ever done what I once had out of curiosity and looked up the word in *The Concise Oxford Dictionary*. Apparently to use it in the vocative and the singular, which was what I had just been up to, could only be either poetical or vulgar, nothing in between. I thought that was very interesting.

'I gather you have *Steve* staying with you,' she said

33

after a pause, quite chuffed at getting over all the various difficulties raised by bringing out this name.

So nothing really awful had happened in between. 'Yes, he dropped in to stay for a couple of days. So it seems. Just turned up on the doorstep. As they do at that age.'

'Such a nice boy. Still working at his writing, is he?'

'Yes, I think so, yes. Plugging away.' It would hardly have been fair to say that Steve had ever plugged away at anything. What kept him going usually was pound-note jobs with gardeners and handymen and dribs and drabs from me.

'Tell me, Stanley, it's dreadfully stupid of me, but I seem never to have taken in just what it is that he writes. Is it verse or prose? Essays? Plays, perhaps?'

'No, it's not plays.'

'How would you describe it?'

'Well . . . '

I tried to remember anything at all about the few badly typed pages that, in response to many requests and with a touching mixture of defiance and shyness, Steve had planked down next to me on the couch one Sunday afternoon the previous winter. But it was the same now as then, really. I had not been able to come up with a single word, not just of appreciation, but even referring to one thing or another about the material. But surely I had managed to tell whether it was in verse or prose? Hopeless.

'Of course, he hasn't shown me a great deal of it.' I looked across and met the old girl's eye and wished she could find a way of coming a little less far to meet me – sometimes you would give anything for a spot of boredom. 'I don't know about you but I'm a complete wash-out when I come up against any of this modern stuff.'

'Oh, I do absolutely agree. But what would you have – '

Susan came in then. 'Sorry,' she said in a half-whisper. I was relieved to see her, as I often was, and it was easy enough to see that her mother felt something similar, say like after spending an unpredictable length of time with a small half-tamed wild animal. When Susan kissed me she gave the top part of my arm the special little squeeze that meant she was thanking me or apologizing or hoping to cheer me up. I imagined she was doing a minor bit of all three that time. She took the dry sherry I poured for her and went and stood with her mother near the china-cupboard. Seen as a pair like this they could look more alike than I cared for, and today was one of the days, with them both wearing darkish skirts and lighter-coloured tops. Lady D would have been in her middle or late sixties but she had kept her figure, and one way or another her hair was almost as dark as Susan's. But then again her eyes were much lighter and she looked less clever, more nervous and not humorous at all.

I drank some of my Scotch and said, 'Any sign of the young master?'

'Oh,' said Susan, 'he – '

She stopped suddenly because the door was thrown open, also suddenly, so that it banged into one of her embroidered stools, though not very hard. Even so, the effect was quite noticeable, especially when nobody came in or could be seen from inside the room. The three of us stood still and said nothing, not in the least like people wondering what the hell was going on. Then Steve strolled round the corner, very casual, I thought, preoccupied but normal enough, scruffy enough too, having probably spent the night in his clothes.

'Hallo, dad,' he said quietly. 'Hallo Susan. Hallo . . . lady.'

35

'Good morning, Steve,' said my mother-in-law rather like a fellow playing in Shakespeare.

'Er . . .' he said, and stopped. I could hear him breathing deeply through his mouth. 'Can I borrow a book?'

'Help yourself, my dear,' said Susan, spreading a hand. 'Fiction there . . . poetry there . . . politics, psychology, what you will . . . Art and so on down there.'

Steve, who had not followed this closely, turned his head towards the bookshelves. The other three of us moved into the window-bow so as not to seem to be watching him looking. We talked about something like the Labour Party or what we might do for Christmas. After a minute or two he moved away from the books and apparently started examining a painting on the end wall. It was mostly blue, but some parts of it were white. As far as I knew he had never taken any particular interest in pictures and this one had hung there all through his dozens of visits to the house. He went on examining it. Susan had no idea – if she had been playing the adverb game 'normally' would have been the one she was doing. Her mother handled it differently, putting all her effort into not running for her life. I sympathized with her at the same time as wondering what exactly it was we three had to be so on edge about. Before I had solved it there was a tearing sound and I saw that Steve was in fact tearing the cover off a book. I shouted out to him. Having got rid of the cover he tried to tear the pages across but they were too tough and he put the remains of the book down on a cushion on the back of a chair. By the time I went over there he had gone. The book was *Herzog*, by Saul Bellow.

'I'm sorry, love,' I said to Susan. 'I don't know what he thinks he's doing. He must be off his head. I'll get you another.'

'It's all right, darling,' she said, 'I'd finished with it, it was just hanging about on the shelves. Lunch in ten minutes,' she called after me on my way to the door, sounding as normal as anybody could have managed.

With my mind on the water-drinking event I checked the kitchen, then briefly the upstairs in general before catching up with my son in the small bathroom, or rather lavatory with washbasin, next to his bedroom. As before, there was plenty of water about – on the mirror behind the basin, into which he was staring, on his face and hair and clothes and on the floor. He had evidently not touched the clean towel on the metal rack beside him.

'What's the matter with you?' I said, trying to sound angry instead of worried. 'What do you mean by tearing up a book like that?'

He just stood there with his hands by his sides and said nothing.

'These things cost money, you know.'

'I'll pay for it,' he said wearily.

'Like hell you will.' Now I was really angry. He was always offering to pay for other people's things he had used up or broken or lost, going on every time as though it was very sweet of him to be so patient with all these smallminded idiots, and then somehow not having the cash on him until I forked out. 'Anyhow it's a waste, and it might have been a special copy, and it might not be able to be replaced, and what did you want to go and do it for in the first place? Are you crazy or something?'

By way of reply he turned on the cold tap and started to slosh handfuls of water on to his face in a tremendous, ridiculous hurry, throwing more of it down his shirt and trousers and round his feet. He did this in complete silence.

I waited till I had stopped feeling angry and said, 'Have

you been to see your mother?' I tried to make it sound interesting, as though his mother had been a film.

At once he dramatically turned off the water and snatched up the towel, and started drying himself, but you could soon tell he had nothing to say this time either.

'If something's upsetting you I wish you'd tell me about it,' I said. 'Or if I've done anything you don't like. I know it sounds dull but I want to help you.'

It sounded dull all right. Perhaps that was what Steve was trying to get across by the way he finished drying his face and neck, peered into the mirror, turning his head to and fro to catch the light, and then started drying his face and neck again. Or perhaps he had really not heard. I tried to think how to go on. At no particular point he said suddenly and in a trembling voice, but just the same like someone continuing a conversation,

'I was hot, that's all. Haven't you ever been hot? What's so peculiar about trying to get cool? All got to be the same, have we? All like you. Anybody who isn't is mad, according to you. Why don't you come out and say it?' He was still looking in the mirror, though not catching my eye in it. 'You want to get bloody Dr Wainwright over and certify me, don't you? Go on, admit it.'

He turned round and stood in front of me, stood about, in fact, not showing the least interest in what I might say back to him. But I began telling him he was wrong and of course I had never even thought of getting him certified, and I would have gone on to appeal to him to forget the whole thing and come and have some lunch, only he pushed past me not all that rudely and went off to his room, still holding the towel. The door slammed.

Susan was waiting for me just inside our bedroom. I shut the door behind us and we hugged each other, with her giving a little half-joky shiver. I told her about the water and the accusation and she listened attentively, arms crossed and lips pressing together. When I had finished she said, 'I waited till he was in the bath and I sneaked into his room and looked in his coat and the chest of drawers and places, everywhere. No passport, no traveller's-cheque stuff, no ticket stubs, nothing. So . . .' She jerked her shoulders.

'So he hadn't come from Spain, or not straight from there. No knowing where he was or how long he's been, well, whatever he is now.'

'Before he had his bath he didn't appear at all so I went up to see how he was getting on, and he was just lying in bed, not asleep, just lying there. Then about half an hour ago I was nearly blasted off my chair in the study by Mahler on the record-player. Not just loud, you know, but absurdly loud. Grotesquely loud. And then of course when I asked him to turn it down he turned it off.' She shook her head a few times.

'Yeah,' I said. 'It must be his sex life. At least it's all I can think of.'

'Oh, I brilliantly rang her flat, having brilliantly but I forget why put its number in my book, but somebody I thought sounded Swedish said no, Miss Blackburn was not there.'

'Didn't they say anything else?' Asking that question was rather dishonest of me, because actually I only wanted to hear some more of what Susan must have thought was a Swedish accent. It reminded me strongly of the Italian accent she had put on the previous evening to tell a story about Toscanini.

'No, in fact I never made out whether Mandy wasn't there just then or on a permanent basis.'

'Oh. Well, I think all we can do is leave him to himself until he snaps out of it. Sorry about that book, by the way. I couldn't get him to say why he'd done it.'

'Never mind. But actually I would rather like another copy if possible.'

'No problem, I'll send one of the girls out for it this afternoon. You go on down now and I'll give it a couple of minutes.'

When I went into the kitchen Lady D swung round on me with an expression that showed clear as a bell that she expected a full report on the case of the buggered-up book. I had used most of that couple of minutes to pour and swallow a stiff Scotch. I wished now I had brought another one with me, that or a brass knuckleduster. Hoping her idea might go away if I said nothing, I took my place at the table opposite Susan, who rolled her eyes slightly.

Fat chance. 'And what did *Steve* have to say about destroying that book?' asked her mother, getting a totally different effect this time from leaning on poor old Steve's name.

'Well, he made it pretty clear that something had just come over him, he couldn't say what. But he was obviously very embarrassed about the whole thing and wished it hadn't happened.' True in parts, I thought.

Lady D gave a kind of one-syllable laugh that in the standard way left it open whether she was coming clean about not believing a word or thought she was keeping it to herself. Mrs Shillibeer helped things along by standing at the cooker doing a marvellous imitation of somebody not listening to what somebody else was saying because of being so completely wrapped up in heating and stirring a saucepan of soup. Susan said,

'Stanley thinks he's had an upset in his love life and I must say I'm inclined to agree.'

'And that licenses him to *rend* apart other people's books?'

I frowned. 'Oh, I wouldn't say that. No, I . . . wouldn't say that. In fact I can't agree at all. Explains it, perhaps.'

'Let's just hope he'll sort of unwind,' said Susan.

'After shedding the gigantic burden of responsibility he habitually carries about on his poor shoulders,' said Lady D with tremendous faces and head-movements as she spoke. Previous to that she had sent me the latest of a series of looks which the chances were she thought I never saw or possibly failed to understand, burning looks, looks that showed she was wondering what sort of bloke it could be that had a son who did diabolical things like tearing covers off books. I stopped trying to think what to say when I noticed that Mrs Shillibeer had pointed her face at me, opened her mouth and started blinking non-stop to show she had a message for me.

'Oh, Mr Duke,' she said, or rather called.

Instead of screaming I said, 'Yes, Mrs Shillibeer?'

'Oh, Mr Duke, would you like me to take Steve up something on a tray?' Her voice climbed the better part of an octave on the last word.

I looked at Susan. 'I don't think so, thanks. Best to leave him. He'll come down and get himself something if he feels like it.'

'Of that there is no room whatsoever for doubt,' said the old girl.

'Oh, I couldn't agree more, lady,' I said.

Mrs Shillibeer doled out the soup and the three of us had lunch. While we were having it I thought to myself

41

that someone else, someone apart from Steve, was behaving unusually, and that was my mother-in-law. It had been clear to me for some time that she reckoned Susan had not taken much of a step up in the world by becoming one of the Dukes, but up to just now she, Lady D, had managed to keep that sort of feeling more or less to herself. But then of course there had not been anything much in the way of reason or excuse or provocation before.

'Are you going in this afternoon?' I asked Susan at one stage, meaning to work.

'I wasn't, why?'

'Well, good, I've got to and I just thought there ought to be someone here.'

'But that'll leave Susan alone in the house,' said her mother in amazement. She had a chain on the ends of her glasses and round her neck so that in between times they sat on her chest and when she was wearing them, like now, the chain hung down in a loop behind and waggled about in a quaint way every time she moved her head, and she had never thought of that.

'Except for Steve, yes,' I said.

'It's all right, mummy,' said Susan.

We never found out what her mother thought of the idea in so many words because just then there was the noise of an assault platoon coming down the stairs and a few seconds later the crash of the street door.

'Would that be Steve?' asked Lady D, doing another variation by putting on no emphasis at all.

'I think it must be,' I said.

'Perhaps when he comes back he'll be in a more gracious mood.'

Soon afterwards I went out and picked up a taxi on its

42

way back from dropping somebody at one of the Jewboys' houses in the Bishop's Avenue.

The phone on my desk rang and a man's voice grunted once or twice and said, 'Is that, er, is . . . is, er . . .'

If whoever it was had really forgotten my name he would have had to do it very recently, since asking the switchboard for me. Another day I might have played him along. 'Stanley Duke here,' I said.

'Ah. Duke . . . you're a shit. A *shit*. Ha. Don't ring off, don't ring off, somebody here who wants a word with you, you . . .'

The words died aw..y in mutterings. Those few seconds had been enough to remind me first of a big fat body, a round dark-red face, a scrubby beard and glasses, and then of a name, Bert Hutchinson, and immediately after that I guessed some of what had happened and felt scared. I was glad I was alone in the office just then.

'Stanley,' said a faint, suffering voice.

'Yes, Nowell. What's the – '

'Stanley, it's Nowell. Could you possibly come round? I can't deal with him at all. I don't know what's the matter with him, I think he must be mad.'

'What's he been – '

'Stanley, you've simply *got* to come round, I can't stand it, it's absolutely terrifying. He's been saying the most horrible things to me.'

'Oh,' I said. That in itself was no atrocity from my point of view. 'What's he doing at the moment?'

'He's upstairs,' my ex-wife admitted. 'But he's in the most awful state. You must come, Stanley. You don't know what it's like, honestly.'

There was a vague kind of bawling in the background during the last part of this, which I thought was probably Bert suggesting some other remarks she could make. I asked her what she expected me to do and generally made difficulties, but I knew I had to go. For one thing, there was nothing to stop me. I checked that they were still where they had been, not in Shepherd's Bush any more but nearer the centre and perhaps classier in Maida Vale. Then I hung up and to show my independence or something rang the High Commission of one of the South-East Asian countries and failed to raise the Commercial Attaché, which was nothing out of the way. Finally I got moving – in the Apfelsine, naturally.

The traffic was a bit hard and I used up some endurance just getting out of the car park. At the lights at the bottom of Fetter Lane I was behind an enormous tourist bus from Frankfurt. The guide spotted me and pointed me out to his passengers as a typical Fleet Street editor. They all seemed to be about sixteen. I tried to give them their money's worth by looking energetic and ruthless, also thoroughly up-to-date in my approach. Or perhaps it was just the car. Talking of which, as I pulled away and again by the Law Courts the clutch was definitely on the heavy side, still, after everything I had done to it. I would have to get somebody in who knew a bit about the subject. Not my field, clutches. When it came to gearboxes, now, I reckoned I could hold my own, even with the paper's motoring correspondent, not that that was saying much. In fact, a good half of my published works, articles as well as letters, had to do with gearboxes one way and another, trade press only of course. So far, at least. But if . . .

No, I must not let myself get out of thinking about what was on the way up. First, though, I was going to go back to that short phone conversation with Nowell. Had she really not named Steve, not laid it on the line that that was who she was talking about? Very likely. It was the sort of thing distracted females did in films – it just went to show how distracted they were. It was also the sort of thing some females did in real life distracted or not, and that went to show, really show, how wrapped up in themselves they were. In a small way. They knew who they were talking about and that was it. Not that they knew who they were talking about and you could bleeding well catch up as best you might – no, just they knew who they were talking about. Another time I might have pretended I thought she was talking about Prince Charles, but not today.

I had never felt I had had too much to do with either marrying Nowell or not being married to her. After going round with her for about six months I had suddenly noticed that I was already well on with a trip that ended in marriage and had no places to get off. Not that I had wanted to. Then after thirteen years and at no particular point that I could see she had gone and set up with this Bert Hutchinson. Between then and now I had done a great deal of thinking about him and how he compared with me, but it had not taken me all that long to decide that about the one difference between us there could be no argument about had to do with him being showbiz and me not being. In talking to people like Lindsey Lucas I would admittedly say that Nowell had gone off with Bert to be got better parts in television by him, but the fact that it had not happened told against that idea – she was too shrewd to be so wrong about what somebody could do for her. No, it was just that Bert fitted in with her by presumably liking to spend as much time as possible with

45

showbiz people and I never had. I could stand spending quite a lot of time with them and looking after myself the rest of the time, only from Nowell's point of view that was unsatisfactory in at least two ways. No prizes for seeing a connection here with her not having been able to run the whole of her and my life whereas perhaps Bert let her run the whole of theirs and even liked it, but that you obviously could argue about.

I had got to that point, and also to the Marylebone flyover, when it suddenly came to me that it was not trouble with or about Mandy or any other girl that was the cause of Steve's behaviour. He had come in for that sort of trouble in the past and it had affected him differently, not in any kind of violent way, more prepared to hang on and keep quiet and tend to make the best of it. That went for how he had handled other kinds of upset. Whatever had happened to him was completely new.

The house was in Hamilton Terrace, stone and dark brick, hard to get into under a quarter of a million. In the garage at the side I noticed one of the first Jaguars, plate impressively DUW 1, well kept but not ridiculous. I pressed a button and heard a chime with a cracked note in it. The door was opened by a girl of seven or eight with straggling dark curly hair and a white dress down to the ground, like a kid in an old photograph. She also had a very boring face with no Nowell in it that I could make out.

'I've come to see your mother,' I said.

'Who are you?' Her voice reminded me of Mrs Shillibeer's.

'Well, I used to be married to her. She's – '

'Do you do commercials?'

'No.'

Shoving past her was the thing, but she was holding the door only a little way open and standing in the gap, and I felt I could hardly trample her underfoot just yet. While I wondered about this I heard a lavatory-plug being pulled and an inner door opened, followed by a sharp thud like someone's knee or head hitting the door, and after a moment the top half of Bert Hutchinson came in sight. I had forgotten – I had only seen him about once before – that he was one of the school that parted their hair just above the ear and trained it over the bald crown, a policy I thought myself was misguided, but only on the whole. Without noticing he pushed a colourful picture on the wall askew with his shoulder.

'What the bloody hell are you doing here?' he asked me hoarsely and at the second attempt, and went on before I could answer, 'Go on, get . . . get out of it, you . . .'

'I talked to Nowell on the phone and she asked me to come round to give her a hand with Steve.'

'That's right, she did,' he said, just as hoarsely. He could see straight away that this made a difference but was far from clear how much. Anyhow, he stayed where he was and so did the small girl, who had to be his daughter and did look rather like him in a frightening way.

'Is he still here?' I said to keep the conversation going.

'Who? Oh . . . yeah . . . fuck . . .' He looked me over, hesitated, then decided to stretch a point and pulled the door wide open. 'You . . .'

'Is that your Jaguar I see there?'

Nothing definite came of that. The hall was stacked with great bulging brown-paper parcels tied up with hairy string. Some of them had been partly torn open to show what looked like blankets and bolsters. It was rather dark and smelt of old flowers or the water they had been in. Not poverty-stricken, though.

I found Nowell in a lounge where there would have been plenty of room for a couple of dozen commercial travellers to hang about for the bar to open. All the pictures, including a large one let into the wall at the far end, were by the same artist or squad and showed one or more sailing-ships having a bad time. Nowell was sitting on a circular couch in the middle being talked to by a white-haired chap in a jacket put together out of suede, fisherman's wool, rawhide and probably canvas. When she saw me she held up her hand with the palm outwards so as to get me to fight down my impatience till she had finished her listening. You could have told a hundred yards off that she was listening, hard enough, in fact, to make any normal person dry up completely in a few seconds. There was no sign of Steve, like pools of blood or blazing furniture.

It must have been a good three years since I had laid eyes on Nowell, either in the flesh or on the screen. She had not visibly aged, though her thick-and-thin look seemed to have become more noticeable. I had often tried to analyse it in the old days, but could still get no further than being nearly sure it consisted physically of a slight permanent rounding of the eyes and raising of the eyebrows plus the top teeth being a bit sticky-out in the English mode. In those old days it, the look, had been one of her great attractions as far as I was concerned, along with things like her breasts. I had not known then that the thick and thin in question was not what she would be at my side through but what she was prepared to battle through to get her own way. On the other hand there was nothing deceptive about her breasts, not then anyhow. Not much about them could be made out today through the top part of her faded dungarees. They and the polka-dotted handkerchief on her head gave the idea that she might be just going to get down to stripping the paint off a door or even hanging out the washing, whereas in fact she would have been easily as likely to be going up in a balloon. There was all that to be said and more, but sitting in the same room with her I found it impossible to be simply glad I was not married to her any more and not to flinch a bit at the thought. Stopping being married to someone is an incredibly violent thing to happen to you, not easy to take in completely, ever.

Funny old Nowell. Nowell? It was amazing, but in all those years I had never realized that of course that was wrong. Nowell was to do with Christmas – there was a carol about the first one. Noel was her name but she or her mother had just not been able to spell it. There were cases like Jaclyn and Margaux and Siouxie where no no one seriously imagined that was right, but this was different. Nowell was like Jayne and Dianna and Anette where somebody had been plain bleeding ignorant.

I sat on and the bloke in the fancy jacket talked on. What he was saying must have been extremely important, because so far he had not had time to notice I had turned up. After a minute Bert came in carrying a glass with a blue-tinged liquid in it, perhaps drawn off from the insides of some appliance. I saw now that his glasses were similarly tinted. He looked over at me round their sides more than through them.

'Listen,' he said, 'have a . . . er . . . Do you want a drink?'

As a matter of fact I did, but I was not going to have one with him. 'No thank you,' I said.

He thought that could not be right and spoke more loudly. 'I said do you want a *drink*.' When I refused again he slumped down on a padded corner-seat some distance off. The little girl, who had followed him into the room, clambered up beside him in a complicated, drawn-out style and started leaning against him and rolling about all over him the way some of them do at that age with men in the family, not sexually quite because they leave your privates alone, but sexually all the same because you would have to take it like that from anyone else. In the meantime the kid watched me from under her eyebrows as though I had to be half out of my mind with jealousy.

After a bit of this I started to feel restless. I went over to Bert and said, 'Where exactly is Steve, do you know?'

He lifted his arm up slowly to point at the ceiling. Nobody tried to stop me when I went out of the room. I reckoned to find Steve laid out in one of the bedrooms and walked up to the top floor, stopping on the way for a pee. The wc had a fluffy crimson mat round its base and another on its lid in case you wanted a comfortable sit-down. The place led off a bathroom with pine panels round the bath and one of Nowell's classy loofahs, looped at the ends to help you do your back, on a bright brass hook behind the door.

Steve was in a bedroom that had large windows, no curtains, bare lemon-yellow walls and the late-afternoon sunshine streaming straight in, so it was never hard to see what was going on in the next few minutes. I thought of Susan's description when I saw he was not only not asleep but not even in the sort of attitude sleeping people get into. Apart from the unmade bed he was lying on I noticed two rather neat piles of sheet-music and a newish bar-billiards table. That set me wondering, a third of a ton of slate and mahogany lifted all this way, and how, and why, but I soon dismissed it from my mind when I took another look at Steve.

'What about getting on home?' I said. 'There's nothing for us here.'

He muttered something I failed to catch, just a few words, rather fast.

'Sorry, what did you say?'

'No, I was just . . .' His voice petered out in a sort of quiet gabble.

I tried again. 'Let's be off. We could take in a beer at the Pheasant.'

'Possessing all the relevant information to the most incredible degree,' he said quickly.

'What?' I said, though I had heard well enough.

No reply. After a pause he suddenly swung his legs round and sat on the edge of the bed so as to face the main window. Then he raised one hand in what might have been a waving movement. Obviously there was nothing out there, but I went and looked to make sure and that was what there was, just a lot of roofs and down below not a soul in sight, a cat sitting on a wall and that was it. When I turned back to Steve I thought his face was not quite the same as what I was used to, not in any way I could have described but enough so that if I had seen him unexpectedly in the street I might not have recognized him for a second. Yes, it was something about the way his features related to each other. There was so much I wanted to ask him, no deep stuff, no more than what he had actually been doing before he turned up the previous night and what he had in mind to do, but there seemed to be no way to start. Another pause.

'Let's get going, shall we?' I said, trying not to sound too jolly. 'I've got the car outside.'

'Do you believe in past lives?' he asked me, in a rush as before.

'Eh? I'm sorry, son, I just don't understand what you mean.'

'You know, people living before and then being born again. Do you believe in it?'

'Oh, reincarnation. No, I don't think so. I haven't really . . . How do you mean, anyway?'

'People that lived a long time ago – right? – being born again now, in the twentieth century.'

'But they . . .' I stopped short – there was no sense in starting on what was wrong with that. 'Say I do believe in it, what about it?'

Steve was staring out of or towards the window. The line of his mouth lengthened slowly in a thin, tight, horizontal grin, and he began to giggle through his closed lips in a half-suppressed kind of way, not a habit of his. Nothing much seemed to be happening to the rest of his face, except perhaps his eyes widened a bit. After a few moments he stopped, but started again almost straight away, this time putting his hand over his mouth. Even though it was not a specially disagreeable sound in itself I had soon had all I needed. I went brisk and businesslike, looked at my watch and turned to the door.

'I must remember to get petrol,' I said. 'Would you keep a look out for a place on the way? I had a full tank on Tuesday, you know. It's all the low-gear work in town.'

He nodded and got to his feet, but then he said, 'Are they still there, those people downstairs?'

'What? Well, they were when I came up. Why?'

'What were they saying?'

'I don't know. Nothing of any consequence, I imagine. Mum was listening to that white-haired – '

'What were they smirking and carrying on about?'

'They weren't carrying on about anything that I could see. They were just – '

'Why are you pretending?' He sounded no more than irritated.

'Steve, I honestly – '

'Don't try and tell me you don't know what I mean.'

I failed to come up with any answer to that one. For the first time I wondered what the horrible things had been that Nowell had told me over the phone he had said to her. She tended to have horrible things said to her more often than most people, though most people would probably not have counted a few of them. One lot had consisted of some stuff about his garden that a neighbour had said to her when he could have been saying how brilliant she had been as the publican's wife in the film spin-off of that TV series. I remembered feeling quite indignant with him at the time.

Whatever Steve might have been saying earlier he seemed peaceable enough now, and when he and I went back to the lounge place we might have been any old visiting father and son looking in to say goodbye. Nowell and the white-haired fellow were not there, Bert and the child were, sprawled in front of the television set, or rather he was sprawled while she wriggled about next to him or on him. A cartoon was showing with the sound turned down so far that you got nothing more than the occasional faint clatter or scream. After a minute Nowell reappeared, having seen her chum off as I had sensed.

'That was Chris Rabinowitz,' she explained when we were still only half-way out of a pretty brief clinch of greeting. The name meant nothing to me, but the grovel in her voice made me think he must be on the production side rather than just another actor.

Steve seemed to take no notice and just said, rather flatly, 'We're off now, mum.'

'Oh, are you, darling?'

There was a big hug then, with her very decently forgiving him for the horrible things. I looked at the television. The cartoon was the sort where as little as possible moved or changed from one frame to the next so as not to overwork the artists. Something went wrong with the hug but I missed what it was.

'Cheers, Bert,' said Steve, and started to move away.

'You must come again soon,' said Nowell to Steve and me, as though the present once-a-week arrangement was nowhere near good enough.

Immediately – though I soon saw there was no connection – Steve turned back to her and said in the same flat way, 'Is he a Jew, that pal of yours?'

'Who, Chris? I don't know, darling. I suppose he is. Why, what of it?'

'Do you get many of them coming round here?'

'What, many Jews? Some, probably. But what on earth are you driving at?'

'They're moving in everywhere to their destined positions.'

'Oh, come on, Steve, don't be bleeding ridiculous,' I said. 'That's not your style at all.' It certainly was not, in fact he would sometimes call me a Nazi for making the kind of mildly anti-semitic remarks that came naturally to someone like me born where and when I was. 'Or is it the way your pals are talking these days?'

'You don't understand. This isn't that old-fashioned shit about Yids in the fucking golf club. None of you know what's going on. They're not ready, see, not even through the whole country yet, never mind some of the other places. But the map is there, and it projects, you know, if you can just get on to it. You want to get your head together.' He seemed to think that this was an important secret and well worth knowing for its own sake too. 'Take warning. When the pattern's complete, the prediction of the ages will emerge. Surely you must have seen something, one of you. Doesn't the colour of the sky look different after dark?'

This made Nowell quite cross. She tried a couple of times to interrupt and finally got in a burst. 'For goodness' sake shut up, darling. I can't bear that sort of poppycock.' That might well have been true – the sort of poppycock she could bear or better, like astrology and E S P and ghosts, was well worked over and properly laid out. 'You've been reading one of these frightful mad paperbacks about cosmonauts or flying saucers or something.'

'No,' said Steve in an agitated way, shaking his head violently. 'No.'

'Of course you have. Or you've been sniffing glue or taking horrible speed. I've got enough troubles of my own without listening to your nonsense hour after hour.' So Chris Rabinowitz had not come up with the offer or prospect he had been supposed to. Without looking at me Nowell went on, 'Get him out of here, Stanley, please, and leave me in peace. I've had about all I can take.'

Before I could say anything he shouted, 'You poor fools! You're in terrible danger!' He looked wildly round the room as though he needed a place to take cover.

55

I tried to get him to look at me. 'What danger, Steve? What from?'

'You have to trust me, dad.'

'How do you mean?'

'You've got to put your whole trust in me, completely. Swear you'll trust me whatever happens.'

'Of course I trust you, lad, we all do, but what do you mean, whatever happens? What's going to happen? Who – '

'No, swear – you have to swear. Mum, you swear first – come and stand over here by me.'

'Don't be ridiculous, Steve,' said Nowell, but she said it without any conviction at all. And incidentally she looked like the way she had looked one time years before, I remembered, when she had wanted a holiday in Morocco and I had said Majorca was far enough.

Steve was shouting again. 'Will you listen! It's going to happen any minute now!'

I said, 'What is? For Christ's sake, what's supposed to happen?'

'I can't explain, you have to trust me.'

Silence fell, but from the way Steve looked it was not going to last long. He was trembling in a jerky way and wincing as though he was cold, and his expression and even the set of his shoulders showed total bewilderment, though the word was not strong enough for a feeling that in this case was obviously as painful as extreme fear. At that point I knew what I had known on his first appearance the previous night, or rather I was forced to admit it to myself. On the other hand I was stumped for what to do. It seemed Nowell was not. She put her arm round his shoulders and talked to him with a loving sort of indignation, taking his part against the world.

'You've had about enough, you poor little thing, haven't you? It really is too bad. You've been under the most terrible pressure. I'm not surprised you're upset. Anybody would be. It must have been absolutely awful,' she said, and more in the same strain.

In a minute or so she had him sitting on the couch and not trembling in the same way. I knew and cared nothing about why she was doing it or what she was saying to herself about it. Bert had no way of understanding what was happening but that bothered him not in the least. His offspring was more up with things, staring while resting her cheek on her shoulder like a kid watching a couple of sweet little baa-lambs. I went over and asked for a phone.

He decided not to trust himself to speak, which I thought showed sound judgement. Kicking over on the carpet his fortunately empty glass he made a last-straw face and noise and pointed at the ceiling as earlier, then flew into a temper and shook his head a lot and pointed at the floor. I found what I was looking for in the next room, which set me wondering rather where Bert thought he was for the moment.

'May I speak to Dr Wainwright? It's Stanley Duke.'

'I'm sorry, Mr Duke, I'm afraid – one moment.'

After a short pause Cliff Wainwright's mellow voice suddenly spoke. He came from one station up the Clapham Junction line from me but he had done a thorough job on his accent, only letting out an unreconstructed SW16 vowel about every other visit. 'You're in luck, Stan,' he said. 'I was literally going out of the door. What can I do for you?'

'It's about my son, young Steve. I'm afraid he's very sick. I'm afraid he's mad.'

'Really? I shouldn't have thought that was on the cards. What's he been up to?'

I did some explaining.

'Oh, yes, well, m'm, slightly hopped up is about what it sounds like to me. Unless he's having fun, of course. No. Ever done anything like it before? You sure? Ah. And I assume he's not pissed. I'd better have a look at him, hadn't I? At home, are you?'

I did some more explaining.

'Fine, no problem, with any luck I should be along in about fifteen minutes. Don't worry, my old Stan. If he turns violent just hit him with an iron bar.'

The phone was a prewar one, or a replica. I went on sitting in front of it after I had hung the receiver back on its hook. The room had probably got itself called the study, or even the den, with a roll-top desk like in the films, a word-processor, a row of theatrical directories and an incredible number of photographs of Nowell – in what looked like Shakespeare, in something to do with Dracula, talking to Princess Margaret, talking to Sean Connery, as a tart, as a nun, on a TV quizshow, on a TV chat-show. The ones I recognized had an out-of-date look. Bert was in two or three of them but there were none of her with Steve at any age.

Words like mania and schizophrenia and paranoia ran through my mind. I tried to remember what I had heard and read about madness and the treatment of it over the years but it was all a mess. I just had the same settled impression as ever that the fellows in the trade had a very poor idea of what they were up to. Now I came to think of it I did recall looking at a classy paperback where a psychiatrist had said that the only actual help they could give you when you went off your head was to keep you comfortable and safe and stop you doing things like killing yourself until you got better of your own accord if you were lucky or for the rest of your life if you were not. Cheers. But he had been making out a case, exaggerating, paying off scores or trying to write a bestseller. Of course he had. The business was bound to look pretty ropy from outside, all wild theories and rich people going to the shrink every week for twenty years and mental hospitals with no roofs, and never mind the successes, the new drugs and therapies, the thousands of patients quietly though perhaps slowly improving. That was certain to be going on. Things were just the same with medical science, you only heard about the scandals and the mistakes and not about the marvellous cures. Well no, it was not the same exactly but there were similarities. And that psychiatrist's book had been published quite a long time ago.

I decided to ring home while I was about it just to say what was going on, but there was no reply – Susan must have slipped out for something. Till then I had not realized how much I had wanted to hear the sound of her voice. Immediately after that Steve shouted something next door and there was a violent noise that was really two noises at once, a crash and a kind of giant pop, and then more shouting and some shrieking. I guessed what had happened and I was roughly right. When I dashed in I saw a lot of glass on the rug in front of the television set and a large hole in its insides surrounded by odds and ends of electronics, also the remains of a puff of smoke. A big grey stone ashtray was lying among the glass. Steve still looked bewildered but not in such a detached way, more as though he was worried at not understanding what the excitement was about. All the other three were yelling,

Nowell at him, Bert more or less in general and the small girl at everybody, and that was the worst of the three. I shouted in her direction, not too loudly but I probably looked a bit alarming. Anyhow, she shut up and so did the other two, only a moment though, in Nowell's case at least.

'Get him out of here,' she ordered me in ringing tones.

I tried to ignore her and tell Steve he was all right. It was not very constructive, I dare say, but it was all I could think of.

'Get him out of here,' said Nowell, bravely sticking to her guns. 'He's raving mad, the boy's raving mad.'

I said, 'Never mind about that. Now just quieten down, will you? Come on, cool it. The doc's on his way.'

At this stage Bert tried to shove himself in. 'You heard, you . . . Out, ha, bastard.'

'Look, old chap,' I said, 'I don't want to find I've got to put a bit of weight on you, do I? And I'm very nearly doing it already, you know,' which was really not much at all but it soothed our Bert's feelings in no time.

Nowell had taken a few steps nearer the smashed set and quite likely it looked worse from there. She certainly seemed more furious on her way back.

'It's ruined.' She was starting to shout again. 'Completely ruined!'

'That's right,' I said, and did what I should have done straight away and pulled the plug out of the wall.

'I'm not putting up with that kind of behaviour in my house. If he's not out of here in one minute flat I'll call the police and ask them to remove him. I won't have it, do you hear me?'

All of a sudden I remembered exactly what it had been like being married to her, a large piece of it anyway – her saying something quite short and uncomplicated that gave me a couple of hundred things to say back, all of them urgent and necessary and with a bearing and all completely hopeless, all pointless. I remembered too how it had felt to start saying them regardless, rather dashing and plucky, like knocking back the drink that you know will put you over the top. The present set were at least as urgent and the rest of it as any, mostly to do with Steve and her being his mother, but with a few here and there about the police and how they might react to the idea of evicting a son from a parental home, plus how serious was she about that, etc. This time I refrained from starting, not actually out of concern for Steve but because I could see clearly what I would only have got as far as dimly suspecting in the old days, that she wanted me to start. And that was because she could be sure of dominating a scene with me whereas she could not with Steve as he was or might be at the moment. After all these years. But that never made any odds.

Some of this I worked out later. I answered her quite quickly. 'Cliff Wainwright'll be here any minute. I'll take Steve then.'

'You take him now. You can wait outside. It's not raining.' She was certainly putting on a wonderful demonstration of somebody having to stand up for what they thought was right.

'Sorry about the telly,' said Steve briskly. 'Only thing to do.' There was nothing brisk about his looks. He was breathing unsteadily and his mouth was trembling.

The cracked chime sounded from the front of the house. 'That one's yours, Bert,' I told him. 'Soon as you like.' With almost no interval he picked up a visual okay from Nowell and went off, followed by little girlie looking over

61

her shoulder and pouting till she was through the door. I put my hand on Steve's arm but he shook it off and turned his face away. 'Nowell, do see what you can do,' I said. 'You were so marvellous with him before.'

I watched her hesitate. Meanwhile I wondered whether perhaps she was taking her current line because Steve had scared her, before deciding that all that scared her was the prospect of everybody not looking at her for five seconds. That was just as she plumped for being distracted rather than marvellous and began blinking a lot and making small sudden movements. By the time Cliff appeared, looking more ridiculously handsome and like a Harley Street doctor than ever, she was well into it, also starting to talk about thank God he was here and so forth. But it cut no ice with him – of course he was used to all that, and not only from her. In some way that was too smooth for me to catch he had her on one side in a flash and after a nod to me was strolling over towards Steve and giving him the kind of casual but wideawake look-over I knew from visits to his consulting room. Steve backed off a pace or two.

'This doesn't concern you in any way, Dr Wainwright,' he said. 'You're not wanted here.'

'Oh, I don't know,' said Cliff, and glanced at the shattered television. 'Was that you?'

I fancied Steve looked uncertain. 'Yeah.'

'Really.'

After nearly a minute Steve said, 'Like I said, I had to,' firmly this time.

'Had to? Bad as that?'

'Yes, I . . . There's something been done to it.'

'What sort of thing?'

'Something been done to it. Fixed. You're going to say

it's crazy, but I know it was recording us. It's happened before, see.'

'What, you mean as it might be on a video-tape.' Cliff went over and peered for a moment into the guts of the ruined set. When he came back he tried to walk Steve to a seat but Steve declined to go along. 'I doubt it, you know. In fact it's impossible. A VTR's quite a bulky affair, you couldn't possible fit one into a box that size.'

'Sophisticated development. Just a microchip.'

'Oh, one of *those*,' said Cliff, sounding very tired indeed. 'Too small to see. I know.' He looked up because Bert had come back into the room, unbelievably carrying what looked like a glass of water. I caught on when Cliff took the glass, produced a pill from nowhere in particular and held the two out towards Steve. 'Here.'

'Look, doc. I don't need any pill. Thanks.'

'Maybe not. Up to you. It's a tranquillizer and I gather you're a bit tensed up by this and that. No lasting effect. It won't – '

'What's your name, *doctor*? Your real name.' Steve sounded unfriendly all right but in other ways he seemed just adrift, half out of touch with what was going on. I was pretty sure he had not connected me with Cliff's arrival, which would have made it seem quite like the result of some conspiracy.

'Oh, get out of it, lad,' said Cliff. 'My name's never been anything but Wainwright. Now you just – '

'Not Isaac, is it? Or Moses?'

Cliff gave me a quick glance which I read as him wanting me to see what I could do. Anyway I said, 'Go on, Steve, knock it back and we can get off home.'

'You keep your nose out of this,' he said without looking at me.

'Its only effect will be to make you feel better,' said Cliff, going on rather awkwardly holding out the pill and the glass.

'Stuff it.'

So everything was in position for Nowell to move towards him slowly, hesitantly, with her arms hanging down at her sides in a way they never did, and stand in front of her son just looking at him, not saying anything, her eyebrows raised a tiny bit more than usual and her eyelids possibly lower and a very slight smile of hope and trust on her lips, which you could just see were apart at the middle but together at the corners. All things considered she was lucky I had somehow not remembered to bring my flame-thrower with me, I thought to myself, then forgot it when he suddenly took the pill off Cliff and washed it down with a gulp of water.

'Well done,' said Cliff to them both. 'We should start getting the benefit of that pretty soon. There is just one more thing, Steve, and then you can relax. Who's behind this business? You know, monkeying with the . . . The Jews, is it?'

'I'm not saying.'

'Right, fair enough, you go and rest for a bit.'

Nowell, with her arm in a protective position round Steve, took him off to the couch where she had been sitting with Chris Rabinowitz an unbelievably short time previously.

Cliff said to me, 'Well, you don't need me to tell you he's disturbed. But there are several possible reasons for it. In my experience the likeliest is a shot of something like LSD. He ever gone in for that?'

'Not as far as I know. Nor even smoked pot. I don't

think he'd have felt he had to tell me he hadn't if he had. No, I just don't think this lot use it.'

'Well, whatever's the matter there's plenty can be done. But in the meantime you and Susan had better stand by for a large dose of boredom and inconvenience, I'm afraid.'

'I reckon we can face that.'

'Ah, you don't really know yet what you're . . .'

He stopped speaking at the approach of Bert, who said quite distinctly, 'Can I get you a drink? Gin? Scotch?'

Cliff asked if he could have a gin and tonic. I hesitated and then said I would like one too. When Bert had gone I said, 'That bugger was pissed five minutes ago.'

'Oh, he still is, he's just making a special effort for me. It's amazing what people will do for doctors, you know. Even today. Barring nobs, of course.'

'Have you met him before?'

'No, but you get to tell straight away. I don't wish him any harm but it would be fun visiting him when he's ill. That sort of hair-do looks great when they've been tossing and turning for a bit and it comes adrift and you get a bald noddle with flowing locks down to the shoulder on one side only. Old Nowell's a wonder, isn't she? Christ, it must be getting on for ten years since I saw her and really she hardly looks a day older. But then egotists always do wear well. Like queers. Interesting, that. Cheer up, Stan boy, you've done all right so far. He'll be okay for tonight, I'll pop in in the morning to see how he's getting on and I'll try and bring a trick-cyclist of some sort along to run the rule over him.'

'Thank you, Cliff, you're being very good about this.'

'Only fairly good at the moment. I had some time to fill in.'

No puzzle there. As long as I had known him Cliff had

been a tremendous hammer of the ladies, quite a reckless one too – he had found himself within shouting distance of getting struck off a couple of times. That made him not all that much different from any other doctor I had ever heard of. It occurred to me like once or twice before that a day spent mucking about with ugly and decrepit and sick bodies might make you particularly keen on collecting a young and pretty one after work. I decided against taking the point up with Cliff there and then because Bert was bringing our drinks over. When he had done that he stayed with us, but apparently not so as to say anything, not at first. But then, when Cliff had told the one about the fellow who was afraid to go to bed with girls because his mother had told him there were teeth down there, and I was trying to think of one to tell back, he, Bert suddenly spoke.

'Do you mind if I ask you something?'

Drinking his drink as I was I felt there was not a lot I could say to that, so I said No.

'Er . . . do you keep a bottle of vodka in the bed at home?'

'No,' I said again, though it took a bit more out of me the second time round. 'Why?'

'I don't know really. No offence. I used to keep a half of Scotch in mine sometimes.'

'Sorry to be so dense, old chap, but I'm afraid I'll have to get you to explain the joke.'

'I think we might as well be getting along if you're ready, Stan,' said Cliff.

When Nowell realized we were off she slowly got to her feet and slowly helped Steve to his. He looked not so much tamed as washed out, emptied, or perhaps like a mental defective. She walked him to the door as though they were going into church, then turned and gazed at the two men who in their wisdom were about to take from her bosom the son she had not quite been trying her hardest to persuade to stay when she had the chance. After that she made a slight effort to prevent herself from hurling her arms round him but soon gave up the unequal struggle. It just so happened that her face was pointing towards Cliff and me at that stage, which meant I could easily spot the tears that were trickling out of her nearly closed eyes, and I thought he probably could too, but then he looked not greatly impressed.

Over her shoulder I saw Bert go back to being drunk – his neck seemed to turn to jelly. Of course, he had stopped making his special effort for Cliff.

'I've got hold of a fellow,' said Cliff when he rang the next morning. 'Name of Nash, Alfred Nash. You might just conceivably have come across it. Well, anyway, he was something of a celebrity in his younger days. Not so much been heard of him since then, in fact he hasn't got a regular job any more and was quite chuffed to be asked to do something. Everybody seems to think he's a very good man – I wouldn't know exactly. I've run into him I suppose half a dozen times in the way of business.'

'An analyst, is he?' I asked.

'Of course he's not a sodding analyst,' said Cliff, quite cross until he remembered it was no use expecting me to know how bad that was or would be. 'No, he's a doctor and a psychiatrist, not a quack in other words. I'd say he was a bit . . . Well, you'll be able to see for yourself very soon because I'm off to pick him up in a few minutes.'

'Are you sure you'll be all right, Stanley?' asked Susan

shortly afterwards. She was wearing a round woollen hat that gave her a trustful, childish look. 'Say the word and I'll hang on till they get here.'

'No no, Sue, you go on in.' Saturday was of course press day at the *Chronicle* and they were all undoubtedly expected to turn up, even though according to her half the reviews and stuff had been sitting in the office since Tuesday.

'It would be quite ludicrous for me to try to tell you not to worry about this,' she said. 'But there is one part to do with it where you can feel absolutely safe and secure, and that's anything involving me in any way. I'll do whatever I can and whatever you want me to. I may not always know what that is and whenever you see I don't you're to tell me straight away without thinking. What I mean is, it doesn't matter if it seems a lot to ask, or even too trivial to ask – you tell me and I'll do it. Now have you got that, darling?'

'Yeah. Thank you, love,' I said, wishing I could find it natural to call her darling at times like the present, up-and-about times. 'And thank you for what you've done already. See you this evening.'

She squeezed my hand – hers was in a woollen glove to go with the hat. I noticed the faint little dark hairs at the corners of her mouth. The previous evening after we had seen Steve safely tucked up, she had spent the best part of two hours pulling me out of a state where I was quite certain I could face nothing more personal and outgoing than watching television and getting drunk – out of that and into allowing myself to be made a great fuss of and finally into bed. I had called her darling then all right.

The street door slammed and immediately there was total silence in the house. When looked in on an hour before, Steve had been asleep or, almost as good, pretending he was. He was going to appear as soon as he felt like it, which would be soon enough to suit me. I felt very reluctant to be in his company – oh, I felt plenty of other things too, and disapproved of that one, but there seemed to be nothing I could do about it and for the moment it was neither here nor there. All the same I had some time to fill in, not much, but some. I could go over the closely argued letter I proposed to send to the editor of the journal of the Classic Car Club on a subject – exhausts – rather outside my usual area. I might work it up into an article – after all, Susan was not the only writer in the family. But when I dug it out and looked at it I found that even to take in what I had been saying was beyond me. So I settled for drinking a weak Scotch and water instead.

I had just decided I would not have another till they arrived when they arrived and put the idea out of my head for the moment. Nash turned out to be about sixty or a couple of years more, tall, pale, moustached, with a better head of hair than mine and a posher accent than the Queen's. He was wearing what he probably called some well-worn tweeds and what was a rather dirty old polo-neck sweater in anyone's language. Cliff took all of two seconds introducing us, I told Nash it was good of him to come over, he told me he was sorry to hear of Steve's troubles, and we were off. My life was getting low on small-talk. For the time being at least there seemed to be no prospect of a drink – I felt shy of suggesting it and Cliff had given me nothing in the way of a lead. Well, it was still early.

I did some filling-in. Nash listened and wrote things down in a notebook, or rather on a new 25p memo-pad with lined leaves. He asked about Steve's early circumstances and history and wrote down some of what I said about that too. Then he wanted to know if there had been any recent emotional upsets.

I hesitated. 'He broke up with a girl – it could have been the day before yesterday or a bit longer ago. But . . . it's not his style to go off the deep end about things like that, and anyway it never struck me as being a particularly serious affair.'

'But it was an affair? Forgive me, but on the rare occasions when I peep into the world of the young I find it about as recognizable as, as medieval Patagonia.'

'He keeps things pretty quiet but from the look of his girl, if she wasn't sleeping with him she was going against a quite firmly established habit.'

Nash glanced up sharply from his pad, as if what I had said interested him in some way he had not expected. 'I see,' he said, paused and went briskly on. 'Ever been mad yourself? Or gone to a psychiatrist or seen a doctor about your nerves? M'm, didn't think you had really. What about your family, brothers and sisters, aunts and uncles, grandparents, any mad people there?'

'Well, there's my mother's sister. She never stops talking.'

'What about?'

'Oh, what she's been doing, where she's been, in insane detail. You can't – '

'No no, merely in foolish and fatiguing detail. Perfectly normal behaviour in a what, an elderly female.'

'But she – '

'Is that the worst you can do, Mr Duke? No uncles who didn't know what was going on, or cousins who sat in a chair all day without speaking or moving? No one they used to say was always rather a funny chap, always a bit

. . . you know. Ordinary people are usually good judges of that, or they were until some lunatic went round telling them it was really the sane ones who were mad. Yes, funny, a bit odd, a bit peculiar, you never quite knew where you were with him, never really knew what he was thinking, you got on well enough together but you wouldn't have been surprised if one day out of the blue he'd said that he'd always hated you. Shocked and hurt, all that, but not *surprised*. Nobody like that at all. Oh well. What about your wife, I mean of course your ex-wife, the boy's mother, Mrs . . . Hutchinson. What about her?'

'Well . . . ' I looked over at Cliff, who made an encouraging face, dilating his eyes. 'Well, I think she is a bit mad.'

This wild understatement had Cliff blowing out his cheeks. 'Why do you say that?' asked Nash. 'In what way? Mad in what way?'

'She can't seem to . . . You mentioned something just now about somebody who can't make out what's going on. I don't think she can do that, not what's *really* going on. I mean she knows your name and what day it is, but she sees it all differently. Nothing's what it is, it's always something else. Her sense of other people's not good. They can be sweet to her, and they can be foul to her, and that's about as much scope as they've got. If they can't be fitted in as one or the other they don't exist, no not quite, they're like Mr Heath or David Bowie, no more than facts. Of course with her personality and everything she just goes on like that through her life. Even if everybody got together and dug their toes in and told her it wasn't like that it still wouldn't do any good. No use telling her to stow it or cheese it or come off it because she really believes it. That would just be everybody being foul to her at once. I'm sorry, Dr Nash, I've said enough.'

'Indeed you have. But the first part was good. M'm. Would you say, would you assent to the proposition that all women are mad?'

Cliff did about ten tremendous nods involving the whole top half of his body with lips pressed tight together and eyes goggling. I said, 'Yes. No, not all. There are exceptions, naturally.'

It was such a gift for Nash to say Naturally back that I had no idea how he avoided it, but he did, just pushed his mouth forward and went on staring at me in what seemed to be his way, not offensively, seeing either quite a lot or not much of anything, it was hard to tell.

'Yes,' he said after some of this. 'We won't pursue the point. I'll be having a word with Mrs Hutchinson. Well. I must say this is a most convenient arrangement, acquiring copious information before so much as clapping eyes on the patient. On other occasions I've found it to be markedly different, you know. Now, Mr Duke, I suggest you go and ask your son to come and have a talk with me. Yes, I'm a doctor if he wants to know, and yes, I'm a psychiatrist. Of course I am.'

I put this proposition to Steve in various not too different forms as he lay in bed in what I thought had to be a mightily uncomfortable position looking towards the ceiling, though his eyes were probably not reaching that far. The room smelt rather, but not as badly as it might have done if he had been really grown-up. I opened a window. I also noticed a couple of new shirts still in their plastic covers and some sets of underclothes out of the chest of drawers – Susan's doing. She had understood straight away that he had nothing to wear but what he stood up in.

After about ten minutes and nothing special about what

72

I had just said or how I had said it Steve got quite actively out of bed. He was wearing grubby underpants and a sort of vest. With the same willing manner he put on his old shirt, his intensely crumpled trousers and a pair of multi-coloured rubber shoes fit for an Olympic track event. I still didn't believe it until I had gone downstairs and into the sitting room with him, introduced him to Nash and seen Nash stare at him in the way I had noticed, and hung on for a moment before Nash politely waved me out of the room.

Cliff had come out with me. On our way down to the kitchen he nodded to me again, not so dramatically as before but at least as expressively. I got us a gin and tonic each and we sat down at the table. The chairs there were supposed to be particularly good in some way, but to me they were straightforward all-wood jobs with slatted or splatted backs.

'We're doing well so far, obviously,' said Cliff. 'Him being so amenable. You should see some of them. But it's not just handy for everyone else, it's a good sign. I can't believe he's really ill. He'll have been sniffing glue or chewing this, that and the other – you see. Anyway, what did you think of him? Freddie Nash.'

I said, 'Well, he's hardly my cup of tea, is he? That voice. And isn't it rather a performance?'

'Oh *Stan*, of course it's a performance, among other things. Doctors are colossal actors, you know that well enough. Worse than actual actors, because they've got more power.'

'What were you going to say about him over the phone earlier? You said you thought he was a bit something but you didn't say what. A bit what?'

'Oh, a bit . . . Well, a bit rigid. Inflexible, kind of style.

73

If that sounds as if he thinks he knows everything then I've got it wrong. Just, when he does know something then that's it. And I've heard one or two of the younger people say there are areas he hasn't kept up with. You'd expect that at his age. But they all agree he's very good.'

'Has he got a wife?'

'Yes, lots. Four at least. He may still be on the fourth, or he may not, or he may be on the fifth by now, I don't know, but it's one of those. Why?'

'Well, I naturally wondered, when he came out with that about all women being mad. Does he believe it himself, would you say?'

'Oh, I see. Christ, after all those wives he can't help but, poor old bugger. Only in a manner of speaking, you understand, in the sense you and I believe it – no, sorry, of course *you* don't think they're all mad, do you? Just most of them.'

Cliff laid great stress on it being me who made the exceptions, as an indicator or a reminder that he made none, especially not his own present wife, one of the few women I had met who could give Nowell a hard game. I remembered an evening not long after we first started to get chummy, which had not been all that long before Nowell had sheered off. Last thing that night, while she and I were getting ready for bed, she had launched into a long monologue which I had thought at first was an amazingly, almost frighteningly clear-headed analysis of her own character and conduct, put in the third person so as to be extra clinical and objective, and it had taken a sudden reference to Cliff being spineless to reveal to me that she had been on about Sandra Wainwright all the time. There was very little from my first marriage that had stayed so clear in my mind as those few minutes.

74

Cliff had gone quiet, probably thinking about Sandra. I said, 'Yes, I didn't actually imagine it was Dr Nash's professional opinion that all females over the age of eighteen were suffering from recognized mental disorders. But then it's not only an expression, not *just* a manner of speaking. There's more to it than simply them being a pest. A lot of them. That's what I was trying to say just now. The ones like that have got a distorted picture of reality. Not as distorted as thinking they're Napoleon, but distorted. More distorted than a bloke who thinks the earth is flat, because you can have a decent discussion of football with him. Their thing covers everything.'

'What? That's right. Absolutely.' He looked at his watch, finished his drink and stood up, so perhaps he had not been thinking about Sandra after all. 'You'll be okay now,' he said. 'He'll take a bit of time yet. When he's through he'll tell you the score so far.'

'What about his lunch?'

'He'll tell you that too. Don't worry yourself on that account. Fellows like that don't wait to be asked anything.'

'Does he drink?'

'No. You know, wine. He won't mind you having a couple, but he might mind you falling down in front of him. Use your judgement.'

Cliff added that he felt sure things would turn out all right and that I was to ring him later, I thanked him and he left. I would have kept him if I had had an excuse. Today I might have welcomed even Mrs Shillibeer's company, but she said her husband made her stay with him all the time at weekends.

There was some of her not-bad soup on the stove, enough for two at a pinch, and in the larder a board of cold meats, a jar of gherkins and some prepared celery and spring onions, and normally just my fancy – not today. I imagined I had anything up to an hour to get through before the next stage was reached. The only thing I could think of to use up some of the time was making myself another gin and tonic, and that used up less than a minute. On a normal Saturday at past twelve-thirty I'd have been somewhere else, at the golf club, at the squash club, at friends', always with people. So how was unaccompanied Duke to fill in? Read? Read what?

Suddenly Mandy came into my head, Mandy's flat with perhaps a Swede in it, perhaps still in it but perhaps by now Mandy as well or instead. The next part was slower. Susan had mentioned the surname. Blackburn. Here was a chance of establishing that there was nothing gruesome or otherwise interesting in Steve's recent past, and I suppose I also had some dim idea of getting a spot of help, though I could hardly have started to think what sort.

Finding the house phone-book certainly used up some time. When it turned out to be missing from its slot alongside the cook-books I searched the kitchen as usual before running it down in Susan's study. No helpful crossed lines or wrong numbers turned up, though. Quite soon a young girl's voice said Hallo with a great deal of alertness and amiability packed into two syllables, English too, very much not the reported Swede, and when I mentioned Mandy I was told she was speaking.

'It's Stanley Duke here, Mandy, Steve's father. I'm afraid he hasn't been too well. How was he when you saw him last?' That should fetch anything worth fetching, I thought, and very likely much else.

The silence at the other end was so complete that I wondered if I had been cut off. After a moment I said,

'Mandy?' and she said simultaneously, 'Who is that speaking, please?'

'Stanley Duke. I'm – '

'Sorry?'

'Stanley . . . Duke. Father of Stephen . . . Duke. *Steve*. You know.' Good God, I wanted to bawl, you were going round with him for four months at least, probably more like six, and it can only be three or four weeks since, etc.

'Who did you want to speak to?'

'To you, Mandy. You are Mandy Blackburn, aren't you? Well then, you remember Steve, surely.' More silence. 'Tall, rather thin, fair, with a slightly crinkled nose,' I struggled on, feeling a perfect idiot, but not knowing how else to go about it. 'Leans forward when he walks . . . Likes Mahler . . . Always cleaning his fingernails.'

'Oh . . . uh . . . ooh . . .' The girl made long remembering noises. Then she said briskly, 'I'm all booked up today and tomorrow and next week.'

'I'm sure you are. I just wanted to tell you that Steve's been a bit poorly these last couple of days, and I was wondering – '

When the dialling tone sounded in my ear I was fooled a second time, and imagined for a moment that something technical had happened. For another moment or more I was filled with rage and amazement, almost with disbelief as it struck me that Mandy had not sounded at all fed up with her own thickness, let alone apologetic – not a bit of it, she was too busy being tickled pink by her powers of recall. To hear her, anybody would have thought she had managed to come up with the name of the pet rabbit belonging to the boy next door but two when she was little.

Thinking of childhood fitted in well. Then, places you

had been to and people you had seen shot out of mind with incredible speed, not necessarily into oblivion but somewhere more remote than the ordinary past, like another life. Steve really had seemed to Mandy very far away. But she still needed a good hiding.

That set me remembering him myself. I turned out not to be much good at it. Innumerable things were in my memory as having happened, but not as full events with visual bits I could play back in my imagination. For instance, I was very clear that when Steve was fourteen I had gone to see him take part in his school's swimming sports, or rather in the finals of them, that he had been in the diving competition and that he had come second in his age-group, but I could not pick up a mental glimpse of the swimming-baths where this had taken place, let alone of Steve in them. When I tried to picture him in his pram, sitting on Nowell's lap, as the boy of eleven he had been when she left me, all I got was a version of present-day him scaled down as required. The few little flashes I had were no more than that, not so much as a face, just a smile, a look. I still had a few photographs, but Nowell had taken most of them with her when she went.

I had just not been able to do any of the *Daily Telegraph* crossword when I heard Nash calling my name from upstairs. His tone of voice made it clear that while there was no crisis on at the moment no delay was needed. My mother-in-law would have handled it in rather the same style.

'Gone for a bath,' Nash explained when I found him alone in the sitting room. 'Most opportune. Some interesting books here. They yours?'

I said, 'No.'

'What, none of them?'

'No. Is he mad?'

'I think so.'

'Oh my God.'

'But most likely not in any settled or irreducible way and very possibly not even for more than a short time. Mad – oh, without any doubt a depressing and frightening word,' said Nash, staring at me, 'but advisedly or not you were right to use it. There's no sphere in which it's more important to call things by their right names.'

'How sure are you, doctor? That he's mad?'

'In one sense I'm not sure at all. There's always the chance, on the face of it quite a fair chance these days with a person of that age, that some drug or other chemical influence has been at work, but you ruled that out earlier, and your son was quite clear on the point, and . . .'

'But my son's mad. He might say anything.'

'He's also frightened. If he had taken anything harmful I think he would say so when asked, and anyhow . . . There are remoter possibilities too. But in another sense I'm perfectly sure. I was sure within five minutes of setting eyes on him. Less.

'One of the troubles with psychiatrists in England is that because of the system here they often don't see a madman for months on end. In my youth I worked in the admissions department of a large mental hospital in Sydney and I saw madmen from morning till night. Fresh ones, if you follow me. And there's no teacher like simple quantity of experience. You yourself, now. Young Wainwright . . .' Nash lingered over this characterization, though without making any point with it that I could see. 'Er . . . tells me you know a great deal about cars. When

79

there's something wrong there, aren't you . . . sure . . . what it is before you establish the fact?'

'Yes, but – '

'Of course there are differences. But go back to the time you describe, when your son appeared late at night. Isn't it possible that you were sure then that he was mad,' – for once, just on that last word, Nash's voice softened – 'or nearly sure, or you might have been sure if you hadn't told yourself you knew nothing about the subject, or you would have been sure if it had been anyone less close to you? Mr Duke? Nearly sure or just about quite sure? Yes? Straight away?'

I hesitated, remembering what Cliff had said about Nash being rigid and the rest, but it made no difference. When Nash answered my first question just now, I knew at last that I had indeed been sure straight away, and that only huge powers of self-deception had kept the memory buried till that moment, through all his wild talk and behaviour – even over the phone to Cliff I had still not meant the word seriously, not altogether. Anyway, I nodded my head at Nash. 'Quite sure,' I said.

He nodded back with his eyebrows raised, then said with heavy emphasis, 'My judgement would be that he's suffering from acute schizophrenia.'

'Oh,' I said.

'Another frightening word. Two, in fact. The acuteness distinguishes not the gravity or intensity of the illness but a stage in its development, an early stage. Schizophrenia itself has of course nothing to do with split minds or multiple personalities or colourful stuff of that sort, which comes in well enough for the films obviously, and in life I can see there must be great advantages in pretending there's somebody else in your head who does all the shoplifting and child-molesting that you wouldn't dream of doing yourself. M'm. Nowadays I'm told chic persons use the adjective schizophrenic to mean something like inconsistent. But then. As to what it is, what schizophrenia is, discussion can be deferred. More important at the moment, it responds to treatment, and I'd like him in hospital for that.'

The last bit came quite fast and I had not considered the idea at all. 'Is that necessary?' I asked at about the third try.

'Desirable. Highly desirable.' Nash looked down at his hands, which were big and rather battered, not upper-class at all at first sight. 'It's only fair to let you know why and how. Briefly, then – your boy hasn't offered any violence to persons so far, but he's plainly shall we say unpredictable and *needs* treatment that'll work fairly quickly. Which in practice means full doses of tranquillizing drugs,' he said with his voice going slightly sing-song, 'which will probably have side-effects which may be alarming and even a little bit risky if not professionally supervised and which may lead the patient to shirk taking his pills, which again can be dangerous. For instance he might – '

Here I interrupted him. I had been trying to follow what he said while fighting off memories of visiting my mother in hospital three years previously. The place itself had not been too bad and she had thought she was coming out in a few weeks – so had everybody else until the last couple of days. What had stuck in my mind were things like the sight and sound of those other sick people everywhere and my mother's feelings of being cut off and not in any control of the situation, and she had been completely clear about what was going on. Steve had been confused and scared in his mother's sitting room, and where he

81

looked like being sent would be worse in some serious ways than where my mother had been, I thought, and I said to Nash,

'Can't he just stay here and go to the hospital as an out-patient? My wife and I could give him his pills and see he took them.'

'Do you really think so? Can't you hear him telling you he's not a child, stop treating him like an idiot, don't stand over him like that, don't you trust him? What you actually have to do to see he takes his pills, to monitor compliance as I'm afraid it's called, is a rather undignified and intrusive business, you know. Much better left to nurses. He'd agree.'

'Surely it can't do him any good to be surrounded by . . .'

'All those loonies. Yes. I can only say it won't do him any harm. No doubt that sounds rather a breezy remark. The fact is that mental illness isn't communicable.'

'But he'll be frightened.'

'He'll be under medication. Tranquillized. As I said. There's really no need to worry about that.'

'What happens then, doctor? Does he get some sort of therapy, or does he just go on being tranquillized? I'm only asking.'

'He gets chemotherapy, which is drugs. As for what you probably mean, psychotherapy, which is corrective training – not recommended in this case. But let me explain about the drugs. They're quite distinct from palliative tranquillizers like Valium and Librium that you may have come across and which are almost useless in treating schizophrenia. Over the last thirty years these, these others have helped a great many patients to recover quickly and well. I realize you may have gained the impression from me or in some other way that all that can be done is keep the patient quiet until he either recovers or doesn't. No, much more than that.' Perhaps he misread or read correctly something in my expression, because he went on to say, 'Or possibly you have ideas of your own on the point.'

. 'How on earth would I have ideas of my own on that kind of point? All I'm doing is trying to take this in. It's rather a lot in one go and I'll probably get some bits wrong the first time round. If that, doing that, sounds like me having ideas of my own it's not meant to,' I said. Christ, I also said, but not out loud.

Nash smiled for the first time, showing a couple of rows of old-ivory teeth and looking like an unreliable dog. 'I really beg your pardon, Mr Duke, but these days everybody seems to think he knows something about the subject, about psychiatry that is, usually after reading a newspaper article to the effect that all the work so far done has been mistaken. A little crushing, you may think. I mean *all* the work? Imagine an astronomer hearing the same. I agree not a close parallel. A jurist. To revert to your son. There's at least one other good reason why I want him in hospital – he needs various medical and neurological tests which would be much better done with him there.'

'Can't he have them done as an out-patient?'

'Yes. Theoretically. But finding the right building, and the right part of the right building, and waiting for the clerk to come back if she isn't there when you arrive, and don't be too upset if it turns out the machine isn't working that day, and fix up another appointment and turn up on time for that, but don't be too sure, don't be too sanguine about its working then either, and don't walk out in a huff if they're rude, and don't lose the form I gave you because they won't do it without, and remember always to leave yourself plenty of . . . well . . .'

'I could take him myself.'

'Mr Duke, I must stress to you that it would be very much simpler and more straightforward, and quicker which is important, if these tests were done in the normal way, with everything organized by the hospital.'

'Yes, I can see,' I said. What I said to myself this time was what it was I could see, or a good half of it – that the ones it would be simpler for in the first place were the doctors, the hospital staff, Nash himself, all of them, the other lot as against Steve's and my lot.

Nash too seemed to have seen something. He said, quietly for him, 'People in your position usually find it hard to face the prospect of their child disappearing for an indefinite period into the shadowy world of mental hospitals, which they don't understand in the way they feel they understand places you go to with something wrong with your inside and have it cut out. They find the notion of madness easier to accept than that of mental illness, which can't be an illness really, can it? Doctors and nurses for that? Something that just comes over you? Then a lot of them feel they'd be abdicating the proper . . . Ah, here we are.'

Steve had put on one of the shirts Susan had got for him, in fact part of the cardboard stiffening it had been packaged with was showing under the collar. I noticed his trousers were very shiny as well as shapeless. His whole appearance and manner seemed ordinary, not worth bothering about, so completely free of strain that just for a moment I thought I was going to tell Nash we were not going to need him after all. Then I caught Steve's eye and he recognized me instantly, which does sound like what he should have done in a way, and it was not that he mistook me for someone else he knew or thought he knew, at least that never occurred to me then. He looked at me in a contented, relieved, friendly way that held not an atom of what gets built up and taken for granted between a parent and a child who get on all right together, different from anything else. After that he gave Nash a polite glance and dropped suddenly on to the velvet settee, soon wriggling into one of his awkward positions.

'Good bath?' Nash asked loudly, rather like somebody talking to a foreigner in a sketch. 'Splendid. M'm, now just, if you would . . . ' He made what were probably encouraging movements with his hand. 'Er . . . just . . .'

Without any more prompting Steve said, 'I told you I couldn't blame her.'

'Yes, you did, but let's go into it again. Why not? Why couldn't you blame her?'

'Well, she couldn't have done any different.'

'Why not? Why couldn't she have done any different?'

'She couldn't for my sake. She had to freeze me out.'

Nash shook his head and drew in his breath. 'I don't see that,' he said firmly.

'She didn't want to know me,' said Steve, with a lot of patience and a look in my direction. 'Did she?'

He really seemed to be appealing to me. 'Not when I spoke to her,' I said.

'You what? You . . . spoke to Fawzia?' That was what the name sounded like.

'I thought you meant Mandy,' I said, blushing like a schoolkid.

'Mandy? That slag?' He sounded quite good-natured, but was a bit bothered or suspicious when he said, 'What was she on about then?'

'I rang her, just to see if she could – '

Holding his hands up now, shushing me, Nash said, 'This freezing you out as you call it, what was the point of all that, it makes no sense to me at all.'

'Well, you know, she was protecting me, wasn't she?'

'I'm terribly sorry, but do you mean she was protecting you by freezing you out? I should have thought . . .'

Steve nodded in a tolerant way, prepared to admit that parts of his story did need some explanation. 'This girl Fawzia, right? She and I had a big thing going, not out in the open, but I knew, just from the little things she said, wouldn't mean a thing to anybody else, and even just the way she looked at me sometimes, it was all there, I just knew. Then she became involved in certain undercover activities, which made her extremely unpopular in certain quarters.'

'When was this?'

'Year ago.'

This seemed to disappoint Nash. He smoothed his moustache and waited.

'So then they get after me, because I know too much. So she starts ignoring me, see, to try and throw them off and to warn me. I know too much not only about her but their systems. Also their organization, which is extremely high-powered, extremely ruthless, and extremely . . . undercover.' Then, coming to the climax of a horrendously embarrassing and pathetic take-off of a hundred would-be brilliant films, he said, 'The gentlemen involved . . . call themselves . . . the chosen.'

Poor old Steve of course belonged to one of the generations which had never been taught anything about anything, and he obviously thought his reference to the chosen was about as advanced and wrapped-up as words could get, well out of sight of a poor bugger as cut off as his dad, let alone any associated other-worlders like Nash. The next moment I remembered him once or twice just about a year before bringing along to the house somebody who could have been a fellow-student of his during his brief stint at the polytechnic, a remarkably unaccommodating female with a short upper lip and a sallow skin and a name very like Fawzia.

With that established, a lot of things became as clear as they were probably ever going to. Jews, or people who might have been Jews or counted as Jews or Israelis, were after him because he had once known – not, I was sure, ever very well – a girl who was quite likely one kind of Arab or another and on that ground could, at the sacrifice of all the common sense and humour in the world, have had them after her too, or something of the sort.

The realization shoved me into a state of combined gloom and boredom. Had Steve really put himself through the whole business of going mad just so as to be able to believe that? At the same time its moderation was a relief – it was only untrue, silly, ridiculously improbable, not mad in itself. There undoubtedly were such things as Arab intelligence agents, even if a female one was a pretty dodgy concept, and presumably Israeli counter-intelligence went around trying to do them a bit of no good. It was another relief that however confused he might actually be he seemed not to feel confused for the time being, nor in the least frightened.

He had been looking at me with cheerful mild contempt, an expression I had never seen on his face before. I tried to remember where he had finished speaking. 'You don't believe any of that, do you?' he asked.

'You've been going a bit fast for me,' I said.

He nodded as before. 'Okay,' he said, and got energetically to his feet. 'We can take a look outside now. Yeah, come on.'

Nash and I followed him to the window, which gave a good view of the street. Hunched up in the slight drizzle a man I immediately recognized was walking along it at that very moment, a man who worked at one of the banks in the High Street and whom I had seen a few times in the Pheasant and who looked like half the other men you would expect to see in places like that. Otherwise there was nothing moving in sight at all.

'There you are,' said Steve.

After a moment I said, 'How do you mean?' because he seemed to think I knew. I wished Nash would join in.

'Joshua,' said Steve.

'What?'

'Oh come on – *Joshua*.' For the first time he showed some impatience. 'He's only just . . . You saw him with your own eyes.'

'I saw a man. What . . . which Joshua are you talking about?'

'More than one, is there? That one's the one that took out Jericho with ultra-sound and saw off the Canaanites.'

He mispronounced this name and I took a second to disentangle it. 'How do you know about Joshua?' I asked. It was nowhere near the most urgent question I had for him, but even now I could not imagine anything that would drive him to the Old Testament.

'There are methods of obtaining the relevant information,' he said, dropping back into his master-spy act for a moment, but soon coming up lively and self-confident. 'Anyway, you saw him, didn't you, what, twenty yards away? Less than a minute ago?'

'You're telling me that that was Joshua out of the Bible out there in the street just now, are you?'

Evidently I was almost there but not quite. 'Well, in a kind of way. You know, that was him born again. They're all that in the key section.'

I had no excuse now for complaining that Steve's new view of the world was short of imagination or scope. When I looked at Nash, hoping for a sign that that sort of thing was to be expected, would soon pass, perhaps even had a nice touch of technical interest to it, there was nothing but a long, serious stare. Before I could speak to him Steve cut in.

'You still don't believe me, do you?'

'I don't see what made you think that was what he was. I don't see how you could tell. I mean you must admit he looked like just an ordinary bloke.'

'What do you expect him to look like, a geezer in white with a long white beard? It's nothing to do with what he looks like, it's who he is.'

'Yeah, but what is it about him that tips you the wink who he is? You can't have – '

'Look, I just know, got it? I know.'

'But . . .' I had seen at the start it was no use arguing but I only stopped now because I could think of nothing to say.

'I'm sorry, it's not the type of thing you can explain.'

He turned to Nash to appeal for support on the point that there were types of things like that. I said to Nash, 'I think what you suggested, I think we'd better do that.' Nash nodded silently. He still looked grim.

'No, I'm not going there,' said Steve as soon as he understood the proposal. He showed no anger or fear but he would not have it. 'I wouldn't be safe in a place like that,' he kept saying. Nash explained that if necessary he could have him put inside willy-nilly. Steve told him he was bluffing, and after a bit I stopped being clear what I thought. I said a lot of things I immediately forgot. A couple of times I felt so hungry I thought I was going to die, then the next moment not at all. Time passed as though it was never going to do anything else. I was sinking into a drowse of apathy and despair when something reminded me of something and I plunged downstairs to the phone. I forgot what I said there too, just like a drunk person, but no matter. 'Your mother wants to speak to you,' I said to Steve when I got back.

He went straight away. I explained to Nash, who merely grunted. He obviously thought it was no time for a chat, turning over his notes with a great rustle of pages and hissing through his teeth, and I tried to hold off but soon I was saying firmly, 'He's very sick, isn't he?'

'Well, we're not quite clear, are we, on exactly when, er matters took their present course,' he said a bit at a time, 'but his illness does seem to have progressed as fast as any I've known, of its type. From your account, and Wainwright's, a remarkable rate of development. And to be so specific, comparatively specific, at this early stage, about his delusion that is – most unusual, if not . . .' His voice died away, and it did seem just briefly that for once in his life he was not sure, or had let it be seen he was not. Then he charged on, 'But very sick in any sense of unusual resistance to being made better, no. At least there's no sign of that at the moment. We're only at the beginning, you know.'

'What causes it, doctor, this sort of illness?'

Nash shook his head, either not knowing or knowing but not saying. 'What . . . triggers it off is often some sort of shock to the emotions. Which means I think that it's always that but sometimes the psychiatrist can't find it or is uncertain about it. In this case the Fawzia episode looks rather a long time ago and the Mandy episode looks rather slight, but one never knows. It isn't all-important to find the shock.'

'He seems less frightened than he was.'

'These things come and go. Large changes of mood from no visible cause are characteristic.'

I thought of that when Steve reappeared, so soon I thought at first my luck had run out and Nowell had failed or not tried to do what she had promised. But I soon saw that was wrong. He had stopped being animated and he looked different, physically exhausted, like somebody who had been up all night. I was sure Nash noticed it too.

'All right, I'll go there.' Steve said that without much expression, but he sounded quite convincingly fed up when he went on to say, 'So I changed my mind. Does it matter why?' The question was for me personally, though I had not been conscious of even asking myself anything on those lines. 'You're getting rid of me, aren't you? That's what you want. Father.'

Those last few words of Steve's turned out to be very easy to remember. They stayed around while I watched him silently – except for eating noises – get through a couple of bowls of soup and some ham and some bread in the kitchen, and incidentally while Nash sat on in the sitting room and wrote a lot of stuff for the hospital and ate Brie and cream crackers and drank a glass of red wine, just what he had ordered actually, though without specifying the rather pricy Burgundy that, feeling a bit of a coward,

I had opened for him. There was a distraction when a young man dressed like a dustman, or so I thought, came to the front door and turned out to be the municipal psychiatric social worker summoned earlier by Nash to take Steve off. He, the social worker, wasted no time, but made two phone calls, handed me a piece of card that had an address and phone number written on it with amazing legibility, made it clear in the same movement that I would not be needed on the expedition and started a move to the door.

'Cheers, dad,' said Steve, not at all hostile now and so a lot more effectively reproachful than he could ever have been on purpose.

'Cheers, son.' Hugs were out, so I said a few things about him being well looked after and me coming to see him soon, and more deep stuff like that.

When the two had gone, Nash said, 'He should indeed be well looked after at St Kevin's,' surprising me slightly – I had put him down as a man who saved his attention for the job. 'There really is a saint called that, you know. Irishman, of course. How he got his name on a hospital near Blackheath I can't imagine. Anyway, it's a cheerful sort of place, not one of your Victorian dungeons. Amusing lot, the Victorians, but when it came to institutional interiors they just gave up. I know somebody there called Dr Abercrombie who's a very good man. I couldn't get hold of him just now, but, er, he's a very good man.'

After that Nash made a whole operation of taking a last look at his notes and bundling them up and into his pocket. He seemed to me to be trying and failing to come up with a hopeful but true remark that also meant something.

'Bit of luck, getting hold of that chap this time of the week,' I said.

Nash thought not, on the whole. 'Saturday afternoon's time and a half. Monday morning's when you won't find them. All day Monday, in fact.'

'Oh yeah,' I said. I could not have accounted for it, but this information depressed me. 'Could you have put him in, put my son in if he'd gone on refusing to budge?'

'Oh yes. Yes. But it's not easy with a patient who isn't grossly mad, mad on inspection so to speak, there he goes waving a great knife, that kind of behaviour. Not at all easy. All these vile rights of the individual, you know – it's becoming more and more difficult to get anything done. M'm.'

He gave me his card, engraved to the nines needless to say, with an address in Eaton Square as well as one in New Harley Street. 'Mr Duke,' he went on, staring at me, 'I do want to impress upon you that I'm most inordinately interested in my subject. So much so that even after all these years I still catch myself wondering how supposedly intelligent people can absorb themselves in these various secondary pursuits. Mathematics. Literature, even. This means in practice that I'm prepared, I'm very willing to talk about your son's case with you at any remotely reasonable time by telephone, in person by arrangement. Such a discussion couldn't fail to touch on points of significance, do you see. Just try to bear that in mind, would you?'

As soon as I was alone I started thinking about what Steve had said when he agreed to go into hospital, or rather just remembering, because I failed to get any actual thinking done on the subject. I stood about in the sitting room, then in the kitchen, where I tried to think about food instead and got nowhere there either. Obviously it was time I settled down to what I always did when I wanted to relax, to unwind, to take my mind off things, to potter through a couple of hours without having to think. Only I was short of anything like that, it seemed, except small stuff like a beer and a read of the paper. How had I managed before and after Nowell left me? It had been different then, I was not very clear how – something to do with being away a lot, changing jobs, having the builders in, and other rubbish I had forgotten after eight years.

On past form on a Saturday Susan would not be back for a fair while, but sometimes she was early, and when she was going to be she usually rang to say, but not always. I was feeling powerfully like ringing her, but was uneasy about making her feel she ought to be home when she could still not leave work. All the same I had moved to within reach of the phone when it rang and made me jump.

'Stanley? Is that you, Stanley?'

It was like something out of a dream, not what that usually means, something marvellous, too good to be true, dreamy in fact, but something very hard to take, not at all vague, most precise, hard to take in too because the thing is wrong in a special way, like black and white at the same time. Anyway, for a moment I really thought Susan was talking to me with Nowell's voice. Then I realized that of course it must all just be Nowell.

'Yes, Nowell, as a matter of fact I was – '

'It's Nowell here, darling. Did it work?'

'What? Oh yes. Like a charm. Thanks very – '

'You might have taken the trouble to let me know.'

'I was going to, honestly, but I haven't had a chance – he's only this absolute second gone out of the door. We couldn't get hold of the chap.' Already without the least sense of strain I had slipped back into Nowell's world, a place where, among other features, the truth or untruth of a statement rated rather low when you came to decide whether to state it or not. Not that you actually bothered to go into that side of it.

'What? What chap?'

'Oh, the . . . the chap at the hospital,' I answered more or less at random. 'Still, it's all done now, thank God. I don't know what line you took but you were pretty good, obviously.'

'Well . . . ,' she said, and in a way I wished I could have been there to see her saying it, 'you know. Look, Stanley, tell me, where have they taken him, how is he, what are they going to do to him? It's all happened so quickly.'

'I don't know any more about it than I did when I spoke to you an hour ago, except they've taken him to – '

'Darling, we must have a proper discussion, it's too absurd. After all, we are both responsible for the poor little thing.'

'Yes of course, but for the moment there's really not a lot to discuss. He's gone into hospital – that's done, as I say. If you want to talk about his, well, his illness then Dr Nash is the fellow for that. He'll be getting in touch with you anyway. He's the one with all the – '

'That's not what I mean. We ought to *discuss* it. You and I. Surely you can see it's an extremely serious matter, and it's a thing we know more about than anybody else, I'm not talking about doctors, and if you want my opinion it's our *duty*, and surely it's a reasonable thing for me to ask in my position.'

'Oh absolutely, but wouldn't it still be sensible to wait

till you have seen Nash and heard what he thinks are sort of the most important points?'

In Nowell's book a discussion was not a matter of views being put forward and argued over, let alone a method of working out what it was best to do about some problem. At the same time it was a cut above your straight chinwag, anyway morally. A discussion had such a serious subject that you could go on as long as you liked about any bit of it you fancied, because you were only trying to get at the truth, not showing off or holding the floor or any of those. The chosen bit could be as far-fetched as you liked too, because these days nobody could be sure what might or might not throw light on this or that. The seriousness also made it all right to be things you were usually supposed not to be in conversation, starting with rude and embarrassing.

For these and other reasons I felt I could really do without a discussion with Nowell about Steve. What I had just said was nothing more than an attempt to hold her off – I had felt like going quite a way further but, as she had reminded me with her last few words, she had been the one who had talked Steve round when my lot could not, twice in twenty-four hours too, and there was plenty of time to go yet.

Until she got to that last phrase about her position, her voice and the looks and movements I could so easily imagine going with it had been chummy, almost cosy, with a definite hint of only-yesterday going on – not her usual style with me. She went back to it when she said, 'After all, this isn't some sort of scientific experiment, darling. It's to do with our son. My son. I don't mind admitting I'm awfully ignorant about all sorts of things, but I do know a lot about him.'

'You certainly do,' I said admiringly, also thoughtfully.

'You can read him like a book. Always could. What was that place in Brittany you took him to a couple of times?'

'What? When was this?'

Her tone had completely changed in that second, but I was too slow to take it in. 'Oh, years ago, he can't have been more than eight or – '

'What did he say to you?'

'Well, he'd obviously loved having you to himself. I was tied up here with all the – '

'Perhaps you hadn't noticed, Stanley, but the poor boy was in the most frightful state. Confused . . . terrified . . .'

'Eh?' For the moment I was baffled. 'Look, Nowell, I don't mean just now, I'm talking about then, when you and he came back to Maida Vale and I asked him if he'd had a nice holiday and he was full of the way you'd – '

'For Christ's sake, any *reasonable* man would have been *pleased* to be helped out of a problem he couldn't cope with himself. I must say I had thought I was doing you a good turn.'

'You were, and I'm very grateful – I didn't – '

'I can see you may be upset but you've no need to take it out on me. There's no point in trying to deal with you in your present mood. Thank you for your information. Good afternoon to you.'

Most of the things old Nowell said and did were funny really. The difficulty had always been in laughing at them, especially when they were coming your way. The dignified-restraint component in her final offering illustrated the point well. At this distance I was unsure how I had taken that type of thing when we were first married – as rather dignified and restrained, probably, though also hasty, perhaps, or confused. I had gone straight from

97

something like that to what I felt now, a desire to chop her off at the ankles, without so much as an embarrassed smirk in the middle.

At the moment any sort of smirk could only have been at my own expense, with first place going to my brilliant attempt to lead her away from the topic of the dreaded discussion. I had forgotten until too late that she was sensitive about Steve's younger days, when she had boarded him out with friends more than she should have, got in unsuitable girls to look after him, and so on. I had only been fool enough to bring these things up once, just before she left me or perhaps just after, but I always might again, she never knew. And then of course when I was baffled near the end of our conversation I knew I had started speaking quicker than before, and a bit louder, and with a certain amount of force or emphasis, and from her point of view I might easily have gone on to set about being foul to her any second, and she could hardly have been expected to take a chance on that. For Nowell, if one patch was dodgy the whole area was dodgy, even if the other fellow seemed to be sticking to the far end of the field. This little way of hers often tended to limit conversation to the here and now.

But when she had gone there I was on my own again. I turned on the radio, a Danish job called a StereoBoy, something I rather wished I had noticed before I bought it, and went not very searchingly over the bands. Most of the stations were evidently playing the same yobbos' war-chant, but even the others were somehow impossible, too far on with what they were doing to be caught up with. I had just started on a second run-through when I heard Susan's key in the door.

I went round the corner into the hall and there she was,

coming down the passage with her briefcase and stubby umbrella and shaking out her woollen hat. Her eyes looked extra large.

'Oh, I am glad to see you, love,' I said. 'I don't think I've ever been so glad to see anybody.'

We stood with our arms round each other. 'There's nothing awful, is there?' she asked.

'No. Well. They've taken him off to hospital. And he's mad, the doc says.'

'Tell me all about it.'

We went into the kitchen, where a woman with a North-country accent was talking seriously about senile dementia. Susan turned her off, or rather, not knowing how to do that, shifted off the frequency, which was good enough for me just then.

I said, 'You're back early, then. Do you mind if I have a drink?'

'Of course not. You sit down. I tried to ring, but the switchboard had blown up or something. Whisky and water?'

'Yeah, lovely.'

When I came to the bit about Nowell and her getting Steve to agree to be taken off, I kept a careful eye on Susan. I took no decision to – I just found I had started to. In nearly four years, longer if you went back to our first meeting, I had never known her say or do anything that showed how she felt about Nowell. I realized this was a pretty big statement to make on any woman's feelings about any other woman, not just her husband's ex-wife, if by anything you meant *anything*. She had obviously found some third way of getting across to me her total hatred, contempt and horror. Her words to me on the subject that Friday night, reminding me that Steve had seemed upset once or twice after visiting his mother, had come over with about the punch of a traffic report. This time round it was the same story – nothing that could show on the tapes, audio or visual, and great waves of umbrage. Fair enough. Still, I thought there was no point in piling it on by going into Nowell's phone-call to me, which had really not added anything, so I ended up with Steve going off in that docile way.

When she could see there was no more to come, Susan said, 'Good. What a relief,' and got up and started to put the kettle on. She had not once interrupted me or even shifted about much.

'Yes, it is,' I said. 'It seems a bit sudden, though, that's all. Doesn't it?'

'Shoving him in on sight, so to speak. Very sudden. But by what standards? If he'd had a ruptured appendix or whatever it is, not sudden in the least.'

'It can't be as urgent as a physical thing.'

'Maybe not – I wouldn't know. I'm just saying, what you mind isn't Steve going into hospital suddenly, without warning – you mind Nash suddenly deciding he should go in. The way you see it, he should have thought about it longer, a serious step like that, gone away and come back again. That's because you don't know any more than I do about psychological things, mental things. They seem like just a branch of ordinary things, don't they? Literature's rather the same, to a lot of people. Anyway, I see no reason why Nash should be less right today than he would be on Monday. I can't remember whether I've ever told you, but I had a barmy cousin once, so I've been through part of this before. Would you like some tea?'

'No thanks,' I said. 'No, yes, I will. Thanks.'

'What have you had to eat?'

'Not a lot.'

Susan washed out the teapot at the sink and carefully dried the inside, a thing of hers. Then she said, 'Those points Nash made about the drugs and the tests and so on, it's much easier to do them in hospital, you agreed with all that, I thought.'

'Yeah. Yes. Didn't you?'

'Oh yes. And that Joshua business put the lid on it, you said yourself. So I don't quite see . . .' Standing behind me, she put her hand gently on my shoulder and went on in a gentle voice, 'What's really bothering you, darling?'

I put my hand over hers. 'Well, it was what he said when he told Nash and me he was prepared to go in – I ought to be pleased because I was getting rid of him and that was the only thing I cared about, according to him.'

'Is that all? I don't suppose he meant it very seriously, do you? And even if he – '

'It's not that so much, I'd just hate to think he was right and I wasn't actually interested in what'd be best for him, only in getting him off my back.'

'Without you realizing it. Give it a rest, Stanley, you're much too self-aware for any of that kind of crap. Also much too bright not to be able to see that what's best for somebody can quite easily be what's best and most convenient for somebody else as well, you for instance. But too bloody sentimental and silly to take it in, to believe yourself. And what's wrong with getting him off your back in the state he's in at the moment? And there's my back to be considered too, you know.' There had been no gentleness in her voice for a bit, but I could hear some of it when she said, 'And too silly to ring me up.'

She leant down and kissed me. With me sitting at the table as I was we were only able to hug each other in a rather badly organized way, but it seemed not to matter much. There was plenty I wanted to say to her, all good, all nice things, only I could not sort them out or get them to sound right in my head, so I made pleased, friendly noises and stroked her neck. In a minute she straightened up and went to make the tea.

Later I rang the hospital number the fellow had given me, and after what I thought was an uncommonly short space of time an Asian voice said Yes, Mr Duke had been admitted that afternoon. But I could find out nothing else whatever, not even whether somebody might tell Mr Duke that his father had called.

TWO

PROGRESS

♀

When I rang the hospital the next day the response was much as before. Another Asian voice, or quite likely the same one, said Mr Duke was comfortable but, it turned out, was not to be visited – not must on no account be or taking everything into account had better not be, just was not to be. After a repeat on the Monday morning I decided unenthusiastically to try and get hold of one of the doctors, but to put it off until after eleven, when there would be no excuse for such people not being on duty.

People like advertising managers of daily newspapers needed to get off the mark a bit earlier. I arrived in my office to find my deputy and our joint secretary already in position, which was right. Everything they told and showed me was very dull except the news, passed on a strip of flimsy that Thurifer Chemicals were cancelling their half-page.

'That leaves them five light,' said my deputy, a capable but non-drinking Welshman called Morgan Wyndham who liked being what he called realistic. 'Five out of eight.'

'I know,' I said. 'He can't do that.'

'He won't be there yet,' Morgan told me when I started to dial the agency.

I ignored him. After the last digit there was a click or two and then a colossal silence, as though I had been put through to the house of the dead. Another try ended the same way.

Morgan looked over from his own phone. 'Was he there?'

'Probably not, but I didn't get that far.' Next time I did a switch in the hope of flushing out the bugs, and got the ringing tone in fine style.

'Penangan High Commission, good morning,' said a girl's voice.

'Is the Commercial Attaché there, please?' I knew that sounded none too clever, but the thing was that like all his pals, apparently, the chap had three names, just one syllable each and, to look at on his official card, perfectly pronounceable as small chunks of near-English. But when I had tried them over the phone a few weeks before, this girl or her colleague, though as English as your hat, had not known what I meant, or so she had said and gone on saying. Eventually she had produced three amazing noises that according to her I must have meant, and I must have, because the right chap at once came on the line. And thereupon became the Commercial bleeding Attaché for ever in my book.

'Just a moment, sir,' the operator was saying politely. I thought she sounded marvellous. 'Er . . . did you want to speak to Mr One Three Five or Mr Two Four Six?'

Of course that was not what she said, but it was no further from it than half the other ways I could have put it. Her question put me in a bit of a quandary. 'What's the difference?' I asked eventually.

'Well . . . Mr One's the old Attaché, and Mr Two came last week.'

'Oh, yeah. Right, give me Mr One, if you would.' This sounded like, or rather probably was, the right chap, and also incidentally a chap destined to go jetting back to Penang at any moment, but there was not a lot I could do with that thought except bear it in mind.

I gave my name and that of the paper, and after a moment a high-pitched voice that made you think of sweet and sour pork said, 'Hallo, yes?'

'It's Stanley Duke, Mr Attaché,' I said for good measure. 'You remember we discussed a possible special report in my paper. I wonder if you'd had a chance to think about it.'

'Ah – Mr Joke. Oh *yes*.' He sounded pretty well overcome with joy. 'Now everything is being arranged. I'm communicating with my government and they're being very interested. Extremely interested. Particularly the Minister of Trade will be coming to Europe next month and will be spending three days in London. He's being very intelligent and very well educated and has visited Australia. Now I think with your good assistance he'll be understanding the commercial advantages of my proposal.'

Mr One tended to speak of his fellow-countrymen as worthy but limited, needing a Western nudge of some sort to fall in with his proposals, of which the latest known to me was the buying of space in the paper to tell its readers, or a couple of dozen of them, about his country's achievements. Actually that particular proposal had come from me in the first place, but I found I could face having the credit hogged.

'You and I,' he tinkled on, 'will be making some arrangements beforehand. We mustn't trouble the Minister with details. Please come to lunch here. I think you like our food.'

'Oh, delicious.' I liked their ginseng stuff too, though delicious was probably not the word for it. 'I'll look forward to that. Well, I mustn't keep you, Mr Attaché.' Then a thought struck me. 'By the way, I gather you have an assistant these days.'

It had not been a good thought. 'Assistant?' said Mr One in a voice like a blast off the Eiger. 'What assistant?'

'I don't know, the switchboard seemed to think – '

'Oh no. No no. I'm not having an assistant, Mr Joke.'

'Sorry, I just – '

'He's being an observer, you understand. We're calling him an observer, you see. Please telephone my secretary shortly to arrange lunch. And please give my regards to your charming wife.'

No light on the replacement question, then, but the stuff about the advertising space was good news as far as it went. Lunch with Mr One, assuming he managed not to vaporize first, would be no huge treat, still, worth it for the experience and for telling Susan afterwards. She had got a mention just now because she had given a small party for the Penangan Cultural Attaché, and he had invited us to a do at his High Commission, and among those present had been Mr One, in on whom I had homed as soon as I had heard what he was, and then Penangans were the sort of people who took a lot of trouble over things like wives.

I glanced up and saw a short bearded man watching me from the doorway, or what might have been the doorway if the walls of my office had come up high enough to contain a door instead of only reaching about as far as the top of this fellow's head. That was as far as the walls of nearly everyone's office had come up since the inside of the whole building was remodelled at some stage in the Seventies. Perhaps he had not been actually watching me, only looking at me, but I felt a bit watched that day.

When I reckoned I had noticed him he said, 'Got a minute?'

'Sure,' I said, standing up behind my desk. You always had a minimum of that much for the Editor, whoever he might be. This one's name was Harry Coote and he had not been in the job long, anyway not as long as I had been in mine, which was what counted, and what made me feel a little uneasy too from time to time. Harry struck me as one of those men who very much preferred their own ideas to other people's on all sorts of issues, including ones like who should and especially who should not be advertising manager of the paper they edited. Of course nobody took a blind bit of notice of what editors thought about that unless the paper was putting on readers, but then rather to my surprise the paper was putting on readers, and doing it at a time when its rivals were giving all their readers cars to try and coax them to go on being their readers a bit longer. And I liked my job – I thought I was good at it slightly more than I liked it, but still.

On my way out I dropped the Thurifer note in front of Morgan. I followed Harry along to his office, which had walls that went all the way to the ceiling, also enough hardware to launch a smallish satellite, also a long tank for tropical fish with no fish in it, no other creatures either, no greenery, no water even, just sand, stones and empty shells, and a light still going that probably no one knew how to put out. In its active days the tank had tipped you off that a great man worked here, along the lines of a flint-glass sherry decanter or an antelope-hoof snuffbox further back.

'How are things?' asked Harry. That just meant he was not yet ready to come to the point, if any.

'Fine,' I said, pretending to hesitate before turning down

one of the dusty, gnarled cheroots he showed me. 'You remember that business about the Penangan report we talked about.' I ran through part of my phone conversation. When the subject had been mentioned before Harry had shown guarded approval. To print four or any number of pages of guff about a distant and irrelevant hell-hole would do nothing, or nothing good, for circulation but it would raise the tone, lift the paper a millimetre up market. More than once I had noticed him saying he thought it was time to improve the paper's image, give it a touch of quality, etc. Perhaps he really hated to have it putting on readers. Anyway, it might be interesting to see his reaction to the nearer approach of the Penangan report.

It was interesting, but not encouraging. 'Yes, well, that's what you get,' he said firmly and vaguely. He wanted to register doubt or disapproval without knowing how. 'Of course, it's nothing to do with *me*.' There he was telling the strict truth, only it lacked conviction.

'Well, we'll see how it goes.' Not easy to quarrel with that either.

'You're, er, you're going to meet this Minister of Trade bloke, are you?'

'I thought I would, yeah. When he comes over.'

'If he does.'

'That's right, if he does.'

Harry's mouth buckled behind the beard with the exertion of dragging air through his cheroot. You could tell they were a cruel smoke just from the look of them. For some reason I thought of what he had been known to do, perhaps invariably did do, when he had you up to dinner at his bachelor joint in Tufnell Park – give you an admittedly not too bad Chinese takeaway meal and make you eat it with chopsticks, real ones though, mind you, bought or stolen on some all-expenses trip to Peking. I had never been asked along myself, but had had the facts on the first-hand authority of the Features Editor, who had heard from somebody else, somebody not even in Fleet Street, that at one of these blow-outs Harry had given them tea to wash it down with, pointing out that actually with any national food you were supposed to drink the national drink, the wine of the country, which in this case any fool could see was not wine. There had been times when I found the tea story a bit hard to believe, but at the sight of Harry now, looking quite upset at the way his cheroot would not draw to suit him, I could manage it all right.

After a short silence he said, 'I've been thinking about you, Stanley.'

I could think of one or two rude answers to that but no polite ones, so I just looked expectant.

'You really, you really *enjoy* doing what you do, do you?'

'Yes,' I said, sounding terrifically certain and relaxed at the same time.

'And you think you ought to be doing it, do you?'

'Without any question whatever. How do you mean?'

'Well, you know, I was just wondering whether you felt you had the proper scope for your talents in the present job.'

'What? What talents?'

He gave a slight laugh. 'Get stuffed, Stanley,' he said, or rather must have meant to say, but what he in fact said was something far nearer 'Gat steffed, Stunley.' That was because he came from up North, so much so that if he ever got tired of editing he could have walked into a job as a chat-show host on any of the TV channels. 'I know more about you than you give me credit for,' he was going on. 'I'm not such a fool as I look, you know.' It seemed a good idea to let that one go too. 'For instance, er . . . Oh yes. Tell me, do you ever see anything of old Nowell these days?'

I had always thought that one of the most appealing things about Harry was his complete openness, if you could use the word to cover being incapable of successful deceit. So I knew straight away and for sure that he had heard not a word about my recent contacts with Nowell – whom many years previously and for a very short time he was supposed to have been in the same digs as – and was just being pushy and nosy in his usual way. 'No,' I said. 'Practically nothing. Why?'

'Oh . . . I always thought it was a pity you two couldn't manage to make a go of it.'

Always? Until he joined the paper, Harry would not have known of my existence much. 'Well, there we are.' I looked at my watch.

'I see Whatsisname, Bert, in the Ladbroke Arms occasionally.'

'Oh, yeah.'

'I suppose you haven't got much time for him.'

'Not a lot, no. Well . . .'

'Oh, he's not so bad when you get to know him.'

I glared suddenly at the fish-tank as though I had noticed something starting to come to life there. Another short pause followed, long enough all the same for it to dawn on even our Harry that the time had not yet come to fill me in on all those good points of Bert's that I had been missing up to now. A knock sounded at the door and the Political Editor put his bald head round it. Harry told him to come on in, sounding quite relieved. 'Well, if you don't mind, Stan,' he said, smiling, 'I seem to have this conference.'

'No, I don't mind, Harry. I really don't mind a bit.'

'Right, see you. Oh, and, er,' he turned his smile off, 'I hope everything's going fine at home.'

He conveyed to me that I was not to not manage to make a go of my second marriage if I knew what was good for me, using so much wattage that something of the sort got across to the Political Editor, a man I knew only from his photograph in the paper, who looked at him and then at me and had started to look back at him about the time I left them together. Outside I just missed butting under the chin, luckily on the whole, a seven-foot female in a knee-length cardigan also bound for the conference. Harry was quite capable, I thought to myself, of believing that what he had been up to back there was showing sympathetic interest in me, kindly concern about someone who was not his responsibility in any strict way but about whom he nevertheless felt a certain this, that and the other. At least he would have said he had been doing that if challenged, gone on saying it to the death too if necessary. But what had he really been up to?

No answer. I had no clear idea why, but I went straight on to do a bit of wondering, for the tenth time, about Harry's sex life. He appeared to have none at all – his name had never been remotely linked with any man's, woman's or child's, though he was seen around with plenty of people. He never went near the subject in conversation – so for instance when his long-ago alleged chumminess with Nowell arose, as it did from time to time, I was at least spared any hint that they might have had it away together, which comparatively few men in that situation would or could have kept themselves from suggesting. He gave nothing away in his clothes or mannerisms or speech. And so on. The consensus was that the bed he kept his distance from had a little boy in it. Of course, it still could have been a big boy, even though Harry must have been getting into his middle fifties by now. After all, you never knew, did you? Not with them.

I forgot about Harry straight away when I got back to my office. No secretary. Morgan made a nothing-to-do-with-me face and at the same time I saw there was a woman standing by my desk. Her back was half turned and for a moment I thought it was Nowell. Then I realized I had been misled just by the hair, which had the right rough texture and shortish cut, though it was rather too dark, and by the vaguely foundry-style rig-out in slate-coloured denim, and it was true that Nowell had been fresh in my mind. I soon saw that this woman was hardly like her at all really, younger, longer in the leg, thinner, with a thin face and a nervous or restless manner. For the second time in a few days I guessed something was wrong without being able to say what.

'Mr Duke?' She had a deep, harsh voice with one or other regional accent.

'Yes. What do you want?'

'There's no need to be unfriendly, surely.'

'So you say.' I felt somehow I had had enough laughs for one morning. 'Now, please tell me who you are and what you want.'

Morgan had been following this, and called, 'She said she had an appointment, Stan. There was nothing in your book, but I couldn't, er . . . ' He left it there. He was a very capable deputy advertising manager.

'Okay,' I said, and nodded to the woman to go on.

She ducked her head and said with souped-up humility, 'My name is Trish Collings, and I'm a friend of your son's, and I was – '

'What's up? Is he all right?'

She stared at me. 'Well . . . that's rather what I've come to ask you, Mr Duke. I thought you might have some news of him.'

'Oh,' I said. Morgan's phone rang and he answered it. 'Now,' I went on, 'how did you make your way here, to this room?'

'Does that matter?'

'Certainly. You're not supposed to be allowed up without personal permission. Standard procedure.'

'That's what I figured, so I got straight in the lift and asked around. It didn't take me long. Anyway, how is Steve?'

'How long have you known him?'

Up to this point she had seemed not to be giving me her full attention. She had kept glancing at, or towards, the photographs and other cuttings that were pinned to the cork runner on the wall by the desk, most of them scattered with hand-written comments. They would have been very largely unintelligible or at best uninteresting to anyone outside a narrow local circle, and even I could have spared a few of them. Now she tore herself away from all that and faced me more squarely. 'I don't see that matters much either,' she said, and I put her down as probably West of England.

'What are you doing here? Why didn't you ring me up?'

'Look, Mr Duke, all I want to know is how Steve is. That's not classified information, is it?'

'Of course not. He's . . . all right. A bit under the

weather but nothing serious,' I said without thinking. 'Why? What have you heard about him?'

'Oh, is there something to hear?'

Across the room Morgan put his phone back. I went over to him and said, 'Look, Taff, could you lose yourself for a few minutes?' I was hazy about why I wanted him to do that – I had no theories to speak of about Trish Collings, if that was her name, except that she was not what she said she was, but even so embarrassment of some sort could safely be predicted. If in due course she came at me with a razor I could call for help from the dozens of people within hearing, run away, etc. Still no secretary, a temporary who was going the right way about making herself even more so than had been agreed in the first place.

Morgan had done quite a good job for him on hiding his astonishment at my request. 'Sure,' he said. 'Er . . . sure.' By the way his eyes flickered I could tell he was starting to wonder too.

'Have you tried him?'

He cottoned on to that instantly – no trouble with anything like that. 'Not reachable, but somewhere in the building, so we're getting warm. I left a message.'

'Great. Well . . .'

The sudden quiet reminded him that he had undertaken to leave. 'Er . . . see you later,' he said, and went out at a near-run.

I started on the female again. 'Now. Who *are* you?'

'Mr Duke, why all this fuss about a simple inquiry after somebody's welfare? What's the matter?'

She spoke, as she had done from the start, in a reasonable tone, in fact with slightly overdone reasonableness. By now we had had quite enough time to finish looking each other over. The female was not all that much younger than Nowell after all, with good features except for that thin mouth, which had something wrong about its shape or perhaps the way she moved it in speaking. I thought there had been sexy bits in her expression part of the time, to show she might be interested in me and inquire whether I might be interested in her, but it was hard to be sure of that because she moved her mouth about even when she was keeping quiet, and also kept shifting her eyes to and fro. Her face was never still. That meant I had no chance of telling whether she was attractive either. What she was mostly looking at was a not very large man with a rather small moustache, probably with a suspicious, hostile look as well and certainly with the nearest he could manage to a deep-frozen eunuch's one.

'State and authenticate your identity in the next ten seconds,' I said, quite enjoying this part, 'or I'll call Security and have you buzzed out.'

'What are you so afraid of?'

'Plenty of things, thanks, and one of them's that you might be off your head whoever you are.'

'Ah,' she said as though she had won a bet with herself.

'Ah? Two seconds.' I moved towards the phone. 'Sorry about the script.'

'All right, you can call off the panic, I've got what I wanted,' she said, still a good deal more mildly than the way I had gone on from the start. 'My name is Trish Collings, and I'm helping to look after Steve at St Kevin's.'

'He is all right, is he?'

'No cause for alarm.'

'Nurse, are you? Or doctor or what?'

'I am a doctor, yes. So – '

117

'I thought a Dr Abercrombie was supposed to be in charge of his case.'

'Dr Abercrombie suffered a small heart attack a few days ago. He'll be off work for at least a month.'

'So are you in charge of Steve?'

'I don't like that phrase, it has the wrong implications, but yes, I am a senior psychiatrist.'

'Really. What identification have you?'

'Oh, for Christ's sake.' She unzipped what looked like a man's black imitation-leather sponge bag and turned through it.

'I'd just like to be on the safe side if it's all the same to you,' I said, I had meant to sound indignant and rather grand, but it came out apologetic. As I spoke I realized I felt it too, and could not quite see why, except there we were and Dr Collings was a woman.

After a moment she passed me a letter addressed to the person she claimed to be, even down to the Trish. It was from the librarian of the British Psychiatric Association, which somehow worsened things slightly for my side. By this time I was fighting hard not to say I was sorry, also wondering whether my uneasy feelings at the sight of her were all accounted for now.

'You didn't give me much of a chance, did you?' I said as I handed her back the letter. 'What am I supposed to think when a strange female barges in . . .'

I had lost her – something in or about the letter had caught her attention. She peered short-sightedly at it while I remembered that the book it referred to had been called *The Parenthood of Madness* and started feeling uneasy again. Then, taking her time, she folded up the single sheet and pushed it back into her sponge bag. 'Sorry?' she said.

'Nothing, I was just – '

'I know, I shouldn't have done it really, but it sometimes helps to catch people off their guard.'

'I see, yeah. Has it helped this time?'

At this piece of repartee she shook her head in a way I thought was more preoccupied than negative – I noticed that whichever it was none of her hair moved. At the same time she gave a smile of a sort, turned down at the corners, not very wonderful to look at, really, but with something awkward or shy about it that I could not object to. She sent me one or two of her short glances but said nothing.

I said, 'How's Steve?'

'Ah,' she said again, but went on straight away, 'He's all right, he's fine, he's just got some problems which we're beginning to get a sense of, we need to know more about him, his early history, all that, I hope you'll be able to help us in those areas.' Where had I heard that sing-song before? 'Which means I'm going to have to ask you to give me some of your time.' Time – toime – West of England it was, the very thing for Long John Silver, of course, but extraordinarily ageing for any young or youngish woman, almost as bad as a southern Irish brogue. 'I thought the atmosphere here would be more relaxed than in hospital.'

'Did you really? Far from ideal, I should have thought.'

As I spoke a phone rang from what sounded inches away, closely followed by another, and a small young man and a bigger older man went by some yards apart with pieces of paper in their hands, shouting back and forth. Further off a voice yelled, calling, swearing, yawning.

Dr Collings seemed to take my point. 'Or would there be somewhere you'd feel more relaxed?'

'There would, quite a few places.' Places like one of the

little rooms at the top of the Bar and Press Club would be private all right but for that very reason not relaxing, not for me, not with this female. 'Er, but I doubt if you'd think they were suitable.'

She frowned. 'Oh? What sort of places are they?' It was obviously nothing to do with the frown itself, but I suddenly realized that her breasts were a size or two bigger than the rest of her. Usually, in fact I dare say every time up to now, seeing a thing like that had me paying the woman concerned much more attention automatically, which in this case meant straight away and without thinking. But the breasts of Dr Collings had no such effect, merely adding up to one more out-of-place piece of her. Still, they were breasts.

'What?' I answered.

'Where are you thinking of?'

'I thought we might go to a pub,' I found I had said. 'If that's all right.'

'Sure, why wouldn't it be?'

'They're usually pretty quiet for a while yet.'

'Fine, fine.'

'There's quite a nice one, well, anyway, just the other side of Fleet Street called the Crown and Sceptre. Not a hundred yards away. Almost opposite.'

'All right. Let's go.'

'Well . . . I was wondering if you'd mind going on and I'll join you in a few minutes. There's just a few things I'd like to get squared away here first, if it's all right with you.'

'Can't they wait?'

'Well yes, in a sense of course they can, but, er, unless you've got a particular urgent bit for me I'd very much like to, er . . . After all, you did – '

'Mr Duke,' she said in her controlled way, 'which is more important to you, your son or these matters you seem to be so interested in? Whatever they are.'

One day quite soon a woman was going to say something very much like that to me, something hardly at all more noteworthy than that, and I would collapse and die without recovering consciousness. I put out a hand, not too fast, and gripped the edge of the desk. 'My son, of course,' I said, 'when it comes to it. If it has come to it you'd better tell me now, hadn't you?'

I thought that was quite good, but before it was half over I lost her again. She walked out of the office at average speed without looking at me. I could think of nothing to do but assume I would find her in the designated pub in due course. Morgan reappeared so immediately that he must have been hanging about in sight of the doorway.

After a quick glance over his shoulder he said, 'Who was that?'

It was undoubtedly a fair question, but for some reason I found it an impossible one to answer in any satisfactory way. 'She's . . . a friend of my son's.'

He waited till he was sure there was no more to come before saying 'Oh yes' in a voice that dripped with disbelief and suspicion. The Welsh accent came in handy for that. There did seem to be rather a lot of accents around that morning, but then I hardly ever came across anybody without one, apart from me, of course.

'Yes,' I said, and gave him a dozen or more boring things to do and make other people do. When I had finished I rang the Thurifer agency again and got the fellow I was after. His story was that not he but someone at Thurifer had gone off his head and I was to stop worrying. So I stopped worrying and rang Cliff Wainwright, who answered at once and in person and sounding quite angry. He calmed down somewhat when he discovered who it was, but went back to being fed up when I asked him about Trish Collings.

'A bit off, you know, this, Stanley, quite frankly. Surely you realize it's most improper for me to go sounding off about all and bloody sundry. *And* I don't possess a card-index system on the whole of the medical profession and areas adjacent as you appear to think. However, by some freak of chance it does so happen I've heard of the bag. Well above average was what was said. Thoroughly in touch, very good with the patients. That can be dodgy, of course. Well, what patients like isn't necessarily good for them. They're keen on not being cut open. For instance. Anyway, there she is.'

'Do you have any other children?' asked Collings.

'No,' I said. 'Surely Steve must have told you that, if you've talked to him at all, as you say you have.'

'Not even by your second wife?'

'No, not even by her. Why?'

'Why not?'

'Eh? Oh, er . . . Nowell said she couldn't face going through all that again.'

'That's not what she said to me. Yes, I spent nearly an hour with her before coming along to see you. She was very helpful.'

'Really? In my experience nothing's what Nowell says to anybody, whether it's you or me or the postman. I mean whatever she said's got nothing to do with what happened. Ever.'

'How long is it since she left you?'

'Eight years. Nearly nine. I'm not bitter, it's just I know her. At least I am, bitter, to some extent, I can't ever see myself not being, but it's much more I know her, that I say things like that about her. It's true anyway. She can't . . . You'll see what I mean when you've seen a bit more of her. Well, you might, I suppose.'

'In fact she did face going through it again.'

'That's right. She wouldn't have not done it just because she'd told me she couldn't or wouldn't. If you remind her that she's said something it doesn't suit her down to the ground at that moment to have said, she says she didn't say it, even if you're fool enough to produce a boatload of other people who heard her say it. Simplifies life no end. She makes the past up as she goes along. You know, like communists. Why are we talking about this, anyway?'

'You still haven't told me why there are no children of your second marriage.

'No, I haven't, have I? I can't think what it can have to do with anything, but you're the doctor. So. Susan was nearly thirty-six when she married me and that's oldish to start having children, I should have thought. She hadn't had any by her previous husband, and presumably she wanted to go on not having any – well, that was what I presumed. She said she reckoned she wasn't cut out for motherhood, which I took as a sign that she probably wasn't.'

'Was that all she ever said on the matter?'

'Just about. I didn't try to get any more out of her. It sounded quite reasonable to me. After all, it's not as if she was the Queen.'

'Did you try to get her to change her mind?'

'Certainly not.'

'Why didn't you?'

'Well, I had no particular, special desire for any more kids. Lots of men would have felt the same, perhaps most of them. No child of Susan's and mine could have been any kind of company for Steve. And I didn't think it was my place to talk her into a thing like that. The woman should decide, and Susan was absolutely definite about it.'

'Is that your usual line, would you say, leaving the basic decisions to your female partner?'

'No, I said in a thing like that, that concerns her more than me.'

'You mean you think the role of the mother is much more important in the raising of children than that of the father.'

'Well, not ultimately, perhaps. I was thinking of pregnancy and confinement and the rest of it. Obviously a young child's going to make more difference to the mother's life than the father's.'

'Confinement. That takes me back. Anyway, what about an older child? Does the mother continue as much more important there?'

'I don't know about much more. It depends. But more, more important. I mean that's the view the courts take, after all, when there's a split-up. It's the wife who usually – '

'I suppose it was your first wife who took the decision to become pregnant?'

'I can't say what happened. She said it was an accident. I was still believing a lot of what she said in those days but of course that was ridiculous. It wasn't my decision anyway, which I take it is the point.'

'Would you ever have taken that decision if it had been left entirely to you?'

'I can't say about that either. Quite likely not. I don't think all that many men actively want children, not when they're twenty-five. Look – '

'What was your reaction to the news?'

'Well, I was pleased in a way. The timing was off, though, financially and that. There's always a case for not having a baby in the next twelve months when you're that sort of age.'

'So really you'd have preferred the pregnancy not to have occurred when it did.'

'Yeah. Yes, I think I would. Do you mind telling me what all this is leading up to?'

'I think we're almost there actually, Stanley. We're close to establishing that you had a negative attitude towards parenthood and resented the difficulties it occasioned.'

'Are we hell! That was just at the start, before I'd had a chance to adjust to the idea. By the time Steve arrived I was as thrilled and excited as, I was going to say Nowell but there again – '

'It's quite common in young primogenitors of high activity – first-time fathers. And it often persists even in association with definite positive behaviour. That can produce some pretty bizarre results.'

Trish Collings started to laugh while she was saying the last part of this and went on after she had finished, her shoulders shaking and her slightly spaced-out teeth glistening. The scale of it went beyond what you normally expected from someone just struck by a witty thought, in a civilized country anyway. When it was over she got up from her bit of bench and without another word walked past me in the direction of the lavatories at the rear of the pub. I was hoping that on her return she would get her questions over and with luck explain the point of them, no insistence there, and then let me ask her about Steve. Well, I said to myself, if one of the first things she wanted to know was how I had felt when I heard he had been conceived, there was probably not so very much wrong with him.

The pub was as quiet as I had said in the sense that there were not yet many people in it, though of course it was noisy as well – I had forgotten about that, as I still often did after all these years, not as noisy as it could be, nor noisy absolutely all the time, but noisy. A fat ginger-haired fellow in – among other things – a whitish tee-shirt and a burgundy plastic anorak, which between them made him look amazingly undressed and dirty and dangerous as well as horrible, was playing the fruit-machine, in this case a new improved model that broadcast at top volume an extract from a harmonium sonata every time anything happened and part of the soundtrack of a Battle of Britain movie in between. In case you were deaf and trying to think, it flashed different combinations of coloured lights on and off like billy-ho. Apart from that there was not much to see by, just a couple of table-lamps with tasteful imitation-parchment shades on the bar and some feeble sun from the street, cut down further by the criss-crossed strips of painted lead glued on the windows.

What with the semi-darkness and being preoccupied I failed to spot Lindsey Lucas until she was almost within arm's reach, and the gritty Ulster tones made me jump. Her hair-do and clothes had their usual neat, slightly dated look.

'When are you going to start managing some advertising? Whenever I run into you you're boozing your head

off in a well-known Fleet Street watering hole. My turn
– what can I get you?' As she spoke she was taking in the
half-full glass of gin and tonic opposite where the Collings
woman had been sitting.

I tried to think and found it hard going. The trouble
was that although I knew quite well that it would be a
good idea to get rid of her and at once, I was so cheered
by the sight of her that the words took their time about
coming. It was not my day. Before I had done much more
than stand up and open my mouth Lindsey's expression
changed in a way that showed that Collings was on the
point of joining us, and I was still turning my head when
she actually appeared. Even now it was not too late to send
Lindsey packing with talk of deal, rate, space, block and
so on, but instead of that I found myself introducing them,
or rather saying their names one after the other and
pointing at each one in turn at the same time, perhaps in
case either of them started wondering which was which.
While my vocal cords went on being selectively paralysed
my eyes were more than up to snuff. They showed me
Lindsey quietly transmitting a claim to part-ownership of
me, but when I looked to see how the other female was
reacting I found her sending the same message back in a
different style, more obvious, jerky, where Lindsey was
smooth, but there. Or so I thought.

That finished me off, for the next half-minute at least.
I went on standing about while Lindsey again offered a
drink, to Collings as well this time, took an order from
her for a single gin and ice and asked me whether I wanted
water or soda.

'What?' I said, having heard perfectly well. 'Er . . .
soda. Water.'

'Are you pursuing that girl?' Collings asked me when

we were alone. Her manner was morally accusing, not at all sexual now.

'Of course not. No. What if I were?'

'But you want her to join in our conversation.'

'No. Why should I? Absolutely the opposite.'

'In that case, why didn't you tell her we were talking privately?'

'I don't know really. I suppose I couldn't face explaining that you were a psychiatrist dealing with my son's case.'

'Oh, *case*. Why couldn't you? It's nothing to be ashamed of. You wouldn't mind telling her your son had broken his leg, would you?'

'No, I just . . .'

'I'd have expected you to be well educated enough not to take that view.'

'It's not a view. I couldn't face going into it with her. Surely you can see that. And now would you mind just telling me what you were getting at with your questions about my attitude to Steve before he was born?'

'Isn't it obvious? You resented him as an intruder. You made him feel he wasn't wanted. Not calculated to foster a sense of security.'

'But that's not true,' I said, trying and failing to catch her eye. 'It just isn't true. I can remember, I didn't resent him when he was born. I wanted him by the time he was born. I couldn't have made him feel he wasn't wanted because I wanted him. Honestly.'

'I don't mean you consciously behaved to him in an unloving way.'

'Oh I see. I thought I was thinking one thing when really I was thinking the opposite. I know.'

Her lips came apart with a little smacking noise. 'Have you ever asked him about this?'

128

'No. Have you?'

'I didn't have to. He told me. There was plenty of it. "Dad was always trying to freeze me out. Dad never really accepted me. Dad had as little to do with me as he could." That kind of thing. Of course you often get – '

'What's the address of your hospital? Out Blackheath way, isn't it?'

'I'm sorry, Stanley, I can't let you see him at the moment. Not just yet. It wouldn't be at all a good idea.'

'How do you stop me?'

'Only by telling you that. But it's enough, isn't it?'

'Yes. Sod it.'

'As I said, this is quite common. And you often find an element of exaggeration, centralizing what are objectively relatively minor grievances.'

'Ah, cheers.'

'I have to get through some more work with you on this session, so can we cut the social get-together short?'

'She won't stay long.'

It was not till then that I realized that Lindsey's eyes were at least as good as mine. She was obviously going to think I was not just with Collings but so to speak going round with her. But Lindsey must not think that – I could simply not bear her to think that. I knew very little about why I felt so strongly on the point, except that the reason had to do with Collings rather than Lindsey. At that moment she was turning carefully away from the bar clasping three glasses in her hands. I should have followed her over there earlier and fed her some plausible de-sexing tale, but it was too late for that, and even at this late stage I could have bounded across the room to give her a hand and dole out a compressed edition, but I thought of that too late as well. Normally I would at least have jumped up to help her put the drinks on the table, but today I forgot.

'Something wrong, Stanley?' asked Lindsey.

I pulled myself together. 'No. I remembered something I should have done. But I can't do it now.'

At this she led off reliably by explaining how she came to have a quarter of an hour to spare, then switched to friendly interest and good manners – no curiosity showing – to ask Collings if she worked in Fleet Street too. This is it, I thought.

'I do and I don't,' said Collings, smiling suddenly. 'I'm in the Accounts Department of the *Sunday Chronicle*.'

'Oh really? Of course, eh, that's where Susan works, the *Chronicle*.'

'Yes, the people on the editorial side, we don't see much of them in Accounts as a rule.'

'No, I suppose not.'

It struck me later that to have Ulster and Dorset or wherever it was coming back at each other in this style was like something out of a very carefully cast radio play. Not at the time, though. At the time I was pretty well too terrified to think at all. I sat there staring at Lindsey, willing her to look my way so that I could twitch my face to signal at least that something was up but, as always in these situations, I might as well have gone to see my aunt.

'In fact I don't know her at all really,' Collings was saying. 'Just by sight. I expect you know her though, don't you? Being a journalist yourself and everything.'

'As it happens I've known her longer than that. Nearly twenty years, in fact. Why?' Lindsey gave the last word quite a shove.

'Oh, I'm just interested. You'll be able to tell me – is it Lindsey? – I imagine she is a very intelligent woman?'

'Christ, you don't have to know someone for twenty years to reach a conclusion on that. Yes, she is very intelligent, exceptionally intelligent, as anybody who's ever talked to her for five minutes is well aware. Including her husband.'

Collings gave one of her hearty laughs and laid her hand heavily on my shoulder. Somehow I managed not to fling it off or bite it. 'Oh, he says the same, but you know what men are, he could be biased, couldn't he? But Lindsey, you mustn't mind me going on like this, I'm curious, but I've heard people in the office who do know Susan say they've found her a bit, well, not standoffish exactly, but very very reserved. What would your comment be on that? Stanley won't mind me saying what I've said.'

That did make Lindsey look at me, but there was no need for signals now. She had gone rather red, which suited her looks no end. Glaring through her glasses, she said, 'Stanley may or may not mind what you've said, but I can assure you that I do. And my comment would be, Fuck off, whoever you are. What's the matter with you? Why don't you listen? I told you she was an old friend of mine. What do you think I am? Be in touch, Stanley. Go carefully.'

She gave me a quick kiss and a squeeze of the hand that reminded me of Susan, and hurried away without another glance. Collings, who had kept up quite a good detached sort of air while Lindsey had been telling her her fortune, twisted her mouth at me as though it had been Lindsey who had behaved oddly or badly. I sat down and for a moment just gazed.

'What the bleeding hell were you playing at?'

'I'm sorry if I've upset you.'

'Me being upset's not the point. What did you think

you were doing? I mean that literally. What did you actually think you were doing? For God's sake.'

'Gathering information,' she said in her patiently reasonable voice.

'Yeah, and a great roaring success you made of it, I'll give you that. You extracted the precious secret that Susan's intelligent and you're where you started on whether she's reserved or not. Terrific. All that at the price of a few lies and a spot of trouble-making.'

'There was information there right enough if you knew what to look for.'

'Oh I get it, you could tell what she meant when she thought she was meaning the opposite or not meaning anything at all. You're a marvel, you are.'

'I have upset you. Please try to – '

'Well I would be upset, wouldn't I?' I stopped for a moment and then went on more gently. 'Look. You're not just a woman I happen to have taken to the pub, you're the doctor who's looking after my son or however you want to put it, and he seems to be very sick. So what do I think when I see you behaving in such a daft and irresponsible and *pointless* way? What am I supposed to think?'

For the first time she met my eyes steadily for something over a couple of seconds. Her own were narrowed while at the same time her eyebrows were lifted. At least that was what it looked like, though admittedly when I tried it later in front of the mirror I got nowhere with making my own face do both those things at once. She also seemed to have drawn in her nostrils. I could not have said what that expression expressed but it was nothing encouraging, that was for sure. I thought for a moment she was going to cry and got ready to start apologizing for everything I could think of, but the moment passed and her face went back to its constant movement. When she began to speak it was in a flat voice without much inflection.

'Now listen to me, Stanley. First of all you'll have to take it from me that my experiment just now wasn't pointless. As regards the rest of it, you'll have to agree that no actual harm was done. That little' Irish girl went off quite charged up with having stood on her dignity, and nobody said anything to hurt your feelings that I heard. But the important thing is for you to reshape your image of psychiatry and psychiatrists, which you've got from people like Alfred Nash. Oh, a brilliant man undoubtedly, made a fine contribution, only trouble he's still stuck in Sydney in the 1950s, and the world's moved on since then. Everything's got much more flexible, there aren't the old rigid categories any more. The way Nash sees the human race, there are mad people and sane people . . .'

'Dr Collings,' I said, 'if I could just – '

'Do call me Trish. The medical title is so compartmenting.'

'M'm, but if you don't mind 1 think I'll stick to Dr Collings, but you can go on calling me Stanley if you want. Anyway. We've talked about me and my first wife and my present wife and Lindsey Lucas and me again and now Dr Nash. Could we talk about Steve? I dare say you haven't finished examining him or whatever you want to call it yet, but you must have some thoughts about him. I wish you'd give me an idea of what they are, if that's all right.'

'Sure.' She gave me a smile I had to hold on to myself not to look away from. 'Let's have another drink, though. My round. The same again?'

She was good in pubs, I thought to myself, promptly naming her preference when I asked her earlier and correctly taking that single off Lindsey to put in her half-drunk gin and tonic. It seemed not to go with the rest of her. Whatever that was like. I groaned quietly. Just when I could have done with a spot of mind-battering the fruit-machine was vacant and silent but for an amplified hum and the general noise-level seemed to be down. There was nothing to stop me from worrying about whether I really had tried to freeze Steve out when he was small. What was it about the idea that was familiar? – not the accusation itself but the type. Familiar from long ago, not the more recent past. Of course! Nowell. It had been a favourite trick of hers to denounce you for doing something or being something that had simply never crossed your mind, so that when it came to answering the charge you had nothing to show, no register of dates and places that showed you doing or being conspicuously the opposite, just a load of denials and undocumented general stuff, no alibi, in fact. But then people without alibis were often guilty.

I had got that far when Collings came back with the drinks. She plunged into business straight off, talking in a much less jittery, uncomfortable way than before.

'Nash's diagnosis of Steve was schizophrenia,' she said, lighting a Silk Cut. 'I just can't accept anything as prefabricated as that. What's at stake here is far from simple. On the information available so far, I think we're dealing with a problem in living, something involving not just him but also the people close to him, especially his parents. You've got to remember first that all kids of that generation have got a lot to cope with, a lot to try and make sense of – unemployment, of course, but also the nuclear holocaust, racial tension, urban pollution, alienation, you name it. They're very vulnerable and they feel powerless, it's a big, dangerous world over which they have no control. Someone like that senses that he's at risk. Then there comes a crisis in his emotional life, like breaking up with his girlfriend, and he's defenceless. So, what does he do? He creates a defence. He doesn't have anywhere to hide, so he makes a place to hide, a place we call madness, or mental illness, or delusions, or hallucinations.'

She paused for a swig, also probably for effect. I felt drunk or something, but asked her, 'Do you mean he's just putting on all that stuff about Joshua and the other fellows in the Bible?'

'Not consciously. He believes every word of it, for the time being.'

'But that's . . . I'm afraid I still don't quite see what he's defending himself against or hiding from.'

'Well, there are various ways of putting it. Escaping from reality, or his own inner feelings, or inner needs might be more accurate. He's trying to keep other people at a distance emotionally, so he puts up a wall, a wall consisting of what the likes of Nash call delusions. In cases like this that's often due to an appalling fear of being hurt. Now at this stage one can't be sure, but I rather think that with Steve it's more that he's afraid of hurting other people. He's a very nice boy, that I do know.' Here she sounded quite defiant, as if she thought I was obviously not going to let her get away with that, and putting me strongly in mind of my mother-in-law. 'Our job is to persuade him to lower his defences. He won't do that unless we can help him to get in touch with his own feelings, including especially his own anger.'

'Get in touch with his own anger,' I said. 'I see. What sort of chance would you say there is of that?'

'It's too early to say. You're anxious about this, I know,

Stanley, but believe me it's most important not to jump to conclusions. This is very tricky and difficult ground. We're dealing with a scared, confused, insecure boy who has to be helped to find out who he really is.'

A frightful feeling that had been growing on me ever since we came into the pub suddenly got much worse, so bad I could no longer pretend it was not there or was really something else. It was roughly that Collings's general style and level of thinking would have done perfectly well for a psychiatrist in an American TV movie but might have looked a bit thin in a Sunday magazine article. And this could simply not be anything like a correct description. I was drunk, stupid too at the best of times, unable to take in ideas of any difficulty. But I had been perfectly sober when I arrived, and Steve talking about Joshua because he was afraid of hurting other people was not a difficult idea. It was not an idea at all.

I told myself it had to be, had to make sense somehow, somewhere. The resemblance to TV must be a mistake, an illusion based on my ignorance, which had made me miss all sorts of subtle points and misunderstand phrases and expressions that were nearly or even exactly the same as bits of drivel but actually conveyed a precise scientific meaning to those in the know, and getting in touch with your own anger and finding out who you really were, etc., were technical terms referring to definite, observable processes. Or Collings's approach was so new that they had not yet worked out a what, a terminology for it. Or she was hopeless at talking about what she did but shit-hot in action. Or something else that made it all right, because something must. Whatever she might say and however she might behave, the bint was a *doctor*.

Anyway, there was no alternative to going on trying to

listen. I went on doing that for forty minutes or so, the stage at which we shunted from presumable technical talk to further inquiries into my early relations with Steve. That part went quite well as far as I was concerned, because I had had time to do some remembering and get my confidence back. I could see now that for some reason, like to fit a theory, Collings was trying to make out that father and son had got on badly or in a distant sort of way. I told her different and thought she seemed to notice. At the end we fixed that I should come and see her at the hospital in a couple of days, Nowell too perhaps.

Back in the office I went straight to something the improvers had unaccountably overlooked, a boxed-in part where you could make phone-calls in private. It was the Sundays' day off and I got Susan at home. Just having her at the other end listening put a lot of things right. She agreed to keep a careful look-out for twitching females with cider-apple accents.

I hesitated a moment over the next, but quite soon had Nash on the line reassuring me it was all right to call. I passed the news about Dr Abercrombie.

'Oh,' he said quietly. 'A small one, you say.'

'That's what I was told. By somebody calling herself Dr Trish Collings, who seems to have taken over from him. She's taken over my son, anyway.'

'*Oh.*' Quite a different noise, and followed by silence.

'Do I gather you know her?'

'I know of her.' A great sigh sounded in my ear. 'You do realize, Mr Duke, that medical etiquette is unmistakable and strict on the point that no practitioner may say anything derogatory about another, or more accurately anything at all beyond the barest facts. So I won't. Say anything at all. For now.'

'I see.'

'She'll probably ask you a lot of questions about yourself. Oh really. M'm. Well, it can't do any harm to answer them. I suppose she didn't say anything about those tests I asked to have done on your boy. No. Of course everything takes time these days. Er, now I come to think of it there's another fellow in that hospital I have some acquaintance with, at least there was two or three years ago. More like five. Fellow name of Stone. He's . . . different from the . . . from Dr Collings. I'll get after him and tell you what I find out. Cheer up, Mr Duke. The boy's quite safe in there.'

My third call broke the run of abnormal luck. Lindsey was out, not back yet. Where from? Sorry. I looked at my watch and thought. From what I knew of her she would look into her office if she could before going to lunch. As I rushed off to look into mine I wondered why it had suddenly got so urgent to see Lindsey in the flesh, too urgent for any rubbish like message-leaving. Oh yes, she must not be allowed to go on thinking or suspecting that Collings and I were having an affair a moment longer than necessary, and stopping her had to be done face to face.

I had wondered whether Morgan Wyndham would be inquisitive or tremendously casual or just determined to delay me, but he was not even there. Only a major disaster could get me now, and before one could arrive I ran out. Rather than wait for the lift I charged down the stairs, along the street, across and along again, and almost banged into Lindsey coming out of the swing doors of her paper.

'Ah,' I said, feeling a great surge of relief. 'Are you lunching somewhere?'

'Yes, but I've got a minute. Right.'

She meant she agreed to a quick swallow in the pub next along but two, the one she and her mates always went to. Like all newspaper pubs it was nothing like the nicest in walking distance, not even the nicest a minute away, just the nearest. Inside, the noise from the people almost drowned the music. There was nowhere to sit, and there seemed to be nowhere to stand either, except in the hearth each side of an unlit gas fire. I bought drinks and carried them over, trying to keep them unspilled by moving three-quarters backwards through the customers, who were huddled along the bar three or four deep and shoulder to shoulder like a crowd waiting to watch a procession go by. The row seemed to have got worse since we came in, but it was too late to go anywhere else and the Crown and Sceptre would probably have been as bad by this time.

'How did you know how to find me?' shouted Lindsey, having sensibly held back till we reached this stage. Then she shouted something else I missed.

'Genius.' I found that at least I could put my glass down on the mantelpiece. 'I had to tell you – '

'Who was that madwoman you had with you just now? What the hell was the matter with her that she went on like that? Do you know your tastes are getting quite extraordinary.'

'That's actually what I came to tell you about, love. Listen, will you believe me if I swear something is true?'

'I might. Try me and see.'

'She and I are not, repeat not, having an affair.'

'Not . . . I've got it. Oh, you're not? She went on as if you were.'

And a sight less subtle on the subject than you were,

darling, I thought. I said, or rather bawled, 'That was just her, I've no idea what she was playing at. But surely you saw me going on as if I wasn't?'

'Well, you would, wouldn't you, in the circs?'

'Maybe. But it's not so, I promise you. It's *not so.*'

'Stanley, have you come all this way just to tell me that?'

'Yeah. Don't ask me why, eh?'

'Oh, come on. Between old friends. What makes you feel so strongly?'

'I just couldn't stand the idea. Of you making that mistake. She revolts me.' I had said the last part without thinking, and it was close, but still not quite right. 'You believe me, don't you?'

'I might if you tell me who she is. She obviously isn't anything to do with the *Chronicle.* I think I get full marks there for keeping my Irish temper in check and not retorting to the insult to my intelligence. And you'll have to tell me too what you were doing with her, and it had better be good.'

'Some check. You went for her like a bleeding pickpocket. Quite right, though, mind you. But what if she'd been on the point of buying an acre of space off me?'

'No serious concern would let a cow like that buy pussy. Fess up now, Stanley – who is she?'

'Who'd you think she is?' I said to hold off the inevitable.

'Christ, I took her for something you'd picked up when you were pissed and were desperately trying to ditch. You greeted me like a hundred-pound note. And then she buggered it up for you.'

'I never get as pissed as that. I wouldn't touch her with yours, if you know what I mean.' Again, true as far as it went. 'And I don't pick up anything when I'm pissed these days.'

'Tamed. Poor old Stan. Now . . . deliver.'

'She's the psychiatrist who's looking after my son Steve who's had a psychological breakdown.' On the way here I had reconciled myself to telling her that, though perhaps not to yelling it at her as I had had to do, but there it was.

'What?' She screwed her face. 'Sorry.'

'My son's in a mental home,' I roared, 'and she's the doctor.'

After a second of shock she laid her hand on my left shoulder and her head on my right. I put my arm around her waist and took her free hand. There was a short pause. When she moved back she looked at me in a kind way I had never seen before, miming the message that nothing much to the point could be said here and now. I nodded.

'Would you like to tell me about it? Some other time?'

I nodded again. 'I'll give you a ring. Thanks.'

Not long after that Lindsey took herself off to her lunch. I got hold of a Carlsberg Special Brew and tried for a cheese sandwich, but they only had Brie and French bread, so I took that. I ate it jammed in a corner with the plate under my chin taking alternate bites of Brie and bread because there was nowhere to put the plate down and spread the one on the other. Then I went back to the office and kipped for a spell in the library. Nobody ever disturbed you there.

I tried to get Lindsey next morning at her office, but she was out. So I tried to leave a message, but nobody knew how to find the person I could leave it with. I had another go in the afternoon, no more successful, and after that sort of gave up. In any case there was less incentive now, after the long cheering chat I had had with Susan the previous evening. On the Collings wordage she took the line that the jargon of any trade was likely to strike outsiders as crude and rubbishy.

'I'd try to forget it if I were you, darling,' she said. 'And the other thing of course is that some of the best people in their line are bloody hopeless when they try to explain it.'

'Yes,' I said, 'I thought of that.'

'You certainly get that with writers. There are all sorts of examples. Oh . . . Yes, Nabokov. You know, *Lolita*. Talks balls by the yard about what he does and yet he's an absolutely super novelist. Wait and see, that's the ticket.'

But when I got on to what I reckoned had been Collings's general approach, as opposed to just her style, Susan was less encouraging.

'What kind of theory?' she asked.

'Well, something like mental trouble being caused or anyway helped on by experiences in childhood, where obviously what the parents did or didn't do is important. I was reading an article by some American the other week that said something like that.'

'Some American will say anything, won't he, if you give him time. So Steve had a breakdown because you took no notice or the wrong kind of notice of him when he was little. Nasty as well as crap. Did she act hostile, this creature? Why aren't you drinking?'

'I thought I'd had enough for a bit.'

'Yes, I noticed you were rather pissed when you came in. You can afford to be a little more pissed than that after the day you've had. Where were we? Oh yes – hostile?'

'More clinical,' I said en route to the drinks tray. 'I don't want to say she was hostile when what I mean is I didn't like what she was telling me. No, but there were definite hostile bits.'

'You said she was sort of sexy but getting it wrong. Did – sorry, you must be fed up with answering questions, but did she . . . issue anything in the way of an invitation to you? It wouldn't surprise me, with such an attractive man.' She beamed at me.

I beamed back. 'Yeah, I thought so.'

'And I presume the lady received a dusty answer. You know when you were talking on the telephone I thought it sounded as if she was taking it out of you for something. I bet that's it. I bet that's it.'

'You seriously . . . you mean because she flies a little kite and I don't want to know, she decides to even up by trying to prove I neglected my son. My God.'

'Oh, I'm sure she didn't decide to do anything. None of it would have been conscious. She'd have said she was doing a perfectly ordinary piece of objective analysis. You know what women are like. You ought to by now.'

'Now I come to think of it she did remind me of Nowell. More than once. But I mean, my God.'

Then Susan said it was only a guess and went off to run up dinner. On further inspection I threw out her guess – doctors were trained not to behave like that. I held firm even though I had in my possession one solid piece of evidence in its favour that was hidden from Susan. It showed great powers of something-or-other to have got there unassisted by knowing about Lindsey's little demon-stration that she had a stake in me, which Collings could not have found at all funny. And I had probably made things worse by if not actually dribbling with lust then at least by making some sign that feelings were mutual. But that assumed that Collings was capable of . . . Sod it.

Actually I had shut up about Lindsey altogether, both today and last Friday. This keeping-dark was required anyway by the regular blanket ban on mentioning as much as the name of one female to another unless it was absolutely necessary. More than that, though, I had told Susan about the affair I had had with Lindsey pretty well straight away, in one of those fits of blurting that come over some men when they fall in love. In the telling I had made it as plain as a dozen pikestaffs that the whole thing had been over before I had ever met her. Never mind – my confession, which was what my harmless bit of reminiscing had turned into almost from the word go, ended up a disaster, needing a pair of Regency candlesticks and dinner at the Connaught. I had forgotten, or perhaps in those days had yet to learn, the rule about comparability, avoidance of. You can let on that you once slept with the richard who sweeps the floors and sells the french letters at the barber's or with a royal, and mostly get away with it, but not when it was someone they were at Oxford at the same time as, even if the two have barely set eyes on each other since. Except perhaps to announce her death I could never again mention Lindsey to Susan.

Over kedgeree and Spanish plonk in the kitchen I mentioned Nash and his reaction to the news of Collings. When I had finished my mention Susan said, 'Old Robbie telephoned today about something and I told him I'd run into a shrink called Nash, because the name had rung a faint bell in my head, and Robbie knew it straight away. Apparently apart from being very eminent in his field he made a terrific splash in the Fifties with a book for the general reader about madness in literature. It seems Cyril

144

Connolly raved about it, but of course he often . . . Anyway, Robbie said he thought he could get hold of a copy for me. Well, it's a fascinating subject.'

I could never have explained, even to myself, why it was that my general estimate of Nash, highish almost from the start and inclined to lift under the influence of today's events, took a small but sharp dive at this disclosure. Of course I kept my mouth shut about that. Later Susan played the hi-fi, Bach and then I thought Nielsen. Later still she did a marvellous job of impressing on me that I was not to blame myself for whatever it was that had happened to Steve. She had hardly started before I became too drunk to remember afterwards any of the individual bits, but the general effect lasted me well into the next day and even took some of the punch out of my hangover. Nothing actually happened that day – two men and a woman told me at different times that Thurifer Chemicals were staying with their half-page after all, and Trish Collings phoned me at work to make an appointment at her hospital at 9 the following morning. Nowell had promised to be there too, said Collings. Fat bleeding chance, I thought to myself, as regards your 9 a.m. anyway. And why 9 a.m., come to that? To show who was boss, said Susan, and I tried not to agree, because I had decided it was better all round to give Collings the benefit of any doubt. Well, almost any.

An alarm phone-call woke me at 7. My first action after ringing off was to grab the usual large jug of water beside the bed and take a hearty gulp. This turned out too late to contain some live creature which had no doubt fallen or flown there, not long before, probably, because to judge by the results inside me there was still quite a bit of flight left in it. I stumbled out of the dark bedroom and hung over the wc for a minute or two, thinking very hard about not being sick and impressing on myself a fact learnt in childhood, that there was enough acid in my stomach to burn a hole in a carpet.

After some long, unaffected groans, a go with the tooth-brush and a hot shower with shampoo I felt very tired. Nothing occurred between then and the time I left the house that would surprise anyone who has ever got up in the morning in London or a similar place. When I took Susan up a cup of tea she again offered to come on the trip with me and I again thanked her and said there was no need.

It was raining busily away when I started on my dis-agreeable journey. I took the Apfelsine through the middle – straight down the hill, along past the office, across Blackfriars Bridge, to the Elephant and into the Old Kent Road. Very likely other routes would have been cleverer, but that morning the thought of even trying to be clever seemed dreadful, not to be borne. At first the traffic was so light that I looked like getting there in about ten minutes, but then an almost stationary Belgian container-lorry, stuck trying to back into a side-turning and so gigantic it must have been built for laughs, put my mind at rest. South of the river I was on home ground, or not far off. By the time I got to New Cross I had come to within five miles of where I had been born and brought up.

For all I knew, this part and that part had been different then, built at different times with different ideas, anyhow not interchangeable. That was no longer so, if it ever had been, unless perhaps you happened to have an eye for churches. Not that I cared, of course – I had left South London for good as soon as I had the chance. And yet in a sense what I saw from the Apfelsine was the same as ever, was cramped, thrown up on the cheap and never finished off, needing a lick of paint, half empty and everywhere soiled, in fact very like my old part as noticed when travelling to and from an uncle's funeral a few weeks back. Half the parts south of the river were never proper places at all, just collections of assorted buildings filling up gaps and named after railway stations and bus garages. Most people I knew seemed to come from a place – Cliff Wainwright and I got out of an area. This might have spared us various problems.

On Shooters Hill I picked up a sign for St Kevin's and was directed across some strikingly unrepulsive parkland through a couple of open gates in a low red-brick wall surmounted by railings. Following further signs I found myself winding through what added up to another park, though this one was in full fig with lawns, flowerbeds, shaped hedges and ordered groups of shrubs, all looking cheerful enough even if fairly well saturated just now. But most of the view consisted of houses, again in red brick, probably of the Thirties, and enough in size and number to shelter a great many people, in fact a small New Town of loonies and their attendants. That sounded like the sort of novel by a dead foreigner that got reviewed in the *Sunday Chronicle*, not with Susan doing the review, of course.

The car park was right at the end, at the back of a one-storey building with a husky-looking creeper trained along it. Having duly parked I walked round to its front, not hurrying because I was early and the rain had stopped for the moment. I turned the corner to find that an ambulance had drawn up outside the entrance and the two crewmen were helping down an old fellow who was going on like a madman in a Bela Lugosi movie. Shock-headed, wild-eyed, wrapped in a grey blanket, he was spreading his hands jerkily about in front of him as he shuffled forward, not actually screaming but crying out in a high wordless voice. The men told him he was fine and doing great. I was trying to look like a piece of the wall and had no idea how he saw me, but he did, and swung and swayed round.

'Hoo-oo!' he howled, pointing a shaky finger. 'Urhh!'

The men quickly soothed him and the younger one steered him through the glass door. The older one came over to me. He had a very long neck and small ears and was blinking and frowning.

'Nothing for it, just got to stare, have we?' he said hoarsely. 'Reflex action, is it? See a nut and goggle like a kid?' He gazed past me and let his lower jaw hang to help to show me what he meant.

'I'm sorry, I wasn't thinking, I was waiting to go in here myself.'

'I mean he's not a bloody freak, you know. He's a poor old man who's a little bit confused and a little bit frightened, and he don't need very ignorant people gawping at him, right?'

'Yeah,' I said. 'My son's in here somewhere.'

'Oh, well I expect you'll learn then, won't you?' He looked me up and down once or twice before letting me off whatever he still had up his sleeve for me, and hurried off into the building, stopping abruptly on the way to light a cigarette.

Something prevented me from following him for the moment. I stood muttering excuses and looking vaguely about, soon catching sight of someone in a white coat who peered out of the entrance of the house opposite, probably a woman, but the white brimmed hat like a cricket-hat made it hard to be sure. Two pairs of eyes met for I suppose two seconds, then the figure threw up both hands and waved them and started towards me, crossing the threshold on widely separated legs. That sent me indoors all right. There was a desk and a girl there, and the ceiling struck me as unusually low.

'I'm looking for Rorschach House,' I said.

She scratched her neck and said without looking up, 'This is it.'

'No really?' I had been fully expecting to be sent on a hike back to the front gate.

'It's over the door,' she said, sighing. 'Was there somebody you wanted to see?'

We went into that and I started walking down a narrow, dimly lit corridor with doors along the sides made from extremely cheap wood and the floor loosely spread with white cotton lengths like the ones decorators put down. I saw nobody and heard no sound before I knocked on a door of similar quality at the end of a section of passage. Like the others it had a number on it but no name.

On request I went inside, and nearly went straight out again on failing to recognize the female sitting behind the metal table with her back to the window. Then I saw that the dark-rimmed tinted glasses, swept-back hair-do and old-style office get-up belonged to Trish Collings – so too with a vengeance did the thin funny-shaped mouth, where I should have looked first. She held out her hand, which I shook, and asked me to sit down, which I did, on one of the kinds of chair you never see in a private house.

There was not much in the room, and nothing personal

or unnecessary, no photographs, newspapers, flowers, books except what looked like text-books and reference works, none of the usual desk-clutter. Except of course there was no desk either, just the bare table with a couple of files, a couple of wire trays, a couple of loose papers, a telephone, a canteen saucer for an ashtray and a white plastic institutional waste-paper basket. Not so much as a typewriter – but a small voice-recorder on a shelf. Strip-lighting gave an effect much more like daylight than any electric light ever did, and at the same time not like daylight at all.

Collings allowed me plenty of time to take this in by finishing, or so far just going on with, the letter or note she had been writing when I came in, my second reminder of the world of the cinema since parking the car. When the wall clock, one of the sharp sort with no face or hands, just figures, showed 09 11 she looked up and said, 'Mrs Hutchinson is late.'

'I know, it's incredible,' I said incredulously, 'I can't think what can have happened to her.'

'Usually on time, is she? I suppose with her – '

'No, I'm sorry, no, she isn't usually on time. She's always late, you see. It's because she's a . . . Er, I don't think we'd better wait for her. Tell me, how's Steve?'

'He's all right, he's quiet, no cause for alarm.'

'Can I see him?'

She hesitated. 'Later. For now you might answer a few basic questions.'

The basic questions started with one about the date of my birth, but its precise hour was not required, which ruled out the casting of my horoscope. They went on with ones about things like whether I had had a serious illness, all from what looked like some sort of form. Necessary for her theory? Possibly. Or then again she could have been softening me up for a sudden really rotten one slipped in after one about my grandparents. If so she had still not got to it when at 09 22 there was a knock at the door and Nowell came in.

She was smiling with demure triumph at having made it on time – well, 22 minutes late was on time unless you were going to start being foul to her. At 10 22 she would have gone on in just the same way, plus being ready, if anyone started being foul to her, to state wonderingly that she was sorry but she had been asked for 10 00. She had on a very upstanding kind of suit in some khaki material, and with her short hair reminded me of the ATS girls I had seen during the war. Collings got up and Nowell went across and I could have sworn they were going to kiss, but without going that far they made it clear enough that they got on famously together. Then they both turned and looked at me. I knew that look, I would have known it even if I had never seen it before – it was the look of two women getting together to sort a man out. And on the way here I had said to myself well anyway, it would be fun to see those two wills battling against each other. My trouble was that I kept mixing women up with men.

Nowell came conscientiously over and kissed me on the cheek. Then she went and sat down on a chair just like mine but ended up rather nearer Collings than me, underlining the two-to-one effect. Intentionally? Not a useful word when talking about Nowell.

'Well,' said Collings in chairpersonal style, 'let's get on, shall we? What I'm trying to do is put together an informal biography-in-depth of Steve so far. I've managed to get quite a lot from him – oh yes, it's not that difficult if you know what to look for – but I've hardly started on you and Stanley, Nowell. Let's go right back to the time he was born.'

She could have meant me but she really meant Steve. The first twenty minutes or so went suspiciously well – at least no physical blows were exchanged. Collings took quite a few notes, which reminded me that I had not seen her take any on the Monday. Nowell went on being conscientious, but in a different style. From the events of Steve's life up to puberty, such as they were, the talk shifted to parental relations. In general, had he got on reasonably well with his mother? On the whole yes, Nowell thought. Did I have any comment on that? No, that seemed fair enough to me. What about how he and I had got on?

'There again,' I said, all systems on full alert by now, 'I think reasonably well.'

'You confirm that, Nowell, do you?'

'I . . . think . . .' said Nowell, dripping with objectivity, 'I think . . . that that's putting it . . . rather too low. Stanley and Steve seemed to *me* to get on . . . considerably better than the average father and young son. In fact I'd go further than that. In *my* view the two of you had a . . . quite remarkably close relationship. Considering how little you saw of each other.'

I stared at her with a sort of grin. 'What? We saw a hell of a lot of each other. Don't you remember how every evening I – '

'It's perfectly understandable, darling,' she said, and gave Collings an I-told-you-so smile. 'Nobody's blaming you. As I say, it was a great success – you got on marvellously well whenever you did actually set eyes on each other. I often remarked on it at the time.'

'This is ridiculous. It wasn't like that at all. For instance, what about those weekends when I – '

'We have here the standard behaviour-pattern in the situation.' Leaning over her work-table and blinking her eyes pretty fiercely, Collings marked the important words by tapping on it with the butt of her black ballpoint. 'Again, it's the norm for young primogenitors with strong external drives, not necessarily producing negative effects.'

Something that might have been the strip-lighting was making a high-pitched humming noise. There was no view through the window, just a flat brownish surface which filled the space and was probably the outside of more of the building, and nothing on the walls, not even a calendar, not even a list or a timetable. All this and the grey paint on those walls made the room seem a long way from anywhere much, like a satellite tracking station in the Mojave Desert, say. I looked over at the two females and saw that, quite naturally really, they were looking at me, Nowell with a hesitant smile and her own, wider-eyed style of blinking, Collings with her usual mish-mash of expressions and what might not have been expressions at all. Much sooner than I had expected, the three of us had reached the point I had foreseen ever since this meeting was proposed, foreseen it intermittently and vaguely and yet with certainty.

Starting with the set of my shoulders, I did my best to look and sound like the very picture of meekness, goodwill, sincerity, tolerance, respect and disposition to admit mistakes, and lumbered off on what had to be done.

'Now I take it the reason we're all here is that we want to do the best we possibly can for Steve.'

'Of course we do, darling,' said Nowell reassuringly,

showing that she really was on her best behaviour, because I instantly saw that opening had been far from brilliant after all – I might easily have been getting ready to tick her off for being there for some other motive.

'For the moment I'm afraid I frankly don't understand just where our, er, inquiries are leading, but maybe I will later, and anyway I'm sure there's a reason and a purpose to them.' In the meantime I was pushing my hands down between my thighs and crossing both sets of fingers.

'You bet there is,' said Collings with a couple of peals of laughter.

I struggled on, addressing myself to her because I had to. 'Obviously, if – er, for the best results we've got to get as near the facts of what happened as possible, it's some years ago now and people forget things, of course they do. But, for Steve's benefit, that's all, Nowell is mistaken when she says I saw rather little of him during his childhood. I could give you the names of friends who would describe to you the situation as it was in fact. Neighbours, parents of school friends. Why, before he could walk I – '

While I was speaking, Nowell had been looking from me to Collings and back and giving little quiet puffing and grunting laughs. Now she said, 'Oh Stanley, you are being rather a bore, darling. You do go on, don't you? And there's no need to, you know. Okay, now it's come up you feel bad about having neglected Steve a bit. Forget it! Nobody blames you. It's normal, as Trish told you. It's all over. Past history, old boy. Now could we possibly all manage to be sensible and get on with the job, yes?'

Having been brought up not to interrupt I kept quiet, against my inclination, until the end of that. When I started, my voice sounded like something off very early radio, or disc, or cylinder. 'In this context I have nothing to feel bad about. It was you, not I, who neglected Steve. One instance. The evening I – '

'Stanley, please.' Collings had got to her feet, and I had to admit, very unwillingly again, that the old rough tones had some authority in them. 'Can I prevail on you not to conduct your private quarrels in this office?'

I said slowly and quietly, and as I guessed afterwards sounding this time incredibly sinister, 'That's not what I was up to, Dr Collings, whatever it may have sounded like to you. I was trying to get the facts straight, not very cleverly it seems, but surely . . . Now presumably you hold some theory or whatever you prefer to call it about the state people like Steve get into being something to do with the way their parents treated them when they were small. Fair enough. But a theory can only give the right answer in a particular case if the facts of that case are properly established. It will give the wrong answer or no answer at all if the information supplied is incorrect for any reason. So in the case of Steve, if the received information says that I – '

'Oh for Christ's sake,' cried Nowell after a leave-this-to-me look at Collings that went on for less than a second, 'Steve isn't a *case*, he's your son! He's a human being, not a bloody motor car! You and your information supplied and theories and answers, I don't know how you can . . .' Etc.

There had never been any hope at all for my side, from how far back you bleeding trembled to think, but in peace no less than in war hopeless efforts must be made. This one had been such a blow-over for the opposition that Nowell had had no need to send in the second wave by asking me why I was being so foul to her, nor Collings to hit me with science. Even so I continued to resist

155

sporadically as the story swept, or rather slouched, on. For instance what kind of school experience had Steve had? How did Collings mean? Had he been a success at school? No, he had not – he had left with a single 'O' level, in biology.

'Were you disappointed with that result?'

'Well I wasn't, Trish dear, I tell you frankly,' said Nowell. 'But then I don't happen to think exams are important. I think what matters is what a person's like. I know Stanley doesn't agree with me.'

'No,' I said, still quietly. 'I think both are important. Sorry, of course that's not agreeing with you. No, exams get you jobs, that's the point.'

'I must say I haven't noticed them getting youngsters much in the way of jobs in the last couple of years,' said Nowell in a concerned, caring voice.

Collings cut in before I could answer that, which was probably just as well. 'So you were disappointed with the result, Stanley. Did you let Steve see your disappointment?'

'You bet I let him see it. It was his second try. I wanted him to have another go, but they – '

'And had you put pressure on him beforehand to do well? Not only for that exam but for earlier ones too?'

'Yes I had. Of course I had. Short of tortures and death-threats, I'd better say. Plus rewards for success. If any.'

'It used to worry the poor little thing to death,' said Nowell.

'And when Steve didn't do well, you made it clear you were disappointed in him, you thought he'd let you down.'

'I was disappointed with the result. I don't think I gave him a bad time, I didn't say anything, but I didn't go round pretending I hadn't noticed either. Perhaps I was a bit disappointed, in him, but you get that. There were other ways he was so much more than I'd ever expected.'

'But surely you must have realized he wasn't academically orientated?'

'I could see he wasn't Einstein, but I still wanted him to do his best. Like English 'O' level. He sometimes talked of being a writer. You'd think he'd have had the interest.'

'Stanley's very keen on writing,' said Nowell seriously. 'His second wife's a writer, you know. She doesn't write a lot but she does write. And he sometimes writes himself, articles for the magazines about cars.'

To my surprise Collings seemed interested in this information and made quite a lengthy note. When she had finished doing that she pushed back her chair, which matched the table and had only one leg, and lit a cigarette. 'Of course with changing social conditions the elitist role of education is passing too.'

'Oh, yeah,' I said.

'Nowadays there's much more emphasis on the social function, training the kids to relate to each other and preparing them to take their places in the adult world.'

'At my school we got that thrown in, just by being there. We didn't attend classes in it.'

'No, and we can see the results, can't we?'

I thought about it. 'Can we?' She probably meant sexism and censorship and things like that.

'Don't you think it's at all important to help kids learn to express themselves and develop their identities?'

'Of course I do. I mean no, not really, and anyway I don't see how you teach that, and that's not what you go to school for. Any more than you join the police force to learn about community relations or whatever. You may pick up some of that on the side but the business of the police is to see to it that people obey the law.'

Nowell had been watching me in a furtive kind of way that somehow made it no more difficult for me or anybody else present to see that that was what she was doing. Other bits of her expression showed how she was slightly thunderstruck to see that her ex-husband was even more stupid or brutal or out of date than she remembered, or perhaps had been able to take in before. She took no interest in politics, but she had been to too many parties in Islington and Camden Town not to know that the idea of the police seeing to it that people obeyed the law, or doing anything really, was a very bad one. So she produced a hissing inwards whistle and gazed wide-eyed at Collings, who managed to convey that she too was shaken by my last remark before saying, 'Don't you find it rather revealing that you see fit to equate the educational process with the British police of the 1980s?'

'I don't myself. I can't see how I would, but I dare say you do. Except I didn't equate them, if the word means what I think it does. I was merely making a comparison on one point, not . . .'

I nattered on a little longer, but I had lost them again. Nowell did one of her controlled yawns, looked at her watch, bounced a hand over her hair-do. Collings pulled her chair back in to the table and put her cigarette part-way out in the saucer, getting it across that the enjoyable frivolous intermission was over and the serious work about to recommence. I wished Susan were there. She would have seen to it somehow that the story Collings went off with was a few kilometres nearer the truth. If that mattered.

So to Steve and sex. He emerged even to Collings as

hopelessly normal, standard, average. She rather surprised me by apparently finding nothing macabre in his slight but visible shyness with girls, not so much as a castration complex. Anyway, she gamely wrote bits down. Nowell came up with a few more of her own-brand facts, but all they did was fill out the picture of Steve spending his early years with his mother in constant attendance and his father at the office, out getting drunk and never remembering his birthday.

At no particular juncture that I could spot, Collings said that that was enough for today, put the top on her pen and gathered up her papers. Nowell glanced over at me. For once in our lives, it seemed to me we were both thinking the same thing, that some kind of round-up so far or tentative communiqué would be welcome. I knew enough about Collings to be reasonably certain that it would never occur to her to wonder whether Nowell and I might perhaps be thinking along those lines, so I spoke up.

Sure enough, Collings was evidently thrown into some confusion by the idea, but she made a quick recovery. 'Well,' she said, 'on the understanding that we're still at a preliminary stage and this is only speculation . . .' For the first time she was addressing Nowell and me more or less equally. 'What Steve needs,' she said slowly, sounding quite thoughtful, 'is to be accepted as he is, and not as other people might wish him to be. That's something that goes very deep in everybody, the need to be oneself. It takes precedence over almost all other drives. So . . . when it's frustrated, the effect can be devastating. Steve is suffering from years of being treated and responded to, reacted to, as if he were someone else, someone quite different, someone created by other people. What we're seeing now is his protest against that kind of treatment.'

By the end of that lot she had gone all the way back to talking entirely in my direction. 'Don't tell me,' I said, 'it's me, I'm the other people you're talking about, I'm the one who's to blame for the state he's in.'

'Please don't think that, Stanley,' said Collings, and Nowell put her head on one side and half-closed her eyes in a way that showed that she was against me thinking that as well.

'Why not, if it's true?'

'Thinking in terms of blame won't do any good. It won't help you to help Steve, which is what this is all about, after all.'

'I ought to have seen it coming, oughtn't I? All the time I was sending him to a private school and getting a tutor in and bothering him about his homework I was actually setting him up for '

'You did it all for the best, darling,' said Nowell.

'Oh, super.'

'I can tell you very seriously and professionally, and without any qualification that you're not to blame,' said Collings. 'Instrumental, perhaps. That's rather a different thing.' After a moment's hesitation she went on, 'I must say it would be a pity if you let concern with your own moral position get in the way of more important things,' and Nowell looked at the floor because she was afraid she took the same view.

'I'm with you there,' I said, and meant it. The trouble was that just then I could see no way of putting the idea of blame out of my mind whatever anybody told me. Without thinking I said, 'Not everyone whose father puts pressure on him to pass exams ends up with schizophrenia.'

'Of course there are other factors. Oh and by the way,

I thought I'd already made it clear that Dr Nash's diagnosis is quite mistaken, I'm sorry to say. If we must use these reductive terms, what Steve's suffering from is something we call a schizophreniform disorder, which may sound similar to you but I assure you is quite different.'

'Oh.'

Nowell did a little forward semi-circle with her head and said in a semi-whisper, 'Do you think I could possibly see him for a moment? Please?'

'Yes,' said Collings shortly. 'He's in Ebbinghaus House, which you'll see on your left as you make for the main entrance.'

'Aren't you coming, Dr Collings?' I asked.

'No, it's a rule of mine.' Again she hesitated. 'You may find some of his behaviour a bit unexpected. You know, unusual.'

'Un . . . usual?' repeated Nowell over a great surge of music on the inaudible soundtrack. 'And what exactly is that supposed to mean?'

For the first time a tiny rift could be seen in the idyllic relationship between those two. Collings said with her laid-on patience, 'Certain physical reactions that are often observed in cases of this kind but people in your position are unlikely to have come across. That's all.'

'What sort of physical reactions?' asked Nowell, taking a pace to one side to head Collings off if she tried to run out of the room.

'Eye movements, changes of expression and so on. Nothing gross.'

Nowell seemed satisfied with that. Collings indicated that she had gathered enough information to keep her happy for the time being. In the middle of doing so she threw me out completely by giving me a really powerful sexy look, one that almost qualified as a leer. At least that was what I took it to be, though given her skimpy control over her face it might almost equally well have stood for impersonal sympathy or moral disapproval. Not that that mattered much either.

A minute later Nowell and I emerged from Rorschach House, whose name was indeed over its door, into watery sunshine. I was again struck by how neat the whole scene was, too neat perhaps, obsessively so, the kind of loonies' garden this lot preferred to head-high grasses, holes dug in the ground and constant bonfires. Inmates strolled on the shaven lawns or walked up and down the weedless gravel paths. Well, I assumed they were inmates, but in these days of any old dress they could easily have been a convention's worth of forensic psychiatrists out for a breath of fresh air after a lecture. Somebody who looked straightforward was approaching, a tall thin woman with a froth of white hair, a tic, a frown and a mouth that moved vigorously, also, as I saw when she was nearer, a copy of the *Journal of Behavioural Psychology* under her arm, which I felt must have meant something, though I was not clear what. I was hungry and I was nearly sure I could have done with a drink, even at whatever time it was, not yet eleven.

'What an extraordinary woman,' said Nowell as we walked, referring I assumed to Collings. 'What did you think of her? Did you fancy her at all?'

'Good God no, and even if I did I wouldn't dream of laying a finger on a dodgy little bag like that.'

'You must be getting old, Stanley. You used not to be so particular. As regards dodginess, that is.'

There was a good deal I could have said on this subject, especially to Nowell, but I gave a peaceable grunt instead.

'I thought it was a bit thick, the way she went on about you being to blame for what's happened to poor little Steve. I hope you didn't take that too seriously.'

'Actually she went on rather a lot about me not being what you'd call *to blame*, didn't she?'

'Oh yes, but that was only what she said afterwards, you could tell she was really trying to blame you. I think that's really mean, it's bad enough to have your son have a breakdown without being told that it's your fault on top of it. Bloody disgusting.'

I moved my eyes to take in her face. Its thick-and-thin look was very much on view at the moment, plus a touch of generous indignation. There had been a time – I could remember it distinctly – when I would have at once asked her why, if that was her view of the matter, she had told Collings those lies about my having neglected Steve in his childhood, and would have been amazed when, instead of answering the question, she asked me why I had suddenly started being foul to her, what was the matter with me and the rest of the list. That certainly made me feel old.

'Well, whatever you may think of her,' she said, 'the bag fancies you.'

'Surely not.'

'Oh yes, darling, I'm never wrong about that kind of thing. So no wonder she gave you a bad time – hell hath no fury, no? Now I'm sorry, Stanley, but I'm afraid I've suddenly realized that after that grilling in that frightful room the thought of picking my way through a bunch of madmen to see Steve doing unusual physical reactions is just too much for me. I'm not like you, tough as old boots, I simply can't face it. Is that awful of me? I'd be afraid of upsetting him. I wonder, could you angelically give him my love and tell him I'll be over to see him in a day or two? And let me know how he is, yes?'

I said I would, and found myself going on to say, 'I should think probably one visitor at a time is as much as he can cope with at the moment.'

Nowell gave me a radiant smile, full of affection and gratitude, and kissed me warmly on the cheek. 'You are a nice man, Stanley,' she said, holding me at arm's length a moment and gazing at me. Then she was off with a spring in her step. I had been sweet to her when I could just as well – rather more easily, in fact – have been foul to her.

I remembered Cliff Wainwright saying once that women were like the Russians – if you did exactly what they wanted all the time you were being realistic and constructive and promoting the cause of peace, and if you ever stood up to them you were resorting to cold-war tactics and pursuing imperialistic designs and interfering in their internal affairs. And by the way of course peace was more peaceful, but if you went on promoting its cause long enough you ended up Finlandized at best. Calling this to mind now somehow helped me to see that Nowell's line on Steve's childhood came out of no sort of hostility, just self-protection, forestalment of the possible and well-founded charge that it was she who had done most of the neglecting. I had forgotten that her whole character was based on a gigantic sense of insecurity, not that remembering that had ever done me the slightest good.

Ebbinghaus House was more of a house than the other place, with two storeys and proper windows. Inside too it was laid out after a different mode. I went into a small ante-room with a linoed floor and a porter's cubby-hole behind a partition drawn far enough aside for me to see that there was nobody behind it. However, there was somebody in front of it, a young black man standing with his hands clasped together, I thought at first over his privates but actually, as a not very searching second glance showed me, just above them, for the time being at any rate. He was rolling his eyes, though not towards me, and opening and shutting his lips about every second. I decided quite quickly against asking him for directions. The partition and a board on an easel were covered with notices, but they all referred to places like bathrooms or the library or to amusements like chess and boxing. Boxing? Here?

I had just given the notices up when a middle-aged woman in some sort of overall and with a pleasant, capable look about her came bustling towards me out of a passage at the rear. I only got as far as drawing in breath to speak to her, because she shook her head at me and in a flash lay down on her back on the lino with her arms crossed over her chest, like a crusader on a tomb. So I stepped over her and left her and the black fellow to it.

The corridor here had a carpet running down it, one of a pattern my mother would have really liked, and a lot of rooms opening off it. Most of them in fact had their doors open to show quite nicely and brightly decorated insides, rather in the style of a mid-market boarding house in somewhere like Worthing or Hastings. Usually there were people sitting on the beds and chairs or standing, some chatting, some reading, some drinking from paper cups, but all the ones I noticed looked as though they were just filling in time and the rooms were parts of one large waiting room – half of them glanced up and away again as I passed. None seemed in any way mad. After going round a couple of right angles and through a kind of arcade of dispensers of soft drinks, hot drinks, peanuts and bubblegum I came to a doorway beyond which a female sat at a desk with papers and telephones on it.

She leaned over slightly in my direction. 'Can I help you?' she asked, meaning what the hell was I doing there and making me wonder whether she had nipped down here from behind the Rorschach House desk.

'My son is a patient here,' I said, and gave his name.

'Wanted to visit him, did you?'

'If possible. Dr Collings said I could.'

The girl, in her middle twenties with pale hair and a great many moles on her face, consulted a list at her side. 'Stephen Duke, was it?'

'That's it.'

'He's in one of the rooms upstairs.' This too seemed to mean something more or other than what it said.

'How do I get there?'

'By the stairs.' Before I was actually forced to ask another question she went on, 'Along on your left.'

I thanked her and she silently went back to whatever she had been doing before. The conversation had made me feel old again, also this time out of touch, high and dry, a survivor from a bygone era.

The stairs were indeed along on my left, a single steep flight ending at a closed door. Here a worryingly incompetent hand-lettered notice asked me to ring and wait. When I rang I heard a pair of feet running away from just inside the door to some remoter part. After about a minute, in other words a longish time, the door opened a few inches and stayed there while a high-pitched voice spoke in a very foreign language, angrily I thought. In the end the door opened properly and a male Asian stood there, Indian or Pakistani, small, middle-aged and without any expression at all. I explained my errand and whether or not he understood he let me in. I just had time to notice that this floor looked quite different from the one below, more like what I had seen of Rorschach House, when he showed me into a small room containing four beds. Three of them were empty and made up and the fourth had Steve in it.

Steve was apparently asleep. He was rather pale in a sort of transparent way. When I said his name his head made a sudden twisting movement and his eyes opened, though if he recognized me he gave no sign. He began to sit up while his head and neck went on jerking sharply backwards and to one side in a way that must have been most uncomfortable, if not painful. His eyes focused on me again for a few seconds, but then they rolled up and sideways in the same direction as his head, which soon followed, along with the shoulder on that side. I said his name again, louder, and he said something back, or perhaps just made a noise, a distressed noise. When he had been taken by another, more marked spasm I hurried back into the passage and called for a doctor.

The Asian put his head out of the next room but one to Steve's. 'Yes?' he said, not sharply, not kindly or in a concerned way either.

'Would you come here, please? Something s wrong.'

He frowned and put his head back in for a moment before emerging and moving towards me carrying a millboard with papers clipped to it and followed by a Caucasian girl of about thirty in a uniform with something that looked like an officer's badges on the shoulders. When the three of us got to Steve his tongue was sticking out quite a long way. The Asian nodded his head as if satisfied.

'What's the matter with him?' I asked.

'He is suffering from schizophreniform disorder.'

'Yes, but does that cover these . . . whatever they're called . . . colossal twitches? Are they all part of the disorder?'

'They're normal.'

'*Normal?*'

'Normal for the patient at this stage.'

'Well, what's he doing in bed? Is that another part of the disorder?'

'He's in bed because he prefers. He spends a very great deal of his time there.'

'But he's much worse now than he was when he came in. He reacted to his name but I doubt if he knew me.'

'In some respects he may indeed be worse.' The Asian spoke with a touch of impatience. 'That too is not uncommon.'

'But what does he . . . Does he go on like this all the time? How does he get to sleep?'

'No no, it's intermittent. It may be brought on by some sudden change in environment, some unexpected thing. Some unwelcome thing.' He was staring at me.

'Like his father coming to see him?'

The fellow did a sort of shrug with his face and looked away.

'Oh my God,' I said.

'Now I'm going to try something.' The Asian took a pace towards Steve. 'Stop that! Stop what you're doing!'

Obediently Steve relaxed almost in the act of twitching and his tongue crept back between his teeth. He caught my eye briefly, then drifted away.

The Asian sniffed daintily. 'It's nothing so terrible. Mainly a matter of attention-seeking, you see.'

At my side, the nurse or more likely sister made a small sound or movement that might have meant she disagreed. She was dark and serious, not pretty but wholesome-looking. Also sympathetic in manner.

'Attention-seeking?' I said.

'Yes, er, my colleague Dr Collings and I agree between ourselves that that is the main thing that the patient is doing, namely seeking attention, though not necessarily in any planned, purposive way. As you yourself saw, the behaviour there is under his control. He can pull himself out of it if he so desires. To my mind, to *my* mind, that rules out the possible alternative explanation, that what we are witnessing is catatonic phenomenon. When he feels a little more relaxed and confident, when he realizes he's in good hands, then we shall see a very great change for the better. Oh yes.'

It struck me that this Asian, quite apart from being an Asian, looked tremendously unmedical, much more like a bloke in charge of loading stuff on to a ship or train, not necessarily in this country, what with his khaki-style shirt worn outside his matching trousers, the row of pens in his top pocket and of course the millboard. Steve, sunk back on his pillows, seemed completely apathetic, more than half asleep. From the sister I got the message that she was going on disagreeing with the doctor.

I said without thinking much, 'It's not his way, trying to make people notice him. He's always been one to keep himself to himself.'

There was a colossal click from somewhere, a roaring whisper and then a loud boxed-in voice that said, 'Dr Gandhi to B1, please. Dr Gandhi, B1. Thank you.' Then a silence that was a bit like being slapped lightly across the face.

I reckoned it was just what you might have expected when the doctor in front of me obviously took his message to refer to him and without hesitation, or anything else, left the room. The sister at once turned to me in a friendly confidential way.

'There's no need to be actually alarmed, Mr Duke.' Her voice sounded like nothing in particular, which was a relief. 'I couldn't have said this in front of Dr Gandhi, and perhaps I shouldn't be saying it to you now, but I've seen patients with those symptoms before, and attention-seeking may come into it, I don't know, but what they mostly are are side-effects of drugs. You see, he's had big doses of this powerful tranquillizer which have certainly tranquillized him all right, but they've also given him those involuntary movements you saw.'

'But don't the others, Dr Collings and Dr Gandhi, surely they know about anything like side-effects, don't they? Or are they using some new treatment or something?'

'No, it isn't that, they know about them. They just haven't recognized them in this case. I mentioned them to Dr Gandhi, you know, said that was what I thought they were, and he said Oh no, and went on about attention-seeking, well, you heard. The thing is, Dr Collings thinks it's that, and Dr Gandhi, he always tends to agree with her. It's not easy for him. She rather . . . I can't say any more but perhaps I don't need to.'

I thanked her and said, 'I've just come from Dr Collings, and she mentioned these reactions, but she didn't seem to think they were all that important.'

The sister looked back at me without replying. She had very clearly defined black eyebrows.

'But those twitches can be no fun at all,' I said.

She nodded. 'And they'd start to clear up in minutes if the drug was changed, not the treatment, just the drug.'

'There's a Dr Stone here, isn't there? Couldn't he . . .'

'He's tried before,' she said at once, 'in the past, I mean. There's a limit to what anyone can ever do. Just, doctors have their patients.'

'I suppose so. But surely if – '

Between being ordered to stop by Dr Gandhi and a moment ago, about when I mentioned his twitches, Steve had hardly moved. Now, having slowly sat half up, he made a clumsy turning movement so that his legs dangled over the edge of the bed, and the twitches began again. They seemed worse this time, more violent, perhaps because in his unstable position they threw him about more. The sister put her arm round his shoulders and told him to stop in a firm and strict but not unkind voice. I said he was all right and similar things, rather like the two ambulance men with the old loony outside Rorschach House about fourteen hours previously. It had no effect, but just when his eyes looked ready to roll up and back in that unpleasant way the tension left him in a couple of seconds, the twitching stopped and he let himself be eased back into a more restful position under the clothes. He had always been a docile sort of chap and still was, even now he was mad.

Soon afterwards the sister went away, having assured me that these attacks would do no lasting harm and that his medication was bound to be changed soon. I wanted to stay and talk to him, but that was obviously not a good idea if I had set him off on a round of spasms just by turning up – perhaps it had been the sound of my voice that had done it again a minute before – so I left. When I inquired, Dr Collings was not in her office. Would I like a call to be put out for her? No thank you, I said, and went back to the Apfelsine and drove to work.

I thought it best to keep out of Steve's way, for the time being anyhow. Phone-calls told me he was satisfactory, nothing more. After turning it over in my mind for twenty-four hours or so I rang Nash. He listened to only a small part of my story before suggesting I might go to see him at noon the following Tuesday. When I asked if I could bring my wife he said I could if I thought it would help, making the helping sound a fairly remote possibility. It would have taken a good deal more than that to get me to leave her behind, not that I expected anything remotely like a replay of the morning at St Kevin's, but you never knew.

Down Rosslyn Hill we rolled when the time came in a brisk downpour. With her ideas about Nash as a literary figure Susan had dressed in a bit of her best in a check suit and black-and-white shirt, but I had allowed for that and knew that she was perfectly serious about whatever might turn up. At the lights at England's Lane I said, 'Have I ever told you about Don Barley?'

'I don't think so. Who's he?'

'Oddly enough, I was just coming to that. Don Barley and his mother lived next door but two to us in SW16 during the war. There wasn't a Mr Barley, I've forgotten why. I suppose things might have turned out different if there had been. I can't really remember what he looked like either, Don. I was only about five at the time and he was seventeen. Anyway, one day Don got a poisoned foot from cutting it on a tin or something. His mother fetched the doctor along. He did the necessary and said he'd be back Friday. He must have rubbed it in somehow that there was absolutely no need for him to see Don before the Friday, Mrs Barley being a bit of a fusspot. Well, Friday comes and the doc turns up, and he takes one look at Don and rushes out for an ambulance, and gets him into hospital right away. And he died there at nine o'clock that night – they hadn't got penicillin in those days, you see. His mother had noticed he was poorly, but the doctor had told her nothing needed doing till the Friday, and doctors (a) knew what they were talking about and (b) you did what they said regardless.

'I can't really say I remember that happening, any of it. I doubt if I was as much as five. But I remember very clearly my mother telling the story, time and again and always in a very horrified way. It was a rotten thing to happen all right, but she went on about it sort of more than that. It wasn't that we knew the Barleys all that well. My mum certainly didn't blame Mrs Barley or anything like that – she always said how awful it must be to have to live with it for the rest of your life. What it was, I think, I didn't see it at the time, actually I didn't see it in full until I started telling you about it just now, what it was, she realized that if it had been her and one of us she'd have done the same, or she easily might have done. My dad would have had more sense, probably, but only probably, and there again he could have been off on his travels. I'm pretty sure his Midland trip used to take the inside of a week. Just right, in fact.

'So if you should think I spent rather a long time making up my mind to get hold of Nash this last time, I don't say you do or you have or you ever will, but if you ever do, or anything else like that, just remember I'm a boy from sw16 whose parents were so much in awe of the doctor that they might have let him die of blood-poisoning rather than do what the doctor didn't order. I suppose I might have reacted against it, but I don't think you do with that sort of thing. Anyway I haven't.'

Susan put her hand gently over mine on the wheel. 'How dreadful.' She was nearly crying. 'Poor Mrs Barley. And I understand about your mother too. But as far as I'm concerned you can forget the rest of it, the last part of what you said. Remember I'm not like the others, Nowell and Trish Collings and the rest of them. I don't think things like that about you.' Now she was cheering up. 'With me you don't need excuses. I say, how terrifically Jewish that sounds, doesn't it?'

'*By* me would be even better,' I said, squeezing her hand. 'There must be an accident or a demonstration or something. They're not moving at all up there.'

But in the end we were being let into 100 New Harley Street at only two minutes past the hour. It was a big old place with eight doctors in it, if as I assumed they were all doctors. Nash's part was at the back, looking out on to a garden with a lot of trees in it now being rained on steadily. The room reminded me of a men's club in St James's, the sort where they keep out the under-seventies. Nash himself was got up in full professional gear, including a tie that was obviously the tie of something or other, no doubt for Susan's benefit, and the same could be said of his manner – bland, almost hearty. Not quite so obviously, but nearly, he found her a good deal better-looking than he had expected to, which I thought was a bit cheeky of him. Susan must have taken that in, though busy at the same time on the furniture, curtains, etc.

On Nash's suggestion I began again at the beginning of

the main Rorschach House episode. He seemed to be paying close attention, not interrupting, now and then holding his breath for a moment and letting it out in a kind of voiceless groan, either as a comment on what I was telling him or because it was a thing he did while he was listening. Susan never took her eyes off me.

When I had reached the schizophreniform-disorder passage near the end of Part 1, Nash came to life and said, 'Thank you, Mr Duke, I think perhaps I've heard all I require to know of that conversation. But you mentioned an earlier encounter with, with Dr Collings in – am I quite mistaken or was it in a pub?' He shook his head slightly once at what things were coming to. 'Can you describe that occasion to me? Not in full, please, just the general drift, or anything that impressed you particularly.'

I tried to oblige. After a minute or two of highlights Nash gave a faint whimper with his mouth shut, like someone taking a nap and dreaming.

'Would you mind,' he said, 'could I ask you to repeat that, Mr Duke? Your son is trying to – what was it?'

'To find out who he is.'

'That of course is an approximation, your paraphrase of a partial recollection of what she said.'

'Word for word, I promise you. Only half a dozen of them, after all.'

'I find that very difficult to believe.'

'It stuck in my mind the moment she said it.'

'Which doesn't mean I can't believe it, I just find the effort rather extreme. Just as – if you told me that a foreigner, say a Frenchman, had said to you, with serious intent as far as you could make out, er, "You English, you are so cold," or a writer, a novelist, a practising one, had solemnly assured you that his object was to strip away the smooth surface of things and show the harsh reality underneath, well, I would quite likely be sceptical, would I not, properly too. Then I might well reflect that somebody, some real person, was bound to pronounce those words sooner or later and it was just a question of waiting long enough and being in the right place at the right time. I'm sure you take the point.'

With a touch more than simple even-handedness, Nash delivered the item about the novelist to Susan. He would naturally have heard from Cliff Wainwright what she did and was, but even so there was more than a touch more than up-your-street to the way he handled it. She chuckled very prettily and did one of those little sweeps of the eyes showing polite sexual approval. All of which was perfectly fine with me.

'There are a couple of further comments I might make at this stage,' he went on. 'Schizophreniform disorder. The Collings woman gave you to understand that it was a condition substantially different from schizophrenia itself. This is not the case. The difference is no more than legal. She clearly, even she clearly agreed with my diagnosis but couldn't face letting you see that. I could have wished to be spared the insult of her confirmation, in fact the danger-flag, the, the, the *tocsin* of it. M'm.

'Now as to the matter of your son's, er, need to be himself, not what . . . other . . . people . . . want . . . him to be, this as the cause of his illness. That's rather surprising in a way. Not fashionable any longer. Nowadays it's more the sort of stuff peddled by quacks and gurus and social workers rather than psychiatrists. But it has the advantage of leading directly to attaching blame for the patient's condition to his parents or parent. Now any decent parent, almost any parent whatever, is going to be upset, harrowed, thoroughly daunted by that accusation and will show it, will very likely protest, make an issue of it, claim good intentions and so on, which leaves the way open to the supplementary accusation that he's allowing his own self-esteem to take precedence over his child's welfare. Checkmate. Or rather, one more to their side.'

I said, 'I didn't think I'd mentioned that part.'

'No, I don't recall your having done so.'

'So how did you . . .'

Nash went into an elaborate dumb-show, sucking in his breath, dilating his eyes, shaking his head slowly from side to side and turning his hands palm upwards on his lap. Then he caught sight of Susan and went back to normal in a twinkling. 'Oh, I've come across that sort of,' – here he faltered slightly – 'person before.'

'But why would anybody play a game like that?' asked Susan indignantly.

'I don't know, Mrs Duke,' he said, having done the first half-second of the dumb-show over again. 'I've no idea. Why anybody should behave in that fashion.'

'There you are,' she said to me, meaning she had been broadly right about Collings.

After waiting politely for a moment or two, Nash said, 'Following your . . . interview with Dr Collings you say you were allowed to visit your son. Tell me about that if you would.'

I told him, a selective version only because I found I had got a bit tired of telling people things. He listened as before, nodding every so often in an as-I-thought way. Susan was as before too.

'This other doctor you saw,' he said firmly. 'Dr Gandhi? Was he, er, did he, er, an Asiatic I take it.'

'Yes.'

Nash sat on for a long time behind his desk without saying anything. He might have been trying to make up his mind to say something he had on the tip of his tongue, or just as likely wondering what was on television that evening. If it was the first he never got there but woke up suddenly and said, 'I can't tell you that your son didn't resent your arrival at the place where he was, I can only tell you that his distressing behaviour wasn't caused by anything of that sort. As Dr . . . *Gandhi* must have known.'

'What?' I said, totally baffled. 'Why did he say it was, then?'

'Why? You'd been making a nuisance of yourself, hadn't you, asking questions and generally using up time he could have spent reading his sex manual. A brilliant method of getting you out of the way.'

'But a doctor doing a thing like that, even a – '

Nash interrupted me by sighing theatrically. 'I've noticed, Mr Duke, I've noticed before that you have an exaggerated respect for doctors. Before it's too late you must learn that doctors are no better at doctoring or about things to do with doctoring than . . . m'm, motor-mechanics are at what they do.'

'Oh no. You don't know what you're saying.'

'The point is clear. Now. One would have to see him to swear to it but I'm sure, h'm, that your son's discomfort was the result of large doses of one of a group of tranquillizing drugs. Not nice to see, no, but . . . no actual harm, the sister was right there, and of course he won't remember any of it when it's over. Anyway, don't worry, I'll get it changed. Yes, I'll just tell Dr Collings. After I've had a look at the boy, naturally.'

'But then she's bound to know I've been on to you, and I thought you weren't supposed to . . .'

'There's nothing to prevent me visiting my patient in hospital, and I also intend to follow up the matter of the tests I asked for, none of which have been carried out, perhaps needless to say, or at least I haven't been told of the results. And then you see I can suggest things to the doctor in charge of his case. And as regards medical etiquette, allow me to tell you, Mr Duke, I'm too old and rich and powerful and fed-up to be unduly swayed by that. You can go straight from here to the Collings woman and tell her I have told you I consider her to be a disgrace to her profession, which incidentally would be saying something, and I won't *turn a hair*. Not that you would of course.' He had got up as he spoke and stood now over his desk with his knuckles resting on its top, as though he expected to have his photograph taken. 'Would you care for a glass of sherry? Mrs Duke?'

'Well, yes, thank you very much, Dr Nash,' said Susan, sounding slightly astonished as well as pleased.

'Mr Duke?'

What Mr Duke would have cared for at this stage was a small tumbler of absolute alcohol, but he had the sense to see that it would not be available and said Yes to the sherry instead. This came out of a cut-glass decanter that came out of an expensive rosewood cabinet with an inlaid top. Some digestive biscuits came too, in a silver-bound barrel, but there Nash must have been joking. Now the room seemed like a don's study in one of the snootier colleges at Oxford or Cambridge. There were certainly plenty of books. Most of them were across the room from me and the light was none too marvellous, but from the look of their jackets a lot of them were not on psychiatry.

I saw Susan giving them a good going-over during the sherry production.

By the time we got to my turn what had been a consultation or something like that had started to turn into something else. Before it could finish doing so I said, 'If my son gets taken off the drug he's on, what sort of happens after that?'

'Of course. Oh, he goes on to another tranquillizing drug that doesn't have the effects you saw but works in the same general way, acting on the so-called neurotransmitter system in the brain and in a great many cases, as I told you, bringing about positive improvement, it's not known how or why. But it does frequently happen.'

I tried to take this in. 'So Dr Collings is aiming in the right direction, so to speak, but so far she's missed the bull's-eye.'

Nash nodded, swallowing sherry. 'Broadly, yes. There's not a great deal of choice in the matter. Electro-convulsive treatment – not much help to us, except with patients so far gone in withdrawal that they're in danger of dying of hunger and thirst because they can't be bothered to eat or drink anything. Neurosurgery – obsolete. Psychotherapy, which is talking to the patient and getting him to talk – appallingly difficult, with the risk of encouraging him to elaborate and naturalize his fantasies. Troublesome, too. Group therapy – useless in my view, likely to be popular with Collings, no matter, harmless as well as useless. Anyway, drugs are easiest and most effective. There we are.'

'But she has all these terrible ideas,' I said.

'Has she? I mean I too think they're terrible, perhaps even more . . . passionately than you do, Mr Duke, but I wonder to what degree she can be said to have them, to hold them. They're to her taste all right, obviously, but then she must hold some ideas or views, or must seem to, to, to do so. It would be virtually impossible for a woman, an individual of that type to say to you, "Your son has schizophrenia, just as that old man said and as any qualified observer could have seen. I'm giving him a lot of drugs to try to make him better. And that's'that." Wouldn't it? Be . . . So she told you your son was trying to find out who he is and a great deal more in the same strain.' He spread his hands in the air.

Susan gave me a cheerful look that said she and I had never thought of that. I wondered.

'There's also the point,' said Nash, 'that, assuming she takes a similar line when talking to your son, going on about his efforts to surmount the difficulties imposed on him by other people, all that, she'll be likely to acquire his confidence, which will tend to reduce his anxiety. However unfortunately in other respects, she is, well, on his side. A supportive approach, as the trade odiously calls it.'

Susan was showing more signs of relief. 'I see that, yes.' I saw it too, and tried to feel relief, but mostly what I felt was a slight sense of being conned. I realized I had hoped, and almost expected, that after listening to my tale with mounting horror Nash would grab the phone or even go tearing out of the building as the first step towards getting Steve out of Collings's clutches and under the care of Dr Stone or some other angel of mercy. All right, not on, but I found it hard to swallow the idea of Collings as a well-meaning blunderer with a duff line in conjuror's patter. At the same time I was reflecting that here I was after twelve years' marriage to Nowell still assuming that unless people were actually lying they meant what they said.

'Is that all?' I asked Nash.

He gave me a sharp look. 'Nearly all of this section, Mr Duke. For the moment I've only one more question for you. Which of the following, if any, would you apply to your son's disposition? Cut off, dreamy, diffident, unintimate, unsociable, solitary, moody, touchy, uncommunicative?'

'Diffident,' I said. 'And a tendency to be dreamy.'

'None of the others?'

'No.'

'Not uncommunicative?'

'No.'

When appealed to, Susan agreed that that was fair. There was no sign that this registered with Nash, but he did come round again with the sherry, which she turned down and I accepted. When he had finished with that he half-sat, half-leant on the side of his desk. I thought he looked clever, grim and crafty, also uppercrust.

'The trouble with discussing schizophrenia,' he began – he was obviously just beginning, 'is that almost nothing is known about it after seventy years of study by some very intelligent men, and a great pack of blithering idiots too, of course. Some of what is known isn't very helpful, for instance you're more likely to develop it if you were born early in the year. North of the equator, that is. The helpful parts are elementary and mostly negative. Schizophrenia is an illness, one in which the brain becomes disordered. The cause has not yet been established, though there's quite a long list of things that don't cause it, like cell senility as I suppose they have to call it, and food allergy and any sort of virus, and anything to do with society. For a time it was thought to be tied up with

182

unhappy families, until someone noticed that there were lots of unhappy families in which nobody had schizophrenia. Heredity comes into it, though it's not known where or how.

'As I told you, Mr Duke, the subject fascinates me, but not as anything but itself. It leads nowhere. All schizophrenia patients are mad, and none are sane. Their behaviour is incomprehensible. It tells us nothing about what they do in the rest of their lives, gives no insight into the human condition and has no lesson for sane people except how sane they are. There's nothing profound about it. Schizophrenics aren't clever or wise or witty – they may make some very odd remarks but that's because they're mad, and there's nothing to be got out of what they say. When they laugh at things the rest of us don't think are funny, like the death of a parent, they're not being penetrating and on other occasions they're not wryly amused at the simplicity and stupidity of the psychiatrist, however well justified that might be in many cases. They're laughing because they're mad, too mad to be able to tell what's funny any more. The rewards for being sane may not be very many but knowing what's funny is one of them. And that's an end of the matter.

'I consider you should know of these matters. Think of your son's illness like a physical illness of the dullest and most obvious kind, after which he may be restored to you undiminished, healed, healthy, or he may be more or less impaired, and the process may be a long one. Meanwhile I'll see to what has to be seen to.'

'Thank you, doctor,' I said, and stood up. At the same moment he looked at his watch and then at Susan.

'I was thinking, if you're not doing anything special for lunch,' he said, looking at me now, 'you might let me take you round the corner to my local, my local restaurant. It isn't awfully good but at least it's pretentious, with the added merit that at this sort of time of day you can just walk in. And from here you can walk to it as well. Two minutes away. It's stopped raining.'

Not for me, in line for a couple of stiff quick ones and a sandwich in Fleet Street followed by a slog in the office. I drew in my breath to explain some of this, caught Susan's eye and said, 'That's very kind of you, we'd love to.'

Nash was delighted. He went and helped her on with her mack as though nobody else knew how to handle a thing like that. She played up to him about the proper amount.

'I see you're an Anthony Burgess fan, Dr Nash.'

'Yes. I find him a very interesting writer.'

That was it. Susan said, 'I didn't notice a copy of *Don Juan and the Lunatics*.'

'Oh, that,' said Nash, pretending not at all strenuously to have nearly forgotten what I took to be the great work on madness in literature, its title now successfully researched. 'Out of print for many years.'

'I'm ashamed to say I've never read it. In fact I don't think I've ever set eyes on it. I suppose there isn't a copy I could borrow?'

'I may have a spare somewhere, I'll have a look. But, er, you mustn't expect too much, you know. I'm afraid you'd find some of the literary judgements ill considered. Where they're not painfully obvious.'

'Oh, I doubt it.' She seemed to think he was a tremendous old tease to say that, then immediately went serious. 'But after what you said just now about mad people being incomprehensible and madness not telling us anything about the human condition, which I thought was absolutely fascinating, well, I just wonder what's left, what you found to say in your book.'

'Internally, in itself, madness is an artistic desert. Nothing of any general interest can be said about it. Like sex. But the effects it has on the world outside it can be very interesting indeed. It has no other valid literary use. But that's by the way. My subject was just how well or, mostly, how badly writers have described madness. As a gardener or a cook might with their speciality. A medical doctor.'

'Mostly badly?' asked Susan in a companionable way.

'Yes. A fellow wants to put some madness into his novel because it's strange and frightening and quite popular. But if he bothers to go into the reality he finds it's largely unsuitable, an unsuitable topic for his purposes. So he gets hold of a pamphlet by some charlatan or crank propounding a suitably colourful fantasy and makes a character kill his wife because he's got an Oedipus complex, or find he's strangled a prostitute while under the impression he was a Victorian sex murderer. Which may be great fun but makes it hard to take the thing seriously. I mean you wouldn't have much confidence in Graham Greene if he tried to tell you Haiti was in the Mediterranean. Good morning.'

The last bit was said to a waiter, because here we were in the restaurant, which at this first sight looked quite modest to me, but then probably Nash was better at detecting pretentiousness than I was. I rather handed it to him for making no bones about enjoying the way the head waiter and the manager practically carried him to his seat at the best table in the place. He had put my mind at rest here and there, and I reckoned I bought his general approach, but I would have had a little more time for him if he had gone pounding off to see after a patient of his in some distress instead of going out to an elaborate lunch and flirting mildly with the patient's stepmother. Still, that part was very likely just me being mildly jealous. And I could see a large whisky coming straight at me.

'Hasn't anybody got it right?' asked Susan when we had ordered. 'Describing madness.'

'Shakespeare got it right. Lear, of course. Cerebral atherosclerosis, a senile organic disease of the brain. Quite common in old age. Periods of mania followed by amnesia. Rational episodes marked by great fear of what he might have done while manic and great dread of the onset or renewed onset of mania. That way madness lies – let me shun that – no more of that. Perhaps even more striking – Ophelia. A particular form of acute schizophrenia, very thoroughly got up – young girl of a timid, meek disposition, no mother, no sister, the brother she depends on not available, lover apparently gone mad, mad enough anyway to kill her father. Entirely characteristic that a girl with her sort of upbringing should go round spouting little giggling harmless obscenities when mad. In fact it's such a good description that this . . . subdivision of schizophrenia is known as the Ophelia Syndrome even to those many psychiatrists who have never seen or read the play. He was content just to describe it, you see. No theories or interpretations. Oh, she says and does plenty of things that mean a great deal to the other characters and to the audience, but she doesn't know what she's saying or doing or who anyone is, because she's mad.'

Our starters came then and I thought we might have heard the last of the topic, but not a bleeding bit of it. I had no great objection to Shakespeare as an author – it was just that I thought he was rather far back as something to talk about over lunch. Also I reckoned I had learnt enough about schizophrenia for one day. Anyhow, in less than a minute and without waiting to be asked Nash was off again.

'The play's full of interesting remarks about madness, among other things, yes. Polonius. A rather underrated fellow in my opinion. To define true madness, what is it but to be nothing else but mad? Not bad. Not bad at all. Not a complete definition, but an essential part, excluding north-north-west madness. Later in the same scene, you remember, he has a chat with Hamlet, the fishmonger conversation, and is made a fool of – the very model of a dialogue between stupid questioner and clever madman as seen by that, er, that, er, that unusual person R. D. Laing – you know, *The Divided Self* and all that.

'But actually Hamlet's only *pretending* to be mad, isn't he? No problem scoring off the other chap if that's what you're up to. Polonius gets halfway to the point. How pregnant sometimes his replies are, he says, a happiness that often madness hits on, which reason and sanity could not so prosperously be delivered of – a remarkably twentieth-century view. If he'd paused to think he might have found it just a bit suspect. But Hamlet in general very cleverly behaves in a way that lay people who've never seen a madman expect a madman to behave. Ophelia doesn't go mad till Act IV.'

The two of them went on having the time of their lives, working their way through Gothic novels and then Dickens, who either left mad people out altogether or was no good at them, though evidently terrific on neurosis. There was something about King Charles's head.

*

'Penangan High Commission, good afternoon.'

'Good afternoon,' I said, and went on to say who I was. 'May I speak to the Commercial Attaché?'

After a moment I heard the dying-away of a phone bell and after a longer moment a hollow voice that said, 'Yes, hallo, yes?'

I said who I was again, but there followed only a rumble that might or might not have been human, followed by more silence. 'Hallo?'

The man – I assumed it was a man – at the other end breathed out heavily a couple of times. 'What . . . do you want?' I could not help being impressed by the quantity of both fear and menace he managed to pack into those four simple words, with a bit of despair added on.

A certain amount of despair came over me as I sweated away at explaining what I wanted, talking about report, supplement, feature, advertisement, publicity in the hope of grazing the target with one of them. Eventually I just ran out.

Another rumble. Then, 'When were you speaking of this before?' I gave the exact date and had hardly got it out when he came back, 'No no, finish, all done, cancelled, cancelled.'

'Does that mean your Minister of Trade has – '

Dialling tone. I rang the High Commission switchboard again and established quite easily that, as I suspected, I had been talking not to my pal Mr One but to his rival or replacement, Mr Two. Mr One had presumably returned to Penang, then. Not yet, said someone on an extension, he was in consultation with Mr Two but was not available.

Cheers most awfully, I thought. Win some, lose some. Well, lose some, certainly. Not that it really mattered, but it would be nice to have something go right for a change. I hoped slightly that it had been panic rather than fury that had made Mr Two bang down the receiver on me.

It was quite late and I was quite tired. I had had another early morning over at St Kevin's, where Steve had turned out to be in more comfortable shape, true to Nash's report the previous day that he fancied he had put the hospital on the right track. Good, but all the same I had found him, Steve, no more responsive than last Thursday, not really. He lay on rather than in his bed and now and then sat up on the edge of it while I talked, but that was all. Already, not nine hours later, I had a pretty poor hold on what I had taken quite a long time telling him, rambling recollections of holidays, places where we had lived or stayed, bits of school, that type of thing interspersed with even less reliable stuff about how nice the hospital seemed and the great strides made in medical science since the war. At just three moments altogether I thought he looked at me properly and perhaps recognized me, but they were only moments. In the room when I arrived, and still there when I left, there had been a small prematurely white-haired man in his forties looking out of the window and making the sort of little grunting, moaning, wincing noises that might have come from a chap watching something like a fist fight in which a friend of his was rather getting the worst of it.

I had made no move to see Trish Collings during my visit, in fact on my way back to the car park I hurried past Rorschach House with my head down. Not much digging inside it was needed to show me that I was afraid that, if I had happened to run into her, she would tick me off for having complained about her to Nash, or for perhaps having done that, which of course was just as bad. Old Don Barley up to his tricks again.

After staring at the wall of my office for some few minutes I left the building. Almost everyone not directly implicated in bringing the paper out had done the same. Quite a few of them would have made their way, as usual at this time, to the Crown and Sceptre. Apart from my own staff I had never known more than a few of them, even by sight, and none was visible now. I carried a large Scotch over to a stool so placed that I either had to face the wall or turn completely round each time I put down or picked up my drink. I solved that one by holding it on my lap.

The racket was colossal, not just a lot of people talking loud and fast but with a kind of ferocity to it I had often doubted if you could find outside Fleet Street. I would stick it while I downed this and another and then go home and take a bottle in front of the telly. Susan was out, spending the evening with her mother, though when she debriefed me earlier over the phone she had said she would not be back late. Still, on the whole things were well placed for Lindsey to make one of her unscheduled appearances. You could say too well placed. She had been on my mind quite a bit over the past days – I had been very touched by her kindly concern when I told her about Steve. Not only that, though. Anyway, it was not she who pitched up at the bar just when I was thinking of leaving but Harry Coote, my short, bearded editor. He looked at me for a moment in the way he had, without smiling or raising his hand or anything, as though he had found out from somewhere that it was quite funny not to smile or anything at times when other people usually did. Then he came over.

'Got time for one?'

'Sure,' I said. 'Large Scotch and water. No ice.' It would normally have been a gross breach of pub protocol to specify the quantity, but that protocol included the clear provision that it was all right to do so when there was a reasonable doubt whether a large one would come as a matter of course. And in this case there was reasonable doubt. But one way or another it was indeed a double that Harry rather grandly delivered to me before taking up a standing position next to my stool. He was short enough for his head not to be so very much further off the ground than mine.

'How are things?' he asked, quite audibly because the uproar seemed to have fallen off a bit.

'Fine.' I could very easily have told him about Mr Two, true, but I kept quiet.

'I suppose you haven't seen anything of old Nowell recently?'

This was routine, Harry playing himself in with me, or it always had been in the past. If it turned out to be different this time, if he started being wise or quietly sympathetic or anything else about Steve, I was off. I said, 'Yes, as a matter of fact I ran into her just last week. Had a nice chat with her.'

'Did you, now? Oh.' No, he had heard nothing. 'Tell me, how was she? How was she looking?'

'Great. She's unchanged, you know. Absolutely amazing.'

'Oh dear,' said Harry, shaking his head, his eyes gone glassy with wonder. 'Makes you think, doesn't it? She's all woman is Nowell, if you know what I mean.'

'I think so,' I said. I said to myself that if I hung on long enough he would tell me he had always thought it was a shame Nowell and I had not managed to make a go of things, but as it was he told me almost straight away and almost in those exact words.

After that he made a great business of lighting one of those rugged cheroots of his, peering at me every few seconds and generally behaving as though he had in mind some tremendously important project or request or revelation which he considered the time was not quite ripe for. This could still have been routine, though by no means a bit you took no note of. He asked after Susan in an intent sort of way, and seemed relieved at the news that she was very well, but I doubted whether hearing so was his whole objective. There was another of the same when he asked for and got my views on the Government's financial policies. After he had given me his I went and bought him a drink, a predictable vodka and tonic. It occurred to me that having a round of Harry's to return was indeed a rare experience.

At my return he intensified his weighty look, then switched off and said casually, 'Going to the Boxes'?'

'Eh? What sort of boxes?'

'Julian and Paula Box.' He seemed astonished when I shook my head in ignorance. 'I could have sworn I'd seen you there. They're on a barge. On the river.'

'Oh, yeah.'

'Why don't you come along? Drinks party. Completely informal. They're a very free and easy couple. Paula doesn't give a toss.' The noise had got up again and I missed the next bit, so he had another shot. 'I thought we could, er, I thought we could have a chat on the way, like.'

After weighing things up I said, 'All right. Where are we off to?'

'Got the car, have you? Oh it's,' he hesitated, 'it's out by Chelsea.'

'Chelsea? Not artists, these mates of yours, are they, or writers?'

'No, no,' he said reassuringly, 'they'll all be in accountancy and insurance and suchlike. No trouble. You'll enjoy yourself, Stanley. You see.'

Outside it was blowing half a gale but hardly raining at all, and there was lots of daylight left. All went well for a time, just one hold-up on the way down to the Embankment and no trouble after that. We slid along the river at a rate that left to itself would have got us to Chelsea in about five minutes, so I held back to give Harry a chance to finish talking about the World Cup and start recruiting me into MI6 or whatever it was he had in store for me. He was cutting it pretty fine, I decided, when we reached the corner of Tite Street and he had still not done with the referee problem.

'Where to now?'

'Well, I'm afraid I'm not much of a navigator, Stanley. Comes of not running a car, you know. The best plan is for you to make for Putney Bridge and we'll think about it there.'

You bleeder, I thought wearily. So much for Harry's famous lack of subtlety. Not that subtlety of a very high order had been needed to con Muggins into saving him the taxi fare to Walton-on-Thames or Reading or Oxford or wherever this perishing barge was going to turn out to be and back, not forgetting the time and difficulty that finding transport at the far end would have cost him in the ordinary way, all for the price of a large Scotch and a slice of somebody else's hospitality. But no getting away from it, I had wanted to come on my own account. It was years since I had gone to a party with any intention of picking up a girl, and a Harry-generation get-together was unlikely to feature many or any girls, just females, and I was someone's husband, but you simply never knew.

We came to Putney Bridge and thought about it, or Harry thought about it, and then we crossed over and went along the A205 until it became the A305, and not much later he made me stop while he thought about it again. After another couple of goes of this and only one wrong turning we reached a yard where a number of other cars were parked and drove in there.

The rain had finally packed up, the wind had risen a little if anything, the sun was shining low down through a hole in a great mass of black cloud and producing the rather unpleasant effect usual at such times. When we started walking there was no sign of the river, but it came into view at the first bend down a long alley. None of the buildings here had probably been touched since the beginning of the century, by human hands at least, though they had certainly got a great deal dirtier, slimier, damper, more battered and no doubt smellier in the meantime. Huge piles of rubbish smeared with oil, tar and soot, from postcard-sized pieces of creased paper to what could have been ship's boilers, went back about as far. I was expecting a trudge through half a mile of mud at least, but when we made it to the waterside there was gravel and then a paved strip, and a long college-type structure on the far bank really looked pretty good after all with the sun on it.

Four barges were moored in line in front of us, moving about quite a bit, it seemed to me, also faster than I would have expected, never mind preferred. Ours was evidently the second along. Harry moved ahead of me across a rope-and-board gangway, which turned out to be all right but not the sort of thing to make sure of not missing. I reached the deck successfully and found two lots of noise going on, a remarkably loud and varied mixture of creakings and groanings from parts of the structure and, further off, the gabble of a party into its second half-hour, loud enough for anybody but without the Fleet Street snarl. Following Harry I ducked through an opening, crossed a narrow platform and, still not too comfortably, went down a short steepish flight of stairs into what, but for the lack of windows, looked very much like the sitting room of a rather well-off house in North London. Clearly the Boxes were living here on purpose, so to speak, and had had the sense to rip out or plaster over every possible trace of what had been there before.

When produced by Harry, the Boxes turned out to be a bit of a mixed bag. He seemed perfectly sound, the kind of fellow who, one minute flat after the last guest had gone, would be in an armchair in front of the large TV set in the far corner, in fact by the look of him I thought he could have done with being there now. She let you know she was the one behind the party, as if you had been in any doubt, and behind a lot else as well, like them being on the barge in the first place. I was given a full and satisfactory explanation of that part and what it entailed.

'I suppose it's not often as rough as this?' I asked after a time. The movement had not eased at all since I came on board, indeed just as I spoke an old boy near by staggered and clutched at the woman next to him, burning his hand on her cigarette, but then he was drinking.

'No no no no,' said Mrs Box, frowning and shaking her head, 'it's only the turn of the tide. Either that or the wind blowing against the tide. Happens quite regularly.'

'Oh, well that's all right then.'

At that she screamed, or rather at that point she made the female sound meaning someone more interesting had appeared, and was away past me without a word or a look. I wondered whether this was her not giving a toss. I also wondered whether the general clearance as regards artistry and writing that Harry had given could be applied to her. She had the look of wondering whether to agree with some of the things you said, and not listening at all to others, that I had noticed in some of Susan's mates.

While I was wondering I took two glasses of Scotch and water off the white-coated waiter and made a drink out of them that was somewhere near what I would have poured myself at home. It lasted me while I made a thorough circuit of the scene that did me no good beyond what I got out of taking a pee in the very nice little toilet I found near what could have been the blunt end. The snag was not exactly that all the women were females, more that they all seemed to be wives or daughters, bar an aunt or so. And establishing the absence of anything pursuable or worth pursuing meant the party was a write-off, did it? Of course not, I could try and get a conversation going. Yes, about cars, golf, advertising, whisky or the price of onions. Oh, and women. Good God. Sometimes I wondered how Susan put up with me.

That last section saw me halfway into another jar. It would be easier if I found someone I knew, even Harry. Had he gone? No, there he was talking to a tall fat man who had his back to me but looked somehow familiar. When I got round to his front I found it was Bert Hutchinson. Yes, Harry and he shared a pub.

'Hallo, Stanley,' he said, and added 'Christ' when the floor dipped slightly more than usual and sent him lurching to one side. Again, the drink could have been helping, but he looked comparatively sober, more so than when I had last seen him, at least. 'You know, people can only take so much of this. If it goes on they'll be throwing up all over the bloody shop. Well, how have you been?'

'Not too bad.' I was going to move on as soon as I decently could, very soon, in fact. 'I haven't seen Nowell anywhere.'

'She's not here.' He spoke flatly.

'Stanley kindly drove me down,' said Harry.

Bert stared at me through his bluish glasses. 'What have you got?'

'Apfelsine. FK 3.'

'Oh, you have, have you? They're very quick, I'm told. What we used to call a quick motor. Dear oh dear.'

'Hey,' I said, remembering, 'haven't you got one of the first Jaguars? I saw it outside your place that time.'

'Yes. I have it, I own it, I possess it, and I derive from that fact such satisfaction as I am able. And that is all there is to be said.'

'How do you mean?'

'How do I mean? How – I beg your pardon, Harry. This is very boring for you. As a non-driver. Lucky man. Who doesn't know what he's missing. Unlike those who once upon a time . . . I'm sorry, I mustn't go on.'

'No really, Bert,' said Harry, who I thought looked a little bit tousled. 'Do carry on. It'll interest Stanley.'

Bert made a great growling noise and then stayed quiet for so long, looking towards his feet, that I started thinking he had forgotten all about whatever he had been going to say. With his head tipped forward like that he gave me a first-rate opportunity to inspect his scalp and the condition of the strip of hair he wore stuck down across it. I reckoned it, the strip, had become both narrower and less dense or luxuriant as the growth area above his left ear declined, but I would have had trouble remembering when I had last seen it close to. Finally he spoke.

'I suppose in a way I shouldn't complain,' he said wisely and like someone completely above the struggle. 'My generation received a wonderful gift – well, earlier generations had had it too, but in a less fully developed form. And the name of the gift was – motoring. For a few brief years after the second war and before the advent of the motorway and all the, all the *vile* things it brought with it,' he went on, in some danger now of losing his calm, 'it was possible to take an evolved automobile on to the roads of Great Britain and . . . drive, by what way and in what way, er, you could do as you liked. No longer so. No longer so. I *have* my Jaguar, I *own* my Jaguar, fuck, Jaguar, but I don't drive it. No sir. Not a chance. It's all over. Thing of the past. Ancient history. Now Stanley, you tell me, am I, has the, is that complete balls? Or what? You be the judge.'

'No, no, Bert, you're absolutely right,' I said. Well, I did think he had a point of a sort. 'All too sadly true.' Admittedly I could have done without the king-in-exile approach. 'Never again.' But it would have been unkind and perhaps dangerous to disagree with him. 'Absolutely right.'

He sent me a look that was not so much kingly as saintly, as though after that affirmation of mine he could face the lions with a quiet heart. Then his glance shifted and he nodded his head emphatically. 'I knew it. There goes one now. Told you, didn't I?'

I turned round in time to see an elderly man who looked like a retired ambassador, hand over mouth, making for the corridor that led to the toilet at an unsteady run that included a glancing collision or two with other guests. This caused comment.

'It could be just the drink,' said Harry, who for the last couple of minutes had been looking from Bert to me and back again in amazement at all this emotion he had had no suspicion of. He looked as if he thought he had missed something important in life.

Bert shook his head just as emphatically. 'Oh no. A fellow that age, he wouldn't be taken suddenly like that, the way a youngster might. No, that was motion sickness and no mistake. Look,' he said in some excitement as a similar chap, white-faced and staring-eyed, stumbled over to the foot of the stairs, 'there's another one. No doubt about it. Not that I'm feeling any too clever myself, let it be said. Ah, bloody good.'

This was addressed to the waiter who had just approached, or more likely was just a reflex reaction to the tray of drinks he was carrying. There were quite a few glasses of Scotch on it, but even so I would not have dared to repeat my tactics under these conditions if Bert had not poured one into another on the tray itself. I did the same. Harry took a white wine rather slowly.

'How did you get here?' I asked Bert.

'Taxi.' He pointed his head at my drink. 'Aren't you afraid of being picked up?'

'They'll get me in the end, I expect. But probably not in the middle of the evening, like eight o'clock, which is when I intend to be on my way. If that's all right with you, Harry.'

'Super,' said Harry unenthusiastically. He had put his wine down untasted and there was sweat on his forehead and under his eyes. 'Think I'll . . . have a pee.'

'You do that,' said Bert, and went on almost before it was safe, 'Right, let's bugger off.'

'I can't leave him, Bert. I brought him here.'

'You bet you did. But what of it? It may be a bit off the beaten track here but it isn't the middle of the bloody Sahara exactly. Three minutes' walk and he can get a taxi. Do the little bastard good. To put his hand in his own pocket for a change.'

'I thought you and he were supposed to be drinking mates.'

'*Christ*,' said Bert, but because the floor had misbehaved again. 'It's getting worse, it's like the Bay of bloody Biscay. I'm not going to be able to stand it much longer. What did you say?'

'He told me he sometimes saw you in some pub in Notting Hill.'

'Unfortunately he does. I grin and bear it. I'm not going to let a little sod like that drive me out of my pub, am I?'

'You were talking to him when I came over.'

'He was talking to me. He thinks he's a buddy of mine. And I don't seem to know anyone else here, except you.'

'Who invited you?'

'I can't remember. It wasn't Harry. Look, what the bloody hell is this, a bloody inquisition? You're like a bloody chick, you are. Actually it is quite interesting. I found I had this very neatly drawn map and all the details written out, you see, so of course I assumed it was them, the Boxes or whatever they're called, and I'd forgotten who they were. Then when I got here I not only didn't recognize them, but they didn't recognize me. Took some getting round, that. The missis turned quite stroppy. I had to tell her I was in TV to quieten her down. A right one, she is. Well, is that enough for you?'

'Quite enough, thanks,' I said. 'I'm going up top. I've got to get some air or I'll die.'

'I'll join you. I'll just get a freshener first.'

Closely following an elderly woman with an enormous backside under some ribbed grey material, I climbed to the deck. It was not quite dark, with hundreds of lights showing on both banks and a few more round me and on the other barges. Out here on the water it seemed very quiet, or it might have done but for the long hallooing retches that came from somebody up at the far end. Half a dozen other figures leant or slumped at various points. I found a secluded spot and had soon taken in all the air I could handle. Having done so I felt just slightly worse. The back of my neck prickled and my mouth kept filling with saliva. There were only three things I could do – leave, lie down or be sick. The first was the one to go for, but I would have to try at least to find Harry first.

Outside the opening that led to the stairway I came across a man of about fifty kicking the corded step below it and biffing at the sides with the heels of his hands. He had obviously given the business some thought. 'I think it's going to rain again,' I said as I approached.

He looked round and nodded cheerfully while going on bashing away and incidentally blocking my path. 'I shouldn't wonder if you weren't right, lad,' he said in an unreconstructed Northern accent. He had a broad pink face and sandy eyebrows and wore a towelling jacket with military pockets and drill trousers. 'Just working off my feelings, like,' he went on, then evidently made up his mind that I deserved some further explanation, because he stopped what he was doing and turned towards me, panting slightly. He was rather drunker than I had thought at first.

'The wife's been being a little bit provoking,' he said in a half-whisper, smiling and screwing up his nose. 'You know, feminine. Now whenever that happens I don't say a word, I come straight outside wherever I may be and I do what I just been doing for two minutes, and then I go back in full of the joy of spring. When I got married I told myself I could be happy or I could be right, and I've been happy now for twenty-two years. Ee, sorry, lad, here I go gassing away and holding you up.' He stood aside, looking at his watch. 'Another . . . forty seconds should see it through.'

I had been away no more than ten minutes, probably less, but the scene down below had changed quite a lot in the time. I thought to begin with that everybody was being sick, then I saw that only quite a small number were or had been, but they were naturally getting all the attention. One fellow had – I turned my eyes away. A woman was – no. Even now there was no general move towards the stairs. The bleeding idiots had stood their ground hoping the whole thing would pass off until it was too late to move a step. If I had been Julian Box I would have been very angry with them, but if he was he was getting no chance to show it, because his wife was giving him a going-over for not stopping them or not holding the boat steady or something like that.

Harry was nowhere to be seen, not in the main room anyway. Literally gritting my teeth and trying to think of rose-gardens I tried the revolting areas round the toilets and shouted his name through the door of each one with no result. In the first bedroom a man was lying with his grizzled head hanging over the edge. The second bedroom was empty – no, there was a pair of legs sticking out from the far side of the bed. They were Harry's. He had helpfully squeezed his head in under to be sick there. Somehow I got him moving. I tried not to look at his beard. When we were nearly at the stairs Bert came up.

'Can you give me a lift, Stan?'

'All right. Lend a hand here.'

There was a hold-up at the gangway, and when he got ashore Harry failed to perk up at once in the usual way of seasick people on landing. He stayed propped up against the Apfelsine while Bert and I moved aside for a pee. The three of us climbed aboard. Bert insisted on going in the back, which called for a semi-climb over the tipped passenger seat, no doddle for a bloke his size even cold sober, Harry got in beside me unaided though unsteady, and we were off.

Bert swore now and then. Harry said once or twice he was feeling better. I kept quiet until I spotted a vacant taxi halted at a traffic-light on our left.

'Get him,' I said to Harry, pulling up and pointing. 'Bert wants a taxi. Quick about it.'

He only just made it but he made it, and came back almost simpering. 'Okay.'

I said, 'I'm afraid it's not okay here, Harry. He's passed out, I can't shift him. Not a hope. Look, you take that taxi, go on. I'll see to him, don't worry.'

'But you can easily – '

'No, it's all right, I'll deal with him. Off you go now, I'll manage.'

There was nothing he could do, especially when I put the window up. The wheels started to turn.

'He's taking it,' said Bert's voice behind me. 'Not much choice, really. Five quid up his shirt from here. That was brilliant, Stan. Real touch of class.'

'It was your idea.'

'I'm talking about the execution. Fantastic. Bloody noble, you were. Anything for a pal.' When he was settled in the passenger seat he gestured towards the instrument panel and said, 'Don't let's do this now. Motors another time, right? Hey, I bet you thought that bugger was seasick, didn't you? Well, he may have been but he'd drunk too much too.'

'Do what? In that minute? We weren't there more than – '

'That's the point. When you go hurling it down it only takes half what it does spread out. When I started talking to him, not so long before you turned up, he was working his way through a bloody trayload of gin and tonics. Just started on the last one as you came along. *And* the rate he was going there'd been other trays before. It was free, you see. Like what, red rag to a bull? One of those. In the boozer we tell him when it's his shout. It's a joke, except we don't think so, and he doesn't think so. How do you stand him?'

'I haven't got to stand him,' I said. 'Good editor, though. Gets the readers.'

'Oh shit,' said Bert in disgust, then shut up for a bit, then suddenly said, 'Five past eight. Fixed up for dinner, are you?'

'No.'

'There's a place I go to sometimes in Soho. Little Italian joint. That sound all right to you?'

'Fine. But aren't you rather pissed, Bert?'

'Not by my standards, old son. Anyway, they know me there.'

They certainly seemed to from the reception they gave him, which reminded me of Nash's at his place, only this one was of course a class or two down the social scale. What was similar was the way Bert basked in it. Pissed or not, he soon saw me noticing.

'Friendly bunch, eh? I come here quite a lot, actually.

In fact I'm quite famous here. I'm not famous in any famous places but I am here.' He drained his wineglass and filled it again. 'Because of the people I'm usually with. I do a lot of TV commercials. More interesting work than you might think. Reasonably well paid, too.'

'So I gather,' I said. This explained several things, including the general impression he gave of prosperity and non-failure. I realized I had known almost nothing about him except that he got drunk and had a first Jaguar.

'You might even have seen the odd one. Er, Prosit lager?'

'What, those two fellows in the helicopter? Marvellous. You did that?'

He looked modestly into his minestrone, which he was coping with rather better than I had expected. 'That's me, yeah. That's one of mine. I do all those. So I'm quite famous in that line, you see, in the business, but you don't get known to the general public there. I don't mind that myself, as I say the money's good, but . . . And then . . . If . . .' He put his spoon down. 'Stanley, I've got to talk about her. Say I can. Say it's all right. Please.'

'I've seen it coming for hours, mate. Go ahead and enjoy yourself.'

'Because you're the only man on earth who'll understand.'

'I wouldn't be too sure of that, but I see what you mean. Anyway.'

'Yeah anyway, but where had I got to?'

'Wait a minute. Oh yes, you don't mind not being famous everywhere, but presumably she does.'

'Yeah, she does. She wouldn't like me being famous everywhere either, but she'd get something out of that, or she thinks she would, or you can't prove she wouldn't, any more than you can prove anything else about her. She reckons if I was a famous director of feature films she'd meet a lot of other famous directors and get parts in their films and that would be some compensation for being married to the likes of fucking me. I said once directors would be much more likely to give her parts if they hadn't met her.'

'You said that? Out loud? To her?'

'I told her. I was cross with her about something. I didn't get the chance of telling her anything else for a couple of weeks after that, but she turned up. It was partly she likes to spend a lot, you see. Christ, you know. She got it wrong about the career, didn't she, but the cash held up all right.'

'You mean she married you to get parts in films?'

'That's right. Like she married you because you were earning a lot for your age. Sorry, Stan. Sounds crude, doesn't it? I suppose it would if I meant she'd planned it and really knew what she was doing. But it's only men who plan things like that. You could fill her with what's that truth drug stuff, that's right, scopolamine, you could dose her up to the gills with fucking scopolamine and she'd still deny it. Another thing she knows without knowing she knows is that she's a not very good actress who isn't very beautiful and she'll be forty-six by the end of the year, so where's she going to go? She's much too neurotic to set up on her own. No, I'm stuck with her. By Christ, you're a long time alive, Stanley.'

'Why don't you get out yourself?'

'You must be joking. Get out? I couldn't face it, not again, not now. I did it before, perhaps nobody told you but I had to get unmarried too, and it bloody near killed me then. And soon enough I'm going to be fifty-three.

But there's a snag attached to what you might call the zero option, which now I come to think of it is a bloody marvellous name.' He laughed, then sighed. 'What? Snag, there's a snag. And I don't mind telling you what it is. It's not much fun . . . living with somebody . . . you don't like much.'

Over a rather good scaloppina of veal and interrupting himself with swigs of Valpolicella Bert told me some of his grounds for not liking his wife much. All of it, or nearly all of it, was familiar territory. Not that that made it any less interesting – on the contrary, it was wonderful to recognize variably sized almost-forgotten offences against common sense, good manners, fair play, truth, all those, with just the names and circumstances changed.

One short section was new. Bert described, believably enough, the way she hated you to be there, within range, in the room when she did some footling manual task like safety-pinning something to something else or tearing a stamp off a sheet and sticking it on an envelope. You were watching her, she said, waiting for her to be slow or clumsy or to get it wrong. Needless to say you were doing nothing of the kind, you had not got as far as taking in what she was up to, but as always you might have been watching and waiting, you could have been, there was no way of proving you were not. It gave me a ridiculous pang to think that I had never noticed her doing that, not as one more tiny absurd awful thing about her but just as a thing about her. I had thought I knew her better than anybody else ever could.

When Bert called for coffee, grappa and cigars it became clear to me, in so far as anything now could, that he was one of that number who could go on when most others had fallen by the wayside, in other words got drunk but had the power of drinking more, perhaps much more, without collapsing, at least for the moment. Also without losing hold of the conversation. He had repeated or partly repeated a couple of his stories, but he was still better than some people I knew cold sober. At the time I had reckoned that his funeral address on motoring could only have come from somebody well on with his last half-hour before blacking out. Not so, evidently. When the grappa arrived he went halfway back to that style for a moment, holding up his glass and staring at it like an actor.

'The great refuge,' he said as though he had just thought of it himself. 'The great comfort. And the great protection.'

'I'll drink to that.'

He scowled at me. 'It's a protection in a way that probably hasn't occurred to you, sonny, as well as the obvious. Now. She thinks I'm pissed all the time, right? You probably think the same, why shouldn't you? But I'm not. Obviously. A piss-artist couldn't do my job. Of course I am *sometimes* pissed, like now, like tonight, partly though not wholly in consequence of a little discussion of a carved walnut armchair, probably early Georgian. Hence also my presence on that fucking barge. But mainly, usually, normally not.'

'You were pretty far gone that afternoon I came to your place, remember?'

'Oh, bloody good,' he said, laughing. 'I take that as a real tribute. By the way I'm sorry I bad-mouthed you over the phone and so on. My line on you with her is that you're a shit, you see. There's no such thing as a safe line on anything with her, as you may have noticed, but I just thought that would be the least unsafe.'

'You mean you weren't pissed at all that time?'

'What? Oh, no no. Couple of beers at lunchtime. I was hamming it up.'

'You hammed it up like mad when I arrived and she wasn't even in sight.'

'Ah, but that's the rule. The rule is, I got to have a rule I'm always pissed there, if not for real then I act it. Too confusing otherwise, too bloody risky too. I work from an office just across the road from here. That's good because she thinks I'm getting arseholes drunk round the clubs. I don't know where she thinks all the money comes from. But that's not interesting, is it? Not so long as it keeps coming.'

'What's the point?'

'Of acting pissed? I'll tell you,' he said in a much quieter voice. 'When you're young, you're ready to fuck anything on two legs. That's almost enough on its own. But as time goes by, you get choosy. You know, if they chat to you about Harold Pinter while you're on the job or they throw their food about and swear at the waiters or you find out they used to work for the Gestapo or the KGB or one of those, well, you notice, it puts you off a bit. And by the time you're fifty, Stan, you're even more demanding. You expect them to be a bit pleasant occasionally, *right*? To listen now and then, *m'm*? To be good company, *eh*? A lot of unreasonable things like that.'

He had not said the last bit very quietly, and he had started to slur his words too. When he went on he kept the volume down but he still talked in a mumbling kind of way. 'If you don't like 'em, you don't want to fuck 'em. And who could like her after they got to know her, after they'd seen her in action? The milkman worships her, but he's new and he hasn't not brought the bloody cream yet. The accountant, well, he's not new, I suppose, just an idiot. She's a . . . she's a fucky *nuck* case, that's what she is. Ought to be put away. For her own protection.'

'Well then, there we are. If you don't want to fuck your wife you have the option of telling her it's because she's such a horrible bloody creature, which actually I wouldn't dare to do, I'd be too afraid of a knife in my guts. Seriously. She could justify anything she did. Unendurable provocation. How do we know it was unendurable? Use your eyes, she couldn't endure it, could she?'

I watched him while he struggled to get his mind round his next, clinching point, ready to help out if needed, but he made it on his own. '*Or*,' he said triumphantly, '*Or* you can be pissed all the time so the matter doesn't arise, ha ha ha. By well-established convention. And for real too, I should imagine. Variation by Hutchinson – be pissed some of the time and act pissed the rest of the time. I must be pretty bloody good at the latter by now because she's never noticed the difference. As far as I can remember, that is.'

'Things must have been all right at the beginning,' I said. 'When you first went round with her.'

'Till we'd been married a couple of years. By which time she'd finally got the message that I didn't really like parties full of T V and film people. She couldn't believe it at first.'

'Was that when you stopped wearing suede shirts?'

'Eh? Sorry, Stanley, I don't get you.'

'Never mind.'

'I heard about your boy. I'd offer to help but . . . but no.' He gave another sigh, one that went into a huge single hiccup. 'If you're going to drive me home, Stan, and my honest guess is you've more or less got to, you'd better do it before I pass out.'

I tried to, but he was too quick for me. Much too heavy, too. It was a judgement on me for the Harry stunt, on Bert as well perhaps. I hauled at his arm for a time, then gave up and went and rang the front-door bell, which clunked as before. Nowell answered it quite soon, wearing a dress which looked to me as though it was made out of a well-known brand of dietary biscuit. I realized I was very drunk myself, nowhere near fit to be in charge of a motor vehicle on any grounds bar necessity.

'Stanley!' she said, all welcoming smiles. 'How nice to see you. Come and have a drink. Bert's gone to a – '

'I've got him in the car,' I said.

Before I could think of a winning way to describe the problem she turned round and went back across the hall. She had started to catch on as soon as I spoke, without showing a wink of surprise or even curiosity about how her husband came to be out with a fellow he always said was a shit. After half a minute or so she reappeared carrying a fat bunch of cushions under one arm and a roll of some thickish material under the other. She seemed definitely shorter than before, and when she passed me on the step I saw she was wearing bedroom slippers, little green affairs with turned-up toes. Her manner had a sort of professional steadiness about it. I followed her into the street with my brain not working too well. The wind was still blowing pointlessly away.

'Where are you?'

'Along here.'

I was parked a dozen yards off, near side to the pavement. She opened the door as wide as it would go, looked at Bert for about a second, took his glasses off his nose and handed them to me, laid out the cushions on the nearest bit of ground, which was damp but not watery, unrolled the roll of stuff, a length of carpet as I now saw, and placed it next to the cushions. Having done that she got in at the other side and, bracing her shoulder against the doorpost, shoved at Bert with her slippered feet until he fell off the seat and out of the car. Then she rolled him on to the bit of carpet and started dragging him along the pavement towards his front gate, a job made easier for her by the suitcase-handle let into the front edge of the strip. I locked the Apfelsine and collected up the cushions, one of which she took off me in the hall and put under his head before turning him on his side. She held out her hand to me for his glasses, which she stowed on a nearby oak chest beside pieces of outdoor clothing like gloves and a child's mack. The last thing was a blanket from the top shelf of the coat-cupboard thrown over him. The whole operation had taken two minutes at the outside.

'You must love him very much,' I said.

'Fuck off, darling.' Nowell stared at me. 'Do you know, I don't think you'd better have that drink after all.' She looked down at Bert and then at me again. 'They say however many times you get married it's always to basically the same person, don't they? Watch out, Stan.'

I drove home in exactly the style of a very very good driver who had had two small glasses of wine with his dinner and was taking no chances but of course not dawdling. And I was lucky. Well, it was still not half-past ten. Quite a few points needed chewing over, though not before the morning. One, probably not the most important, was whether Bert always or even sometimes got himself given the cushion-and-carpet treatment when he was only acting pissed. Another came from what Nowell had said. Had she only been talking about drink?

THREE

RELAPSE

♀

Steve was worse when I saw him next. He talked, but not to me or to anybody else who was there. I could not make out half of what he said and the rest made no sense. His mouth was very dry, with the drugs presumably, and there was a crud or something of what looked like half-dried-up saliva sticking to his teeth. He obviously had no idea of where he was or what was going on, and the way he moved his eyes, which had dilated pupils, made me think he was seeing things that were not there. Still, he seemed calm.

On the next couple of visits his hallucinations, if that was what they had been, seemed to have blown over, but nothing or very little was getting through to him. That was what I thought, anyway, and Susan agreed the day she went with me. So it came as quite a surprise when Trish Collings rang up that evening and said she was transferring him to the St Kevin's day clinic, which meant he would be spending his nights at home, and would I please come and fetch him at 5.30 tomorrow. His condition had significantly improved, she said.

I held down any desire to cheer, no longer knowing what I thought of Collings. 'Since this morning?' I asked.

'The improvement has become obvious since this morning, but it's been taking shape for some time now.' As before, she sounded extra west-of-Winchester over the phone, bursting with cricket and cream teas. 'Anyway, you'll be able to judge for yourself very soon.'

When I got to her terrible office she started explaining about how it was up to me to arrange for Steve to be brought to and fro. I interrupted her.

'Aren't we going to wait for Mrs Hutchinson?'

'I didn't ask her to attend. This is between you and me, Stanley.'

'Oh, so when it comes to getting something done I'm not such a disaster.'

'Will you please try to contain your aggression towards your ex-wife at least while you're here.'

She spoke quite stroppily. I apologized, and she went on to caution me against assuming that Steve was now completely and permanently cured, and put it on record that she was not a magician. After that she talked about what a bad thing it would be if I or anybody else, but particularly I, showed any resentment towards him for any upset or inconvenience he might unintentionally cause. She also warned me against thinking that quite run-of-the-mill possible bits of behaviour on his part, like smashing crockery or staring into space for a couple of hours at a time, were really abnormal violence or withdrawal respectively. If anyone, me for instance, got it across to him that that view was being taken, then he would become more alienated.

'May I ask a question, doctor?'

This set her off on one of her merriest guffaws. When she was able to she said, 'My, we are being formal today.'

'Well, I thought so. Anyway, just, if he's done so well in hospital, and there are likely to be these difficulties at home, wouldn't the logical thing be to keep him here?'

Her mouth slid sideways. 'That's a bad question if it means you're thinking of the disruption likely to be caused in your routine and your wife's.'

'Of course I'm *thinking* of it,' I said, glad that as I felt just then I was indoors and sitting down. 'That's natural. But in another sense I'm also *thinking* of my son. Parents often do think of their children in ways like that.'

'I'll accept that,' she said, doing so with suspicious willingness. 'Perhaps you have been taking a balanced view of the situation. Yes, in some circumstances continuing hospitalization would be the answer, but here we have to consider the long term. What we're all trying to do, you'll agree, is get Steve to be able to stand on his own two feet, and the first step towards doing that is to allow him out of the artificial hospital environment and into the community, as far as possible at the moment, when he's ready to spend his evenings and nights with family, and I think he is ready for that.'

'I see. Can we look forward to a steady improvement?'

'Hopefully yes. But in these situations there's always the possibility of relapse. That's why I stressed the importance of responsible handling.'

'I see,' I said again. 'One more thing if I may. I've got a wife at home and I'm no unarmed-combat expert myself. How likely is he to get violent?'

'Now here again that sort of thing can't be ruled out, but any purposeful violence is much more to be associated with psychopathiform disorders. Steve may well appear threatening and alarming without engaging in any violent behaviour at all.'

'Well, that's something, I suppose.'

She told me a bit more about what to expect, none of it markedly confidence-building, and at the end of it said in a voice that was quite gentle by her standards, 'I expect you're looking forward to having him home.'

My God, I thought to myself, if anybody ever looked

off their bleeding rocker then this was it, never mind what Nash and his lot might say. She was sitting hunched up at her table clutching a fag in her right hand, opening and closing her left hand, smiling unsteadily at me with the left side of her mouth and blinking her left eye. Her head jerked a couple of times. The nearest thing would have been out of an award-winning Mexican movie made in black and white on purpose and called *Las* something. If she bothered at all she probably read my expression as embarrassed paternal feeling. At any rate she got up after a minute, nodded at me and went noisily out of the room. When she came back she had Steve with her.

'Hallo, dad,' he said, and shook my hand. He was looking me in the eye and smiling. 'How are you?'

'Hallo, son, I'm fine.'

'Is everything all right?'

'Oh yes, absolutely.'

I was very nearly sure that I would sooner have had him as I had last seen him than as he was now. He, his normal self, would never have shaken hands with me like that without a private signal that of course the whole thing was a joke, an act, an imitation, anyway not what it seemed to any idiots who might have been watching. And he had met me eye to eye right enough, but if he had not just called me Dad I would have said without recognizing me, certainly without the least touch of the humorous warmth I had always had from him on meeting and whenever we were at all specially aware of each other for a second. Again I wondered whether I would have instantly recognized him out of context, and fancied the proportions of his face had altered in some small but unmissable way.

'Isn't it nice to see him looking so well, Stanley?' said Collings.

'Yes, it certainly is. Well, Trish, if there's nothing more for the moment we may as well be getting along.'

'No no, you're free to go,' she said, and choked back another peal of merriment, unless I imagined it. 'I'll just walk you to the entrance.'

It seemed a long hike to the hall of Rorschach House. The lengths of material underfoot, which on my last visit I had thought must be for something temporary, were still there, only more crumpled and stained than before. I was dying to be rid of Collings and at the same time dreading being alone with Steve. Her farewell when it came was fully up to standard for embarrassment, with a terrible roguish bit about it being au revoir not goodbye for him and her.

The car park was in weak sunshine. 'Well, how did they treat you back there?' I asked, and when I got no answer, 'All right, were they?'

'Yeah.'

'What was the food like? Okay, was it?'

'Yeah.'

He had spoken so lifelessly that I was filled with a sudden panicky suspicion – he had indeed not recognized me, he still had not the slightest idea of what was happening, he had simply had it drummed into him to address as dad the man who turned up and to go wherever he was taken. No, that could not be, that was daft, he was simply nervous, confused, frightened, shy of committing himself or saying more than he had to. He would talk all right when he had settled down and felt safe.

There was not much sign of that for the first couple of days. On arrival he said Hallo to Susan quite nicely and shook hands with her, a bizarre sight if I ever saw one, but after that he only spoke without being spoken to when he wanted the coffee jar, an extra blanket, a light for his cigarette, the time of day. He ate little, read nothing, watched television, took long showers, left the television on, left the shower on, left the lights on. I could find nothing abnormal about any of this, nothing unusual, and yet it was different. The most different part came first thing in the morning – so far from having trouble getting him up I found him fully dressed sitting looking shell-shocked on the edge of his bed or on the broad sill of the big window on the landing. But he certainly seemed calm.

About the third evening early on he said to me quite normally, 'Just popping out to get some Marlboros.' Susan was there too.

It was the first unnecessary thing he had said for a long time. Partly because in a very unimportant way I was fed up with having to give him lights every ten minutes and partly to provoke some sort of reaction I said, not at all crossly, 'You might as well buy yourself a few boxes of matches while you're about it.'

I got my reaction all right, also noticed that he had some sort of grasp of the state of affairs. He glared at me with astonishing hostility, showed his teeth in a way I had never seen before and said in a sort of choked-up or choked-off voice, 'Don't you fucking dare talk to me like that, you bastard. Who the bloody hell do you think you are, giving me your fucking orders?'

Knowing at once there was no point in it I still said, 'I wasn't giving any orders, I was merely making a sugges-tion.'

'Like fuck you were. You were trying to make me into part of your bloody little police state, weren't you? You're just a pissy little dictator. You don't care about anybody but yourself and other people can go and jump in the fucking lake.'

'That's not true.' Susan sounded pretty cross herself. 'Your father sweats his guts out for you. Look at the way he – '

He turned on her so savagely that I got to my feet. 'You keep out of this, you fucking bitch,' he said with shocking sincerity. 'You've done enough, pushing my mother out and now you won't let me go near her, you bloody . . .'

'She's not there,' I shouted. 'I can't get hold of her. She's not around.' I had phoned three or four times on my own account and only got an answer once, from a foreign voice that said helpfully that Mrs Hutchinson had gone to London. Not that Steve had so much as mentioned her until this moment since the evening I first fetched him. But it was no use going into any of that.

With a growl of hatred and disgust he took a step towards me and jerked his fist in the air, but then shoved past me and hurried out. Susan and I stood without moving until the front door slammed, on which we clung to each other.

'That's not his way,' I said, trying to remember something of Collings's about helping him to get in touch with his own anger. Was that what I had done?

'No, well he's not himself. He's all in a muddle, poor little thing. He probably feels bloody awful from all these drugs and things and when you're like that you lash out at whoever's nearest. Come on, darling, let's have a drink.'

After ten minutes or so we heard the door slam again and after another moment a burst of working-class music from the television. When I went in last thing I found a semi-circle of used matches round Steve's chair, one of which had burnt the carpet slightly. It seemed not much to be bucked up by.

*

The next day Susan's mother came to lunch. So did Alethea, Susan's elder sister by half a dozen years. Alethea had been married to a doctor, a chest man at a London teaching hospital who had run off with one of the cleaning women there. I still thought that was a pretty peculiar thing to have done, though not as peculiar as before I met Alethea. She had gone white early, wore her hair in a short bob and, with her tallish, stooped figure, looked a bit like a country parson in an old number of *Punch*, dressed differently, though. When I turned up, rather late on purpose, she greeted me quite heartily and made a great thing of insisting on a full double kiss in the continental mode.

'Stanley dear, how marvellous to see you, it's been absolutely ages.'

'Lovely to see you, Alethea,' I said, only just managing not to burst out laughing in her face. Although we had met a good dozen times over the years I had never learnt to be altogether ready for the way she talked, which sounded to me like a fellow trying to get you to hate and despise the upper classes by ridiculously overdoing their accent. My mother-in-law looked quite startled at the way I came rushing over to embrace her. Susan was out of the room.

'And how are things going in Fleet Street?' asked Alethea. 'Have you had any good scoops lately?'

'I'm not on that side of it,' I said, 'but nobody gets much in the way of scoops these days because – '

'They're pulling down the whole of that lovely William IV terrace just round the corner from where I am,' Alethea told me. 'You remember, on the north side of the square?'

Her mother answered, not that I had any objection. 'Oh darling, they can't,' she said, with a quick glance my way to check that I was not grinning with satisfaction at this news. '*Not* the one where Sickert lived?'

'I'm afraid they can, darling. I've a number of friends locally, as you know, and I hear on the best authority that it's all coming *down* and a block of flats and a supermarket are going up. Damn-all chance of stopping it.'

'People like that will do *anything*,' said my mother-in-law.

'Terrible,' I said. 'Terrible.'

'Of course you're all right round here, aren't you, Stanley?' said my sister-in-law. 'All these rich socialists with their Georgian mansions, nobody's going to lay a finger on *them*, oh dear no, don't make me laugh.'

Good advice, that last bit, I thought, successfully remembering what it was like. 'Yes, they have been quite reasonable, actually,' I said. 'There's a place in Flask Walk called – '

'They're stopping the season-ticket arrangement for those concerts of the Friends of the Baroque,' said Alethea to the old girl and me more or less jointly. 'Something I don't really understand about the laws about charities. Apparently there is or was some loophole that some little bureaucrat has cleverly managed to close.'

'A magnificent achievement. Obviously a man destined for the highest office.'

Lady D had let me off that one, but I went and poured myself a Scotch anyway. While I was doing it Susan came in and we had a quick exchange – all well, no news, lunch in ten minutes. I took the sherry round. We had an item on the duty on wine and another on the Royal Shakespeare Company. Then there was something about the Saab wanting its boot repaired and I pricked up my ears, but before we could be told about the latest slow-motion bump good old Alethea cut in. She made sure there were only the four of us in the room and said into a minimal pause, 'I rather gather . . . poor Steve . . . has been a little . . . under the weather lately.'

'He's better than he was,' said Susan. 'As I told you, they let him – '

'Is it . . . some sort of breakdown?'

'Evidently they don't use that word,' I said, 'but yes, that's what it seems to boil down to.'

'Poor you, how frightfully worrying for you both.'

'Has he been behaving violently again?' asked Lady D.

Alethea twisted round on her. 'Behaving violently? How do you mean, darling? What sort of thing?' Now was the time I could have done with hearing about the terrace or the tickets, but it was obviously too late for anything like that.

'Well, when I was here three weeks ago he flew into a rage about nothing in particular that I could see, grabbed a book of Susan's off the shelves and tore it to pieces, and then rushed out of this house and round to his mother's, where he proceeded to smash the television set to fragments.'

I said, 'A very distinguished psychiatrist – '

'But that's nothing very terrible or extraordinary,' said Alethea, really disappointed.

'I quite agree, darling, exactly my own view of the thing,' said Lady D, causing me to blink slightly. 'But then of course these days everything has to be . . . Stanley,' she went on, and lifted her head up in a confidential way, so as to let the world know we were all on the same side, 'is that boy really to be regarded as ill, would you say?'

'Well, he's not physically ill, lady,' I said. 'As regards mental illness I have to leave it to the – '

'Mental illness?' said Alethea. 'What sort of thing?'

'I don't think Stanley wants to go into any of that,' said Susan.

'Just in the family, darling.'

'*No*, darling.'

'What does Steve do with himself here?' My mother-in-law swung her glass out of the path of the sherry bottle. 'How does he get through the day?'

'He gets through the day at the hospital. As regards the evenings here he just sits in front of the television. No trouble to anybody.'

'And no good to himself, it appears. I suppose he'd die rather than go for a walk. Does he never help Susan in the house?'

'Well, there's nothing really for him to do, darling,' said Susan. 'I have two people coming in and I'm not going to put him on to papering the best bedroom just for the hell of it.'

'So he never so much as washes up a teacup,' said the old girl, sending her elder daughter a glance of wonderfully covered-up horror and getting back one of the same sort.

'There's a machine for that, as you know.' Susan was beginning to fidget.

'Which requires to be loaded, I believe.'

'Darling, Steve's in a very strange state, he's not just another idle teenager with a fit of the mopes. He needs to feel sympathized with and that nobody's trying to get at him.'

'And it would be *getting at* him to induce him to perform some portion of his share of household tasks. I see.'

'Surely there are simply dozens of things he could do in the garden,' said Alethea.

'*Please*, both of you,' said Susan, getting up. By now

she was quite agitated. 'We're going through a very nasty time in this house at the moment and we don't need lecturing on how to run it. Really we don't. So could we / please drop the subject.'

'I'm sorry,' said Lady D in one of the plenty of ways of saying that without doing any apologizing. 'I was only thinking of Steve and what a shame it would be if he were actually encouraged in his . . .' She took a long time over that one. 'Slackness,' she said eventually. 'But of course I quite realize that it's much too late to talk along such lines,' she said with her voice beginning to die away, 'and that these rather unhappy strains in his character probably go back to his early training and the unfortunate influence of his mother,' she said with the last word coming through strongly enough and a glance at me that left no real doubt in my mind that the mother she was thinking of was rather bald and had a little moustache and drove an Apfelsine.

'Shall we go down to lunch?' said Susan. When the other two had finally cleared off she said to me, 'I don't know what happened, darling, honestly. That's about as bad as I've known her. Alethea being there comes into it somehow, I've noticed it before. But . . . part of it was to do with concern about Steve, I would like you to believe that.'

Yeah, I said to myself. And some more of it was to do with making out that what was wrong with Steve was nothing more than a severe case of being lower class. Not all of it, no.

When I got back from the hospital with Steve the following evening I could see Susan had news for me. I waited till

226

he had settled in front of the TV with his usual coffee and slice of bread and honey, then followed her up to our bedroom. What she had was something to show me rather than tell me, a square-cornered length of metal or heavy plastic about four inches by an inch by half an inch with a roughened surface. It looked like the handle of something, which was what it actually turned out to be when I pressed a stud at one end and a stout pointed blade shot out of the other.

'In his chest of drawers,' said Susan. 'Not even covered up. It wasn't there yesterday. I look every morning.'

'Quite right. But when did he get it? Unless he was keeping it somewhere else before. And even then . . . Must have been at the other end, out near the hospital. I just drop him there, you see, I don't bodyguard him all the way to the ward. It's quite a walk to the shops. Not impossible, though, I suppose. Anyway here it is, eh?'

'Must have cost a bit if he got it new.'

'I gave him fifty the other day. I can't have him coming to me every time he wants a packet of fags, can I?'

'What are we going to do?'

'I don't know.' I clicked the knife back into its hilt. 'I honestly don't know. Well, we can confront him with it.'

'No need for that, we can just ask him what it's for. Can't we?'

'That's confronting him with it. Or we can throw it away. That's confronting him with it as soon as he finds it isn't there instead of now.'

'Well, what about confronting him with it?'

'Yes,' I said trying to think whether concealed possession of a flick knife would count as normal or abnormal in

Collings's book. 'We can predict his reaction from what happened the other day. Rage, curses, accusations of spying, and so on.'

'Which can be faced.'

'Oh, sure. But . . . It's a pity about the spying. I support you on it, I mean if you'd asked me whether you should look through his things I'd have said go ahead. But if you look at it it is very much the sort of response that . . . Well, that Dr Collings said would alienate him.'

'So you're in favour of putting it back.'

'I can't see what's to be gained from not. We know it's there now, and he doesn't know we know. And it's not as if it's the only knife in the house. Those non-stainless French kitchen jobs of yours, you could tackle a bleeding elephant with one of them. I suppose we could lock them up. You're not really with me over this, are you, Sue?'

'I just think if you said very casually and calmly that I'd happened to come across it when I was – '

'Then he'd fly into a rage and accuse us both of spying. Don't forget he's Nowell's son too. Can you imagine how she'd behave if you casually and calmly told her you'd happened to come across something in her handbag? Of course, she is a . . . er, we all know what she is. I'll check this with Collings in the morning.'

Collings said putting the knife back was right – Stephen had probably only got hold of it in the first place so as to feel secure. In case I went for him with a hammer, I said to myself but not to her. Further reports would be welcome. His action on being encouraged to take a shower, which was to take a shower so thorough that he used up all the hot water and made me late for work, had its annoying side but hardly seemed worth reporting.

At the start of the second week he took to going to his room earlier than before, at ten o'clock, nine o'clock, straight after arriving home. That time, feeling a perfect idiot, I sneaked up about eight to spy out the land. The light was on in the room. One or two slight sounds told me nothing except that he was not in bed. Reading? Conceivably but not much more. Looking at dirty pictures? Quite possibly. Staring into space? Quite likely. I left it and Susan and I forgot about him for the whole evening, until we heard him coming down for his late-night snack and our conversation, which had been bounding along before, soon petered out.

Five days after the knife incident Susan again had something waiting for me when I got home. In the bedroom she handed me some sheets of cheap lined paper covered with Steve's familiar and terrible handwriting. 'It was on the little round table in his room,' she said. I thought she looked tired, rather pale anyway. 'He must have meant us to find it there.'
'What is it, a letter?'
'You'd better read it.'
I sat on the edge of the bed and she settled herself next to and partly behind me in one of those kneeling or squatting female positions with her arm on my shoulder. Although terrible enough, full of unnecessary loops, leaning, falling over and straightening itself up again, the writing could mostly be read, and the spelling mistakes were plentiful, but the intended words could mostly be rescued. Put right as far as it could be put right, Steve's message went like this:

Light years ago in the secret heart of the galaxy an Element created itself. For centuries it had no name, then ancient Atlantean physicists discovered it with scanners and named it POTENTIUM. But when Atlantis perished neath the waves the secret of POTENTIUM perished also.

More centuries flew by on the wings of time, until Lemurian mystics got to know about it in dreams and visions sent by MITHRAS, but when they went and told their king he was displeased and had them slain. So alas the secret was lost once more.

Then as NOSTRADAMUS had predicted the Alchemists brought POTENTIUM back into existence, but no man knew what it would do.

Then one day the great AVERROES was experimenting on some POTENTIUM by bombarding it with Photon Particles and this mutated it into an isotope that could live in the human brain.   REJOICE! HENCEFORTH MAN WAS ARMED AGAINST EVIL.

POTENTIUM IS THE SOURCE OF THE SPIRIT THAT FIGHTS FOR GOOD.

> The element that had no name,
> Through the centuries it came,
> Through all the smoke and flame,
> POTENTIUM God's gift to man,
> By his great plan,
> The war against evil began,   EVIL
> Against those who live for greed,   LIVE
> To smash their vile creed,   VILE
> And make them all bleed,   LEVI
> POTENTIUM gives the power,
> To strike at the right hour,
> And all the evil devour.

Atomic Number 108
          Symbol Pt
               Atomic Weight 303
                    Valency Number 99
                         Rainbow Metal

THIS IS A DEMOCRATIC DOCUMENT OF GREAT
IMPORTANCE CREATED FOR THE PRESERVATION OF PEACE
                         AND THE DESTRUCTION
                         OF THE WICKED

HAIL POTENTIUM THE POWER OF THE LORD

Underneath the text there was a drawing of a person with
a beard stretching out an arm towards some buildings that
seemed to be falling down among small figures probably
intended to be human beings. It, the drawing, was done
in ballpoint and I thought showed very little talent.

I had just had time to take this in when Susan gave a
sort of shrieking gasp right in my ear and I looked up
rather quickly to see Steve standing by the door, which I
could have sworn had been shut, and glaring at us. He
might have been there for a couple of minutes. When he
saw us see him he came towards us in a determined way.
I jumped up.

'What are you doing with that?' he said, or rather
snarled.

'Reading it. That's what you meant us to do, isn't it?'

'Fucking snooping!'

'You left it lying about,' I said, and tried and failed to
get the energy together to go on about people having to
go into his room to make the bed, etc.

The next moment, probably just by chance, his manner
changed. All menace left it. He looked alert and preoccu-

231

pied at the same time, like somebody trying to remember something or to hear a distant sound. He soon gave this up and focused on me with his mouth hanging open. Slowly he closed it and pressed the lips together until his expression was one of smothered amusement, also shyness and a modest kind of pride, reminding me of how he had looked at me the first time I saw him walk. Then he broke out into laughter, completely amused and amiable, no awful side to it at all in itself. The trouble was I could see nothing much that was funny in what was actually happening or what was there in front of us. I tried to make out he was laughing at me and Susan for being serious or stupid or worried or frightened, or at himself for being angry just now, or anything like that, but it was no good. Nash had talked about schizophrenics being too mad to know what was funny. I stood there longing for a drink till Steve jerked his head back and scampered out of the room.

Susan had come up and taken my hand and now she put her arms round me and squeezed. 'Stanley, I'm scared,' she whispered.

'Not much of a treat, was it?'

'No, I mean I'm still scared. All that . . . *mad* stuff about Atlantis and alchemists and smashing the evil ones, it's like . . . I don't know.'

'Bleeding ridiculous.'

'Darling, it's not just ridiculous. That boy, he's very seriously disturbed.'

'We knew that,' I said. 'I'll discuss the matter when I've got a glass in my hand and not before.' When I had, and we were in the sitting room with the door firmly shut, I said, 'Sue, love, listen to me, now. This thing is just an old piece of sci-fi, that's all it is. Tripe, in fact. I thought it had gone out. Plus the sort of stuff you get through the post from the green-ink brigade – you know, the pyramids one minute and lasers the next. The thing's not worth taking seriously, really.'

'He believes it,' said Susan. 'He thinks it's true.'

'Oh, come on. Believes it? It's like a kid scribbling. Doodling.'

'There's violence there. To smash their vile creed and make them all bleed. I suppose that's more doodling.'

'I'd say maybe he was trying to get a rhyme, but then I wouldn't know about a thing like that.'

'The destruction of the wicked doesn't sound very funny to me.

'Well, he wasn't going to threaten to let their dog out and knock over their pint in the pub, was he?'

This was the moment where she should have looked up at me and smiled and said she was sorry to have gone on like that, and I would have said of course I saw why and more in the same strain while saying to myself, in this case, that although Steve's document might not be worth getting steamed up about it was a long way from reassuring in itself. But instead of that she went on sitting there on the grey velvet settee in one of her grey cardigans and dark skirts, pressing her lips together, her head down in a way that showed off the blackness and glossiness of her hair. I felt I was a long way from knowing what she was thinking, not that I would have gone round claiming I regularly did know.

Partly to break the tension I said, 'I'd better give Nowell a ring.'

Susan looked up then and no mistake. 'Why? What for?'

'I'd like to tell her about this just now and, well, the

general situation. I should have got hold of her earlier.'

'What for? What can she do?'

'Nothing, love. I don't want her to do anything, I just want her to be informed. She probably doesn't even know he's here.'

'I dare say she doesn't,' said Susan sharply. 'She never takes the slightest interest in him.'

'Look, I'm not calling her in as a consultant, all I'm after is putting her in the picture so if he does act up, like walking in there out of the blue as he's quite liable to do, she can't complain she was kept in the dark. Okay?'

'Yes.' Susan sighed and blinked apologetically. 'You know, it's hard going on being reasonable all the time when you're feeling a bit shaken up.'

'Oh, absolutely. Listen, Sue, I'm sorry all this is happening, and it's sort of none of your doing.'

'It's none of yours, either. Forget it, darling.'

'No, you know what I mean. I don't really feel I can leave him alone in the house much for the moment, but you can go out. You must go out on your own a bit more.'

'I don't like going out without you.'

'Then we must have a few more people in.'

'Don't worry, there's always plenty to do here. And you're here, aren't you?'

'It's not much of a life for you.'

'Yes it is. We'll make sure he doesn't get into the bedroom again, darling.'

When I tried the Hutchinson number it answered immediately. I remembered feeling very slightly baffled when there was no answer before – what if I had been somebody who might have had work for Nowell? But no point in going into that now because it was Bert at the other end.

'Stan here. Hold on a minute. How did you get away with it the other day, going out on a blind with your favourite shit?'

'No problem,' said Bert with his mouth close to the phone. 'I told her she had to be joking at first, then I couldn't remember anything about it, could I? Well, it wasn't all no problem, because it still didn't look good. But she was over the moon that morning because Chris Rabinowitz wanted to talk to her about an idea he'd had. She can be quite agreeable when everybody's doing what she wants at once. Remember? Anyway. Was I all right that time? When I look back, it starts getting a bit vague over the veal.'

'You were fine. Not that I was in much of a state to judge.'

'Not offensive? . . . Good. Hang on, I'll get her. Ah, you . . . shit,' he said, his voice getting louder and further away at the same time, fuzzier too. 'You bloody man. Ha . . . darling,' he continued with a quite impressive off-mike acoustic. '*Darling*, it's that, er . . .'

Nowell came on the line full of simple wonder and pleasure at hearing the sound of my voice, but changed it to sincere puzzlement when I seemed to think she might want to be told what Steve had recently been up to, where he was, etc. When I actually started to tell her she switched again and stopped listening. How she got that across on a non-visual circuit without saying anything or making any other kind of noise I had very little idea, but the fact made me realize I must have seriously underestimated her acting ability in the past. Then something I said about the flick-knife business evidently broke through, and she came over all motherly – to me, not Steve.

'I'm very glad you've told me about this, Stanley. You did quite right. *Of course* it's an upsetting, disturbing thing, suddenly coming across *a knife* hidden away like that.'

'Actually it wasn't – '

'Anybody who wasn't upset, even a bit *frightened*, in those circumstances would have to be rather stupid. Fair enough. But darling, you mustn't mind me saying this but it's really not very sensible to *go on* being frightened because of it.'

'I'm not – '

'Because a lot of young boys go in for that sort of thing you know, having a knife and so on, it makes them feel big. They've no intention in the world of *using* it. And as for *Steve*, I'm quite staggered you think he might take a cut at you, or Susan. I mean surely.'

'I don't – '

'He's such a *gentle* creature, always has been. I don't believe he'd be actually violent to anybody, however frantic or worked up he got. It's just not in him.'

That was more or less how I felt myself, but hearing her say it almost made me want to change round. 'M'm,' I said.

'But I want you to be quite certain of one thing, Stanley,' she said, and her voice started to tremble slightly with thick-and-thinness, so that I could visualize every last millimetre of her expression. 'If ever you need me, if there should ever be anything I can do, you only have to say the word and I'll be there, depend on it.'

'It's good to know that.'

Speaking at three times the speed and steady as a rock, she said, 'You must understand quite plainly that he's not coming here, Stanley. I won't have it, I've got to think of

Joanne,' their daughter, presumably. 'It wouldn't be fair on her. Surely you can see that. I'm sorry but I really have no alternative. Goodbye.'

I got it almost straight away. Although I was pretty convinced that my last remark had sounded quite all right, devoid of any hint of malice or sarcasm, I could always have got it wrong, and in any case from Nowell's point of view I might easily have been having malicious or sarcastic thoughts, and I might even have been getting ready to be foul to her about not going near her son while he was having a not very good time. Well, this was the sort of thing that helped me to go on not making any mistakes about my first wife, like spending a few seconds every couple of months wishing she had not run off with Bert.

The next morning I told Collings about the potentium stuff and she told me it was normal. That evening Steve started whispering to himself as he sat watching television, or rather with the set turned on. From the way he kept pausing and looking attentive I reckoned he was having a conversation with a voice inside his head. While a journal-ist on the screen talked about and tried to illustrate the decline of bits of Liverpool Steve listened to this other voice, disagreed with what it said, disagreed quite strongly but consented to listen further, made a couple of reluctant admissions and finally caved in. For five minutes nothing more happened, but then he started disagreeing again and I went upstairs for a stiff Scotch.

The morning after that I drove him over to St Kevin's as usual. At first he kept quiet, also as usual, but about halfway there he said or muttered, 'Leave me alone,' not for my benefit. For the rest of the journey he said the same thing or variants of it every couple of minutes, plus excuses like there was nothing he could do about it. If he had been on the end of a phone trying to get rid of a bore he would have sounded completely normal. At last we arrived.

'See you tonight, son,' I said when he was getting out. Twice before when I said it or something similar he had given me a terrific bawling-out for treating him like a child and so on, but I found it was impossible to let him just go off in silence.

Today was different. He bent down to get a proper look at me and said, 'Goodbye, dad,' shut the door and moved off.

I watched him cross the car park, head slightly forward as always, and pass out of sight. Should I have gone with him to the ward and to hell with his objections? Should I now find Collings or that Gandhi bloke and tell them about the whispering? Well, presumably they knew already or soon would, unless he put it on specially for me, which I doubted. And it was probably normal anyway.

The thought of him saying goodbye like that came back to me several times in the next few hours, especially when I got back to the office after a rather long lunch break and Morgan Wyndham handed me a slip of paper and told me to ring that number urgently – the St Kevin's number with Collings's extension. He then took himself off as though the thing was his own idea, one which another time would have earned him a lot of marks.

I got Collings in ten seconds flat. 'Hallo, Stanley,' she said like a real old pal. 'What have you done with that boy of yours?'

'No jokes if you don't mind. What's up?'

'Well, that's what I was wondering. Where is he?'

238

'You mean he didn't – I brought him in as usual.'

'Well, we haven't seen him here. Any idea where he might have gone?'

I tried to think. 'His mother's. He went there before once. I told you.'

'No reply. Or from your home number. Of course he might be there all the same and not answering. Anywhere else? . . . Right, I'll let you know if anything turns up.'

'Hey, hold it, hang on a minute.'

'Yes?'

I had been desperate to prevent her ringing off, but now I could find very little to say. 'Er . . . he will turn up all right, will he? How long . . . ?'

'If he's still loose tonight we'll set things moving in the morning. Don't worry, Stanley, they very seldom come to much harm.'

'He's been talking to himself.'

'Yes, he has aural hallucinations. Very common with disorders of this kind. Usual, in fact.'

At least she had not said normal. 'He wasn't doing it or having them before yesterday as far as I know. I thought he was supposed to be getting better.'

'He is. You should have seen him on his first couple of days here.' This would have been a good moment for one of her horse-laughs, but it failed to show. 'Anyway, I warned you not to expect his progress to be smooth.'

'You said he might have a relapse. Is that what this is?'

'I simply can't say at this stage, Stanley, I'm afraid. It depends what he's doing. If he's just sitting in a park somewhere, which he probably is, then there's not much to worry about.'

Except for him being rather wet and cold in the kind of drizzle I could see through my window. After Collings I rang home. Still no reply, which meant nothing. Before I did anything else I had to see a punter about a quarter-page. I saw him, though without result, and got home just on 5.30. When I let myself in the phone was ringing. I took it in the kitchen.

'Mr Stanley Duke?' a man's voice asked pleasantly.

'That's me.'

'Oh, it's the Metropolitan Police here, sir, Superintendent Fairchild speaking. I've got a young fellow with me who says he's your son. Name of Stephen. Is that correct?'

'Yes. Is he in trouble?'

'Well, I'm very much afraid he is, sir, yes. He's in our custody at the moment at the Jabali Embassy, where I'm speaking from now. I have to ask you to come down for a short interview.'

'Jabali? That's Arabs, isn't it?'

'Yes, sir.' He gave me an address near Regent's Park. 'Just down the road from you, really. You'll be making your own way, will you, sir?'

'Yes – can you give me some idea of what's happened?'

There was a short silence. When the Superintendent spoke again it was in a slightly different voice, one that made him sound bored stiff with what he was saying. 'I have to tell you there are diplomatic aspects to the matter which preclude it being discussed over the telephone.'

'Oh. Is my son all right?'

'Oh yes, sir,' said Superintendent Fairchild quickly and unreassuringly.

I had a quick drink. Of course I did. Not being a blithering idiot I never even considered taking the Apfelsine and phoned for a minicab, a quicker bet than a black cab hereabouts and in the rain. But I was idiot enough not to remember the flick-knife till the driver had rung the

240

doorbell. No knife, at least nowhere I looked in my top-speed search. All the way down the hill I told myself that Fairchild would have taken a different tone over a stabbing, and got nowhere.

The embassy turned out to be one of a row of between-wars houses of upper-bank-manager status, rather small for St Kevin's but in a similar style. In a back corner of the hall a uniformed constable was standing outside a closed door. He let me into a sort of waiting room newly decorated and furnished in an extremely down-market Western way. There was Steve, presumably Fairchild, also in uniform, and an Arab in a three-hundred-quid suit.

Steve's appearance was a shock, but at the same time a relief after what I had been imagining. He had the makings of a black eye, a bashed nose and a cut lip and had probably been crying, perhaps still was in a small way. 'Hallo, dad,' he said, not at all cheerfully.

The Superintendent seemed about my age, tall when he stood up, with red-grey hair and a clean-shaven gloomy face, rather a good-looking chap. After introducing himself he nodded at the Arab and said, 'This is Mr Fuad.'

'Major Fuad.' The man spoke in a stroppy way. Arab or no Arab, seen close to he looked incredibly Jewish to me, but who was I to judge?

'All right – Major Fuad. Er, Major Fuad would like to advise you of certain circumstances relating to the present matter, Mr Duke.' Without actually waving his arms about, the Superintendent signalled to me that this was something that would have to be gone along with.

'I see,' I said, and sat down on the indicated hard chair and waited respectfully.

In quite good English, but speaking at a pitch of disrespect no Englishman would have dared to use in front of another, even to a foreigner, Major Fuad said, 'You must realize that under international law this embassy is deemed to be part of the sovereign territory of the Republic of Jabal and that intrusions upon it will be treated in the same spirit as intrusions upon the republic itself,' and more in the same strain. He had a small moustache which made me wonder about my own. He also reminded me of somebody, but not because of the moustache. Superintendent Fairchild watched him with an expression on the far side of contempt or distaste, more like continuous quiet amazement. I kept nodding my head at what Fuad was telling me, or rather while he told me. Finally he said, 'I call upon you to see to it that your son understands these considerations in future, because it seems that those of us here have been unable to do so. Will you undertake to carry that into effect?'

'Yes, Major Fuad, I'll do my best.'

'You would be well advised to. Tell your son he may not get off so lightly a second time.'

'I will. Now may I ask what's happened?'

'Superintendent?' Fuad handed the ball over but went on to listen closely to the next part.

'Well, sir, it seems in brief that this young man called here earlier this afternoon and asked to speak to someone in Intelligence. He was taken in to see, er, Major Fuad's assistant and told him he had information about the activities of Israeli secret agents in this country, in London. When questioned about the source of his information he began to talk wildly, became violent and had to be restrained by the official and one of the guards here. At this point the duty PC was called in and he fetched me along.' Fairchild's manner sharpened. 'That's not quite all, I'm afraid, Mr Duke. Your son had this in his possession.'

The flick-knife right enough. I looked at it and kept my mouth shut.

'Did you know your son was in the habit of taking this kind of weapon round with him?'

'No,' I said, thanking God for the form of the question.

'I see, sir. Now you do know, it might be sensible to discourage him from carrying one in future. For one thing, as you're no doubt aware, such weapons are illegal. They may not be offered for sale, bought, possessed, borne on the person, anything. You and he have Major Fuad to thank for asking us to overlook the offence. Perhaps you'd like to dispose of this.' He handed the thing to me and stood up. 'I have some further questions which I'll put to you in another place. Thank you, Major Fuad. We're all grateful to you for your restraint in not taking the matter further. And now we won't keep you.'

I did my best, not a very good best, to imitate a man being grateful, got in return a glare of hostility with nothing imitation about it, and left the room with the others.

Outside in the hall, the Superintendent said to Steve, 'Are you all right, sonny? Do you want a doctor?'

'No, I'm all right.'

'You sure, now? You didn't get any nasty kicks? What do you say, Mr Duke? Do you think your son should see a doctor?'

'I reckon we can leave it for the moment.'

'Okay, fine. There aren't any further questions actually, sir, but there is a little more to be said, later, when we've run you home. I'll just have a word with the PC a minute.'

I squeezed Steve's arm and muttered that he had had a rough time and he nodded and looked at the floor with his mouth open. It occurred to me to wonder what he had

243

told those Arabs. About Joshua and the rest of them milling around Hampstead? No wonder they had asked him to name his informants. What was he thinking now? About which embassy to try next, possibly, or something as far out as the rim of the galaxy, where Jews in phylacteries and Star of David teeshirts sat in intersystem ships tuning their hyperspatial receptors to his brain currents. The cleverest thing I could think of to say to him was not to worry and we would look after him.

When we got to the house Superintendent Fairchild sent his driver to the pub and made a phone-call in the kitchen. Susan was terrified at the sight of the police uniform, but I soon calmed her down and told her what had happened. I called the hospital and spoke to Dr Gandhi. Should I bring Steve in for the night? Unnecessary since he appeared calm – but bring him all the way in the morning. Agreed. Steve side-stepped me when I went to comfort him, asked for and was given aspirins and slouched off to his room without another word.

'I owe you an apology for that ragtime carry-on down the road,' said Fairchild when the three of us settled in the sitting room with our drinks. 'But there was no help for it. Now I expect you'd like to know what really happened down there, wouldn't you? Right.'

He was facing me directly. 'All okay up till the point where your lad starts giving them funny answers to their questions. So he's a joker or a nutter or an unbelievably useless would-be infiltrator, but anyway he's not what he says he is. So they set about working him over out of habit, till one of them remembers they're not supposed to do that, even if this is the Jabali . . . Embassy. Then they call in the PC and say it was the boy that went for them in the first place, and there we are. How do I know? There wasn't a mark on either of the two I saw, Captain Abdullah or whatever he calls himself and some goon. And that knife, it was closed-up in his pocket when the PC searched him. They hadn't even done *that*, would you believe it. You'd have thought at least . . . I don't know.' The Superintendent shook his head and sighed in professional vexation. 'Oh no, I know those fellows of old.

'Because – I'm not an ordinary copper, I belong to a special corps that does all the security on the embassies and what-not. Now, you see, Mr Duke, my standing orders say that whenever possible I must promote cordial relations between their side and our side. Cordial relations. What that means in this instance, there's that Fuad knowing full well his side have made a bit of rubbish, an error, and the thing these blokes can't stand is losing face, right? So we all pretend he's the one with the grievance, and we have you down to be given a going-over on behalf of your son, because he's too young and helpless to be worth a going-over, you know, to get any real satisfaction out of it. And you heard me being grateful to him, Fuad that is, for not pressing charges when he knew I knew what I knew. So now he's won that one we'll have cordial relations for a bit. Meaning instead of him being unbearable on purpose he'll give us a dose of being unbearable not on purpose.

'Oh, it's a funny old job sometimes. You'd hardly credit it – I have to get into this clobber every time I put my nose inside the door, else they go on about not showing proper respect. Nothing wrong with Fuad going round in his fancy suits, of course. It's all right when they do it, you see.'

'But he can't think he's really won,' I said.

'Not a bit of it, Mr Duke, not a bit of it. As I say, he

knows full well. But he *seems* to have won, everybody goes on as if he has, and that's all that worries him. These fellows, they're like,' he glanced at Susan and away, 'like children, really, aren't they? Just big talk,' he wound up vaguely.

Susan was sitting with her legs under her on the grey settee. Now she straightened her back and said quite fiercely, 'I don't see why that pair of bastards should be allowed to just get clean away with roughing up poor Steve.'

The Superintendent reacted unfavourably to the swearword, though I could not have said what he physically did. But he politely turned in his seat towards Susan, giving her his full attention for almost the first time since they had met. 'Oh, they won't, Mrs Duke, far from it,' he said decisively. 'Our friend Fuad will see to that. I must say I'd quite like to know what he's got lined up for them, just out of curiosity. No, I understand your concern for your son, but I can – '

'Stepson.'

'I'm sorry, I just assumed. Oh yes, those two'll be taken care of all right. Thank you, just a drop if I may, I really must be going.'

Saying something about putting the meat in, Susan took herself off – we were having a couple of neighbours in that evening. Fairchild conscientiously looked round the room, nodding to himself once or twice.

'Are you a writer, Mr Duke?'

'Not really, Superintendent. My wife is. I'm in advertising myself.'

'M'm.' His face seemed to go slightly gloomier. Then, making it as clear as daylight before he spoke what was coming up, he said, 'Your boy, I take it he is, er . . .'

'Yes, he's disturbed. He goes to a day clinic at a psychiatric hospital. They say he's improving.'

'I thought it was that pretty well straight away. At first I thought glue-sniffing or one of those, but then I thought no no. You get to recognize it. You know, if those fellows down the road were any good, they'd have got on to it and just turfed him out before he could start making a nuisance of himself. They'll never learn, I'm afraid.' He paused and hung out another sign. 'That knife of his, now. You'd seen it before, hadn't you?'

'Yes, but I didn't know he was taking it around with him. I or rather my wife had just come across it in his drawer.'

'And you left it there? What a silly way to behave, even for someone who didn't know that weapons of that sort are illegal. I mean as I say, I'm quite satisfied in my own mind that this afternoon that knife never left his pocket, but nobody with any gumption would bet on a thing like that in advance, surely to God.'

'I see that now, but the hospital people were on at me not to let him feel – '

'Misprize common sense at your peril is my motto. Well, it's not my place to go on about this, especially when I'm drinking your excellent whisky. Which I must now very reluctantly tear myself away from.' He got to his feet, drained his glass and gave me a look. 'Bury that nail-file good and deep, eh?'

I followed him to the front door. He put on his uniform cap, making himself look quite grimly official, and seemed to be thinking something out. Finally he said,

'You know, Mr Duke, from a personal point of view, speaking just for myself you understand, the Major Fuads of this world have got one thing to be said not *for* them at all, just *about* them. They do seem to have got the women problem sorted out nice and neat. Whether you like it or not. Well, here I go. Thank you for your hospitality. Say good night to Mrs Duke for me if you would. And good night to you, sir.'

He hesitated for a moment, then turned away. While I strolled back upstairs to get my drink that last mention of Major Fuad got it across to me who he had reminded me of. I winced and groaned to myself and felt bad, all in vain – it was Nowell, no question, not just the tune being more important than the words and the no nonsense about forbearance towards a helpless victim, but also the sort of substitutional effect, saying A and meaning X, or rather talking about A but *really* talking about X, and not caring who knew it – especially that. At the same time I realized I had started to wonder whether I ought to ring her and tell her about the dust-up at the embassy. Not now, that was for sure – perhaps in the morning, from the office.

'What a horrible bugger, that policeman,' said Susan when I joined her in the kitchen.

'Is he, was he? What was wrong with him?'

'Oh, the ghastly bloody complacent way he could see through everyone and know exactly what happened out of his vast experience.'

She was being pretty definite about it, but I held on a bit longer. 'Well, with a bloke like that, I should imagine experience would be quite a reliable guide.'

'And the way he sneered at me for being your second wife. Fucking cheek. Who the hell cares what *he* thinks?'

I had been looking fairly closely at the Superintendent at that stage in the conversation, and I had seen nothing but a passing embarrassment. Still, it was probably not an interesting enough point to be worth a mention, so I made a semi-agreeing noise instead.

'Incidentally,' she said with a look that failed miserably to convince me that what she was going to say would be incidental, 'it wasn't such a good idea to let him have his knife back, was it?'

'No, it wasn't. Your friend the Superintendent said the same sort of thing. I just didn't think of him going and doing a thing like that. Good job he didn't actually *do* anything.'

'According to that cop.'

'Well, yes.'

She came over and put her cheek against mine. 'Bit frightening, isn't it?'

'Yeah. And awful. Let's have another drink.'

The next morning Steve was nowhere to be found. His bed had been slept in, in fact I had seen him sleeping in it when I looked in last thing. He had evidently made himself a cup of coffee. We reckoned or hoped he had gone out to buy cigarettes, though five to eight seemed a bit early for that, and there was rain about and he had not taken the mack I had lent him, but none of that counted for much. If buying cigarettes was all he was up to he would be back by 8.20 at the latest. 8.20 came and went. I could think of nothing to do but get on with shaving and dressing.

Half a dozen decent-sized trees stood in a line in the bit of garden at the side of the house, elms that had somehow escaped disease. As I shaved, the mirror in front of me reflected a view through the window of the upper parts of two of these elms. I was working my way round my moustache when I caught a movement in one of the two. As soon as I went over and looked I saw Steve standing on a branch next to the trunk about thirty feet from the ground. He was holding on to and also leaning on another branch in a position that was probably quite comfortable for the moment. I tapped on the window and after an eerie interval he turned his head and caught my eye. The light was poor but good enough to show me that he was very pale. I collected Susan and we rushed out and round.

It was not actually raining all that hard just then, but there was a lot more to come in the sky and a gusty wind was blowing. In just his shirt and jacket and trousers Steve was going to be wet through before very long and thoroughly chilled, unless he already was after however long he had been up there. Some rooks or crows were flying about near the tree-tops and cawing a good deal, perhaps because of him. He watched us approaching as though it was barely worth his while. When I asked him what he was doing he took no notice, in fact he looked away and seemed to stare into the next garden or the one further, where there might have been something interesting going on for all I knew. His hair clung to his head with the wet.

I decided it would be impossible to climb the tree to a height where I could hope to get through by talking to him face to face, and pointless to go up to any lower level. So I stayed where I was and said all the things you would say in the situation, or as many as I could think of, and no doubt some more than once. Susan went in and fetched the mack he had left behind, and then I did do a climb and managed to loop the thing over the branch he was standing on. He ignored it. A little after that he pulled himself forward and I thought for a moment he was coming down, but he was going up, up to the next tier, so to speak. I stepped back for a better view, remembering rather late in the day that he had been given to this sport as a young boy and had once, on holiday in Wales, climbed some horrible height like seventy feet to get to a bird's nest, not to take the eggs, just look at them. Now I saw him find a fork and another bit that between them made a kind of seat where he had no need to hang on to anything.

'He could be up there all day,' I said. 'What are we going to do?'

'I don't think there's anything we can do.' Susan had pushed her hair up and under a red mackintosh hat with a fairish brim. It made her look French or Italian, anyway not English and absolutely not like her mother. 'I can't imagine what would make him come down while he still wants to stay there.'

'We can't just leave him there to get wetter and wetter.'

'It looks as if we'll have to, darling. We're not helping him by standing about here getting wet ourselves. I'm not being callous about it but he'll come down in his own good time. When he's had enough.'

'Oh sure, but when's that going to be? He's mad, love. He's probably got voices telling him to stay there for forty days and forty nights.'

'Maybe, maybe not. Didn't one of those doctors say something about attention-seeking? Anyway, it's their job to sort it out.'

'But surely to God . . .'

'I think we ought to try leaving him to himself. Taking no notice.'

'Hey, dad!' called Steve, so unexpectedly that I jumped. 'I couldn't do anything else. I didn't want to come up here but I had to, where I can't be looked into. I kept giving things away in the house, even when I was asleep.' He was shivering and making hissing noises between the words. His voice came out odd but distinct in the damp air. 'I didn't mean to but I just couldn't help it. I haven't got to be awake to be tapped because the storage circuits are always active, but there's got to be conduction too and that means metal or stone at ground level. I can always be looked into if there's that and I don't even know when it's happening. The street's nearly as bad even with the location tuning. But up here I've got all this insulation with vegetable matter and the gap's too wide to jump at normal power. I just hope they don't realize what's keeping them out. With stepped-up power I wouldn't even be safe up here.'

His cheeks were shiny with rain and probably tears as well and his mouth was turned down at the corners. I could not imagine a better example of a person full of fear and misery. I called to him, 'Please come down, son, I beg you. Just for your dad. Please.'

He shook his head and turned away, his face crumpling.

'I'm going to ring Nowell,' I said to Susan.

She stared at me for a couple of seconds and then said in what I thought was a cheerful voice, 'I hope you're joking, Stanley.'

'No I am not joking. I told you about the way she calmed him down when he got violent at her place that time, and talked him into going into hospital over the phone. Well, let's see if she can work the trick again.'

'Surely you know how I feel about her.' No, there was nothing cheerful here.

'I fancy I've a pretty fair idea, though you've never actually said. I understand all that, and in the ordinary way of course I wouldn't dream of letting her get within

252

a mile of you, but this isn't an ordinary situation. Your feelings are very important to me, make no mistake, love, but just at the moment Steve's feelings are more important. And his state. Now you must be able to understand that.'

'Yes, I understand,' she said, and turned round and went back into the house.

For a moment I felt a pang of a kind of fear I had not even thought about for nearly ten years. Then it was gone. I called to Steve that I would be back and left him there.

I got through to Nowell straight away. When I did I realized I had been half or a quarter hoping she would be unreachable. As soon as she understood what was required of her she started thick-and-thinning away like nobody's business and after doing enough of it to last me, or herself, said she would come at once.

'Great. Don't – ' I said, and stopped.

'Don't what, darling?'

'I was going to say don't break your neck, then I remembered you don't drive.'

She sounded a bit puzzled when she signed off, as well she might. I had been going to ask her not to queen it too hard over Susan, but then it had flashed on me that it was very much the wrong time for being foul to her.

Exactly as I put the phone down the doorbell rang, as if she had found a way of literally coming at once. But of course it was Mrs Shillibeer's early morning. She was wearing a pale blue plastic mack with a hood and resembled an enormous child.

'Hallo,' she said in her geriatric-minder voice. 'Horrible weather.' She mouthed the words so that if I was too deaf to hear them I stood a fair chance of lip-reading them.

'Oh, yes, it is,' I said with a slight quaver.

'Mrs Duke upstairs?' she went on, actually pointing.

'I shouldn't be at all surprised.'

I could hear very little sting in the last one, but it was the best I could do at that moment, and probably just as well. I went out and told Steve his mother would be here soon and saw him nod. Then I went to the bathroom and finished shaving, and then to the bedroom to finish dressing. Susan was there. The whine of the vacuum-cleaner came from somewhere under our feet.

'Has she arrived yet?'

'No,' I said. 'I'll come and tell you when she has.'

'I don't want to set eyes on her.'

'Oh, fair enough. I shan't be bringing her up here.'

'How long will she be around, do you think?'

'Not long, I'd say. If nothing happens in the first few minutes then that's it, probably. Anyway, she won't want to hang about.'

'I've got things to do in here, clearing out drawers and so on, so I shan't be wasting my time.'

It was sporting of her to throw that in. All the same I would have settled for a smile or two. Not that she was cold or I had done any better myself. The two of us had been relaxed but not intimate, like people who had worked in the same office for years without ever having met outside it.

I was in the kitchen trying to eat a yoghurt when Mrs Shillibeer barged into the room. Her forehead looked amazingly huge compared with her chin.

'There's a man in one of the trees out there,' she gabbled, no geriatrics now.

'Yes,' I said, 'I know.' My mind was a total blank. I had not stopped thinking about Steve or him being in the tree for more than five seconds at a time, but somehow it had never occurred to me that this female was going to have to have something said to her on the subject.

'What's he doing? Who is he?'

'He's my son.' This slipped out a second before I got to ideas about branch-lopping, man from the Council and so on.

'The one who's staying here? The one you . . . What's he doing up a tree?'

'I suppose he just felt like it,' I found I was saying. Perhaps I really had gone senile.

'*Felt* like it?' she asked indignantly. 'In this weather? What's the matter with him? On drugs, is he?'

Here was my out, but I was too thick to recognize it. 'Nothing like that,' I said with conviction, realizing as I said it that this was not even true in any literal way.

'What is it then? People don't go sitting in the middle of a tree in the pouring rain like that, not if they're . . . normal. What is the matter with him?'

I coughed. 'He's . . . upset. Confused. Unhappy.' Nobody hearing the words could have believed they were honestly spoken.

'That hospital's not just for anxiety and depression,' she said, suddenly gone all calm and wide-eyed. Susan and I had worked out that that was the best story to cover any unforeseen puzzling or perhaps alarming bit that might have emerged. But it was no use this morning. Mrs Shillibeer had guessed the truth, near enough anyway. 'He's barmy. I'm not having that.'

She started to fling out of the room but then froze and, while I watched in fascination, retraced her steps to where I sat at the table, moving with ridiculous caution like somebody imitating a burglar. First looking over each

255

shoulder in turn she bent forward in my direction and gave me a slow wink.

'I'll tell you this much,' she said in a throaty undertone about as far as possible from her usual mode. 'It's a relief, that's what it is. I've been dying to get away from this job almost since I first started here, that's almost two years now, not that long after you moved in. The money's good quite frankly and my husband would never have let me walk out of here just because I didn't fancy coming. But now I've got a reason, see. He knows I've got this thing about loonies. So I'm off the hook at last. Whoopee.'

'Why don't you like working here? Not because of me, I hope?'

'Ooh no, not you, Stanley, you're a darling, you are. No, it's that stuck-up cat you married. What did you want to go and do that for, a nice guy like you? Have you ever noticed the way she talks to me?' Actually I had, but I kept quiet. 'No reason why you should. Oh Mrs Shillibeer, would you very kindly, very sweetly chop up these shallots, not too fine, you know the way I like them, and tell me when you've done them.' It was – of course – an unkind imitation but not quite an unrecognizable one. 'Never once talks to me like a human being. It's not much to ask. And that mother. And that sister. You want to watch the mother. That's the way Susan'll end up. Well, she's most of the way there already, I reckon.'

Mrs Shillibeer seemed again ready to be off. I said, 'Are you going up there now to tell her some of that?'

'Christ no, what do you take me for? I'm much too scared of her. I'd sooner cross my husband. And that's saying something. Good luck, Stanley love. I'm afraid you're going to need it. Oh, and I hope your son gets better soon. They can do a lot these days, you know.'

She went out in the same sort of style as she had come in, getting into trim for the action. Instantly the doorbell rang. It was Nowell. Who else?

'Darling Stanley.' A warm hug came my way, one full notch below sexiness but no more and accompanied by the usual good smell. 'Am I going to be asked in?'

'Of course. I . . .'

'Is he all right? Will he be all right for the next two minutes?'

'Yes.' I took her into the kitchen, which was all she seemed to want. Much against my expectation she showed no interest in her surroundings. 'Would you like some coffee?'

'No thanks,' she said, not sitting down. 'Stanley, I want to say this. I know you think I've behaved pretty badly over Steve and his troubles, not doing my fair share and all that. Of course you think so. And in a way you're right. The thing is, I've got troubles of my own. Or rather Joanne has. You've seen her, so perhaps you've some idea of how difficult she can be. Difficult, that's hardly the word. It's a full-time job just keeping an eye on her. Not long ago I had to take her to Portugal for a week because she wanted some sunshine. It may be all my fault in the first place but there's no point in arguing about that now. As you can imagine, I don't get any help from Bert.' The mention of this name had a knowing look packaged up with it. 'There it is. She's got me and Steve's got you. Simple as that. I'll lend you a hand when I can but mostly I can't. There we are.'

Again, it was not the moment to query any of this or boggle at the idea of a human being who could make Nowell have to do things, so I was sweet to her instead. Before I had quite finished somebody came tearing down the stairs and went out by the front door. Nowell ignored this completely. I told her to hang on a moment and went up to the bedroom.

Susan was sitting on the bed with about five hundred waist-belts on the counterpane. I was a bit flummoxed on how to open the conversation but she led off straight away.

'Mrs Shillibeer has gone. Walked out.'

The way she spoke these half-dozen words sounded incredibly and horrendously like what I had heard in the kitchen five minutes before. I was reminded in a more disagreeable way than usual that snobbily or not I was quite tickled by being married to someone who talked like that. 'Yes,' I said, 'I heard her.'

'She said you told her Steve was mad and mad people frighten her. She had a mad brother. What the bloody hell possessed you to tell her?'

'I didn't mean to. It just sort of . . . She guessed. I wasn't ready for her.'

'You knew she was here, you let her in. A clever man like you.'

'I'm sorry, I got flustered. We can discuss it later. Nowell has arrived.'

'I can't understand why you didn't call the hospital. They must have people who are used to dealing with this sort of thing.'

'Perhaps I should have, I don't know. I will if this doesn't work. Anyway, she's here now.'

'Well . . . good luck,' said Susan with a smile that came and went.

Whether by good luck or not, it worked. Nowell took her previous line about what a rough time he must have been having and in less than five minutes Steve was down, soaked to the skin, pale, shivering, wretched, but on terra firma. Nowell hugged him, but he seemed unresponsive and had nothing to say for himself. Having called off his performance, though, he was keen enough to get back indoors, and without fuss set about obeying instructions to go up and take off his wet things.

I walked Nowell to the door. Her behaviour had impressed me rather. As well as hiding all curiosity about the house and its contents she had not once mentioned Susan's name or raised the subject without actually referring to it, something she was very good at, and at no stage had shown any triumph or complacency at getting Steve to quit his perch, just pleasure and relief. True, she had more or less blamed me personally for his wetness, coldness and lack of topcoat, but I could think of quite a few people who would have taken that tack.

At the threshold I said, 'Thank you for coming so quickly. That was a damn good show just now.'

'Think nothing of it. Just a knack I have.' Then she gave me a look that signalled the advent of something in bold. 'You're a good chap, Stanley,' she said very earnestly. 'No wonder Steve's devoted to you.'

'Oh.'

Here it came. 'I miss you, you know. Do you believe me?'

'Why not? I miss you. Every day.'

The warmth in my voice took her by surprise, and me too a bit. For an insane moment I could see her seriously wondering why I had said that, how much I meant it, what it might indicate for the future – then it passed, and the Eternal Woman once more looked out of Nowell's eyes. She threw her head back, kissed me lightly on the cheek and tripped away to a waiting taxicab whose driver was doggedly picking his nose.

I was glad I had said what I had. I had indeed meant it, though it was not a complete statement of the case, perhaps not even accurate as far as it went. But if you could miss somebody, feel somebody's absence, without ever wanting to be with them again, then yes, I missed Nowell every day. More to the point, I had been sweet to her in spades, which was not going to come in unhandy when Steve climbed on to the roof of Buckingham Palace or hijacked a jet.

I got him into a hot bath now and went to the bedroom and said, 'All over. She talked him down and she's gone.'

'I know.' Susan had moved on to long thin strips of different-coloured material the purpose of which was very difficult to guess. 'At least I gathered he was down. Is he all right?'

'Well, he's better where he is than where he was. I don't know what more you could say.'

She was still on her limited-friendliness tone, the nearest thing to a female freeze-out I had ever had from her. But when the time came to take Steve off we held on to each other for a fair time, with her seeming not to want to let go as if I were off to the States or somewhere. At the end she gave me a smile, a real one this time. So that was all right.

When I had escorted Steve to Dr Gandhi's manor I went in search of Collings and found her in her room. She was looking really rough that morning, with her hair got up to remind you of carefully prepared paper. I told her about Steve and the tree and she said it was part of the pattern.

'Look, it may be part of your pattern, Dr Collings,' I said as quietly as I could, 'but it's not part of mine or my wife's. We're not used to handling this kind of thing.'

'I understand that.'

'Terrific, but could you do something about it? We're getting near the end of our resources.'

'Of course it's a period of great tension and distress for you both. It would be far from unusual in this situation for your marriage to suffer severe strain,' she said, ready with more technical data if they were needed.

'I dare say it would. I wasn't actually thinking of that side of it. What I was driving at, my wife and I don't know how to deal with someone like Steve. We've managed so far but any moment he might do something we couldn't cope with. Would you please take him back in as a full-time patient where there are trained people to look after him. In his interests.'

'It's in his interests to stay as he is, believe me, Stanley. Do you want him to be a hospital case for the rest of his life?' She went on to describe a few of what she called hospital cases in some detail, and if she wanted my honest agreement that the general run of them would have been as well or better off dead she could have had it for the asking. There was more than a touch of overkill here and I wondered where we were due next. At the end of her cases she said, 'I hope you'll agree it's worth a lot of sacrifice to make any of that less likely to happen to Steve.'

'Oh, absolutely,' I said, letting myself off a question about how much sacrifice and how much less likely, and another one about how likely in the first place.

'He must be helped to live in the world, to make a successful transition to family and community.' On she went about that while I grew more and more uneasy. As she spoke she looked more steadily at me than ever before. This part was so boring that when the punch came I almost missed it. 'These current difficulties are all part of the process of adjustment to the withdrawal of chemotherapy. A progressive – '

'Chemotherapy? That's drugs, isn't it? You mean you've taken him off drugs?'

'Drugs are a crutch, an artificial support. He's got to learn to do without them if he's ever going to live any sort of normal life.'

'But he's *mad*. You should have seen him when he was up that tree. Not just the loony stuff he was saying but the way he looked and everything. He wasn't in a difficulty or adjusting, he was raving bonkers, poor fellow. He was in a *state*. Anyone could have seen.'

'It's very difficult and painful for him and that's why he needs all the understanding and encouragement you can give him.'

'Please take him back. For a bit. He's not ready.'

'You must let me be the judge of that.'

After a bit more along the same lines I came away, trying not to feel scared about what might be in store. Just after starting back I remembered the flick-knife, still in my pocket. I had not exactly forgotten it but so far kept finding I was short of a good place to dump it. Now I soon had one – the river off Blackfriars Bridge. When it was gone I felt a glow of relief, which was not very logical but well worth having on a day like today.

That afternoon, while I was on my way back from an advertising agency somewhere off Oxford Street, an accident up ahead kept me sitting in a traffic block for forty minutes. On my desk in the office I found a note from Morgan telling me to ring home – urgent.

'How long ago was this?' I asked, dialling.

'Oh, getting on for an hour. It was your wife.' He hesitated, then said, 'She sounded a bit upset.'

After half a dozen rings a man's voice spoke at the far end.

'This is Stanley Duke,' I told him.

'Stan, it's Cliff. I'm afraid there's been a bit of a dust-up here, old son. All under control now, but you'd better get along as soon as you can. I'll stay till you come.'

'Anybody hurt?'

'Nothing that can't be taken care of.'

When I got home by taxi and let myself in I found a trail of blood, drops of it the size of a 10p piece, running into the kitchen. 'Up here, Stanley,' said Cliff's voice.

Susan was in her usual chair in the sitting-room. She was pale and had a fair-sized bandage on her left forearm. There was more blood on the carpet and furniture, not a great amount but quite enough. I hurried over and we hugged each other. She said she was all right. I asked what had happened. Cliff answered. 'Steve came at her with a knife,' he said.

'Oh, God. Where is he? Where is he now?'

'In his room. With a shot in him that'll make him not want to go anywhere for quite a while.'

'How bad is the arm?'

'Well, it's nasty, but it's not, it's not bad. In the fleshy part, no major blood-vessel punctured, I've put three stitches in, under a local anaesthetic of course.' He spoke in a dead sort of way, almost as though these details bored him. 'There'll be a certain amount of pain when it wears off and for a couple of days afterwards. I'll leave some pills for that. And I'll look in tomorrow.'

When he had said that I quite expected him to leave,

but he stayed where he was, standing by the empty fireplace. I had pulled a stool up to Susan's chair. 'Tell me what happened, love,' I said. 'If you can bear to.'

'Oh, I can bear to. I think the worst part was the fright at the beginning,' she said, a little quietly for her but well under control. 'You did take him to the hospital, darling, did you?'

'Yeah. Right to the ward.'

'I didn't even know he was in the house. The door just burst open and he came rushing in with this knife shouting that I was a bloody bitch who'd driven his mother and father apart and wouldn't let him see his mother. Like that bit of hostility last week, you remember, only this time he meant business, and I just had time to get to my feet before he . . . struck at me.' She started to lift her left arm to show how, but winced and used the other one instead. 'I tried to catch his wrist but I didn't manage it properly, and he cut me.' I squeezed her hand. 'And I thought I was done for, but then he stopped, I don't really know why, perhaps it was the sight of blood, anyway he dropped the knife and gave the most awful sort of groan or moan, an absolutely harrowing noise, and then he simply ran off and I heard his bedroom door slam, and it was over.'

She had not actually started to cry but she was not far off it. I thought she was being pretty good. 'Thank God for that, anyway,' I said. 'What knife was it?'

'There,' she said, and there it was on one of the low tables almost in front of me, though I saw it now for the first time – a kitchen knife from downstairs with, as I knew, a sharp point and edge, now with dried or drying blood on it, some of which had leaked on to the sheet of newspaper underneath. 'Well . . . I went down to the kitchen and tried to get you, and couldn't, and then I got Cliff, and he sweetly said he'd come straight away, and I sort of hung about near the front door, ready to run, until he arrived, and there we are.'

'I know it's a bit early but I'm going to have a drink,' I said after a moment. When I looked at Susan she shook her head. 'Cliff?'

'No thanks, I've got to get back.' But he still made no move.

'So then you turned up,' I said from the drinks tray.

'Yes, I turned up,' said Cliff. As soon as he started to speak I knew that he was not at all bored, just choosing his words carefully, and also that there was something that had not been mentioned, something to do with him – actually I had known it almost since coming into the room. 'I put in the local,' he went on, 'and that was going to take a few minutes to work, so I went up to have a look at Steve. There he was, lying on his bed, not asleep, but quite relaxed I thought, you could almost say torpid, but after what Susan had told me I was taking no chances. I gave him Valium intravenously, which is pretty quick-acting. He didn't object.'

'Didn't he say anything at all,' I asked, 'why he'd done it or anything?'

'Oh, he said something. I asked him why, why he'd attacked his stepmother, and he said he didn't know what I was talking about. He'd let himself in and come straight up, thinking he was alone in the place, he said.' Cliff snapped the catches of his bag. I fancied his hands were shaking. 'He said he hadn't done it.'

A horrible pause followed. What felt like a hundred thoughts went through my head in two or three seconds, bits of remarks about Steve from Nash, from Collings, from Nowell, cloudy memories of Steve himself when younger, sharper ones of Susan the other day, this morning, and behind it all something I could neither face nor define. At last, very late, I said, 'Amnesia, presumably.'

'Does rather suggest that, doesn't it? Yes, it's quite common in these cases.' He sighed, scratching his head elaborately and sending a thin shower of dandruff on to the shoulders of his incredibly dark green suit. 'Well, that's it. I shouldn't say much about this to anyone, but then I don't suppose either of you will want to. Except of course to the people at the hospital, Stan, when you take Steve in in the morning. It's quite likely they'll want him back in full-time, I suppose. Yeah, and better let them know where he is now.'

'What did you say, you suppose they might want him back in full-time?' Susan asked. 'But surely, I mean after a thing like this they must, mustn't they? Or has he got to murder somebody first?'

'If you're talking about legal committal, I can assure you it wouldn't be at all easy. Not really worth a shot, in fact.'

Cliff had still not sounded his normal self and Susan had spoken so faintly I could hardly hear her, almost without expression too, a new voice for her as far as I was concerned. Shock, that would be. Fatigue. I felt dazed, like with a very bad hangover, wanting to start using my mind on what had been said and what seemed to have happened but unable to get there.

Now Cliff handed over pills and gave instructions about them and other things and I tried to listen. When he started to leave I went with him.

He kept well ahead of me all the way down the stairs and nearly to the front door. 'Nasty,' he said as I opened it. 'Look, er, it might be as well if Susan went and stayed somewhere for a couple of days while we sort things out with the hospital and so on. Just to be on the safe side. No need to worry tonight but she ought to be out of the way tomorrow. So long, Stan. I'll be in touch.'

I rang the hospital, but could find nobody who gave any sign of having heard of Steve, so without a lot of hope of success I left a message at the switchboard. In the teeth of a whacking reluctance I went back up to the sitting room, though once there I landed up at the drinks tray without any trouble at all. Susan was sitting in the same position, her injured arm on the arm of the chair.

'What did Cliff say to you?' she asked in the same tone as before.

'He said tomorrow you ought to get out for a bit. Stay with someone.'

'Did he really.'

'Can I get you anything, love? What about a nice cup of tea? Tomato sandwich with the skins off? Do you good to eat something.'

She looked at me with her eyes half-closed and her mouth drooping and said in another voice I had not heard before, low and level, 'You little bastard. Swine. Filth.'

I was so surprised I knocked a bottle of tonic water over with my elbow, and yet I had been fully expecting it. 'What have I done?' I said.

'You think I gave myself that cut, don't you? Three stitches there are in there. I'd like you to see it.'

'But I don't, I don't think you gave yourself it.' I had no idea what I thought.

'I was watching you when Cliff told you Steve had said he didn't know anything about it and you stood there weighing it up. Weighing it up.'

'I wasn't, there were just some things I couldn't help – '

'You believe what somebody says your deranged, deluded, fucking raving maniac of a son said instead of what your wife tells you happened. You see what that makes me, don't you?'

'I don't believe – '

'Or rather what it reveals about what you think of me. You think I'm so neurotic, so self-centred, so . . . unprincipled that I'd expose that boy, that poor madman to being locked up and Christ knows what and I'd put you through it and suffer all that pain myself just to . . . just for what? Attention? Is that what I was after?' She spoke in the same level tone.

At least I had the sense to see that this was a question with no good answers.

'And you think I'd do that. As well as tell a lie on that scale. That seems to me about the worst insult one person can give another. And I'm not having it.' She stood up. 'I'm off. And I'm not waiting till the morning as your friend suggests, I'm leaving straight away. Catch me hanging on here with someone who thinks I'm like that.'

I stood up too. 'You're not fit to travel, you need rest,' I said, and got out of her way as she moved towards the door.

'I'll risk it.' At the door she stopped and turned round. 'If anybody wants me they can get me at my mother's. Though you'll be wasting your time if you try me there yourself. I suppose you think that's funny. Yer, ass right, the wife's gorn orf to er muvver's,' she said in a very poor imitation of perhaps a Hackney or Bow accent as much as anything. 'Just up your street, you lower-class turd. I don't know how I've put up with you for so long, with your gross table-manners and your boozing and your bloody little car and your frightful *mates* and your whole ghastly south-of-the-river man's world. You've no breeding and so you've no respect for women. They're there to cook your breakfast and be fucked and that's it. So of course nothing they say's worth taking seriously, and when one of them says something quite important and serious and a man says something different then you believe him even though he's out of his mind. Oh, I wish to Christ I'd found out about you sooner.'

I watched her saying this, looking as brainy and nervous as ever but not humorous any more and nowhere near vulnerable. Her eyes were wide open now, though blinking pretty fast, and I had seen them more or less like that a thousand times, but if she had ever before had her lower lip pushed forward as it was at the moment then I had missed it. She had taken a few steps back into the room from the doorway and stood there with a brown striped cardigan thrown over her shoulders and her right hand clasping her left elbow just above the top edge of the bandage. This set my mind running on whether she had had her arm in the sleeve or not when . . . but I pulled guiltily back from that. I was still dazed and could think of nothing to say. Well, I said 'Cheers, love' at the end.

'*Love*,' she said through her teeth, and made for the door again.

'Are you coming back?'

'I shan't be able to take everything with me in one go if that's what you mean, so yes to that extent.'

She said this from outside the room. There was no one I wanted to see and nothing I wanted to do. Except have another drink, of course. By the time I had seen to that I was into my second minute of having no wife.

Had she really stabbed herself? What a perfectly

ridiculous sodding question. Who ever heard of the assistant literary editor of the *Sunday Chronicle* stabbing herself a bit and saying her barmy stepson had done it to pay her husband out for thinking the barmy stepson was more important than she was? But perhaps she had. And of course perhaps she had done it to make the stepson seem barmier than he was, more violent, so violent he would have to be shut up and her life could go back to normal. But that would have been calculation in pursuit of comfort – too squalid to suit a woman like Susan, a woman who might incidentally let an innocent party in for damage while following her ends but would never make that damage her aim. If she had done it, she had done it for ego, as in her own scenario, not for peace and quiet. Wow, I thought to myself – I had come quite far quite fast too. Could she have done it? Surely not the woman who had put so much into cheering me up when I needed it, who had only the other day seen off her own mother and sister on my behalf. But perhaps she had. Could Nowell have done it? Perhaps. Probably. Yes. But what of that?

At least one fact needed establishing. When Cliff said Steve had said he knew nothing about any attack, had I really – what had she said? – had I weighed up the chances? Not a lot – it had been far more a matter of telling myself in a completely slow, thick way that that was funny, what Steve said had happened was different from what Susan said had happened. And when I tried to do some weighing a moment ago I had not even been able to start. Never mind, at the time in question had I looked as if that was what I was doing? That depended not only on how I had behaved but on who had been watching. But what was absolutely bleeding certain and inescapable was that I could have been weighing up the chances, which was the same as I could easily have been, which meant I might even have been going to be foul to her. Good God. Surely not.

I was going through this for about the fifteenth time when the doorbell rang. Having got half-way across the room I remembered hearing the phone give its little end-of-call chink a few minutes earlier and reasoned that a minicab stood below, so I went back to my chair, not before I had topped up my drink. Almost at once I heard Susan coming down the stairs and in a moment she appeared in the doorway. She was carrying the large red suitcase she always took on holiday and was wearing her round woollen hat and gloves. I got to my feet so as not to show unwilling, but she just stayed where she was and looked very seriously at me. If I had had a bit more time I might have gone over to her and confessed to or admitted anything she liked – as it was I too stayed put. There was no knowing, then or later, what was going on inside her, from profound sorrow to wondering whether it would be all right to touch me for the cab fare. Anyway, the bell rang again and without saying anything or changing her expression she went out, and soon enough the street door slammed.

Later on I went and looked at Steve, but he was obviously out for the count, so I came down again and had another drink or so. About 4 a.m. I woke up in my chair and went and drank a couple of litres of water and got into bed.

FOUR

PROGNOSIS

♀

First thing the next morning I took a cab down to Fleet Street and drove the Apfelsine slowly and dangerously back to Hampstead. I wished I had a headache or anything else like that, out where I could see it so to speak, instead of how I felt. Steve was still half-full of the sedative Cliff had given him and I had a hard time getting him to get up. When he finally came downstairs he ate nothing, not that he had done much different on previous mornings as far as I could remember, but now I was in charge of breakfast I noticed more. I managed a glass of apple juice and most of half a bowl of posh continental cereal with nuts and raisins that had been cunningly turned the same dusty white as the cereal itself. On an ordinary day I would have said that of course I preferred this sort of thing to any old eggs and bacon or sausage or kipper in the world, but now, again, I remembered that neither of my wives had been the sort to fancy cooking their husband's breakfast, never mind what the second one had had to say on the point the previous evening. I drank a lot of Lapsang Suchong, which I really did quite like and which helped the other stuff to stay down.

When the time came I told Steve so and went and had a pee and collected my gear. He had not appeared, so I went back to the kitchen and found him in exactly the same position as I had left him in, sitting near rather than at the table with his shoulders hunched, hands clasped and head down. I wanted to fetch him a thump that would lay him full length on the floor, in the first place for not doing what he was told, but also for being a bleeding pest, being dull, being off his head, being around the place all the time without a word to say for himself or even a glance to spare, and taking over my life and mucking it up. But instead of thumping him I shouted his name. He looked up very quickly and just for a second I saw him as he always had been before that first evening he came to the house, but then almost at once his face changed in ways I had no hope of making out and went back to being something different, more different than it had been, I thought, with a funny sort of twist to the corner of the lower lip. I told him we were off, quietly now, and he got up straight away.

As always it was a relief being in the car because people often said nothing to each other in cars, and anyway there was the driving to be done. After a few minutes, though, I started asking Steve what he had been up to the previous day and he answered after a fashion. He had walked out. He had got on a bus. He had arrived home. What time? No idea. He had gone to his room. Susan had been in the sitting room, had she? No idea. What had she said to him? From here on the answers stopped coming. It looked as if I was never going to know any more about that afternoon.

I had one last shot. 'There must be something you remember,' I said. 'Never mind how trivial.'

He seemed to reflect for half a minute or so, then nodded slowly. 'Actually there is something.'

'Let's have it then.'

'You're not going to like it,' he mumbled.

'Don't worry, I'll manage.'

'Promise not to be angry.'

'Of course. I promise.'

'Well,' he said, staring in front of him, 'I remember being born.' I just managed not to drive into the side of a bus. 'What?' I said. 'I remember being born. Everybody's done their best to make me forget by telling a different story. Mum says she brought me into the world and you say you're my father and I don't really blame either of you – you probably believe it yourselves by this time. And everybody else believes it and no wonder. But I've had the message so often on television and in ads and the street names and the names on shops and even the labels on bottles of sauce and things, so many times I can remember it, actually being born. Well, I say born, attaining consciousness would be better, more precise. It was like a great light being switched on.

'Yeah, I was put together by these alchemists using the philosopher's stone.' He was smiling cheerfully now. 'Kept in a vault in Barcelona till needed, then triggered off by radio beam. And here I am, ready to begin my task.' At that he looked guilty and nervous, as though he felt he had let slip something important. 'Er, I want to thank you for all your kindness, Mr Duke. Oh, and I think we should go on calling each other father and son in public. For security reasons. You understand.'

I pulled in to the side of the road and stopped behind a van delivering a lot of eggs. I spent five minutes or so trying to get myself to think that it was all just part of his madness, nothing to do with rejecting me or his mother, while thinking under zero pressure that whatever happened or was said in the future I would always feel I had had some hand, somehow, in bringing about his condition. Nobody could prove the contrary. Perhaps nobody could prove anything of importance. Having reached this conclusion I drove on, since I was going to have to some time.

When Steve and I eventually reached Gandhi's pad Gandhi was not in, it. But Collings was, which would save me a walk. Also in attendance were the sister I had seen on my first visit and since, name of Wheatley, the white-haired moaning loony I had also seen before, not actually moaning at the moment, and another with no teeth who was new to me.

Almost straight away I said to Collings, 'It looks as if he stabbed my wife. Took a knife to her. Nothing too serious.'

She followed it up in a flash. 'Looks as if?' she repeated. 'Did he or didn't he?'

'He did,' I said without thinking at all. To believe anything else was ridiculous again. 'I just wasn't there when it happened. But he did it.'

'Are you sure?'

'Of course I'm sure.' This time it was more that I spoke before I could think. 'There she is with a gash in her arm. What are you talking about?'

She was hardly listening, looking into Steve's face, looking at his eyes, feeling his pulse. 'This boy has been sedated,' she said.

'You bet he has. That was Dr Wainwright's doing, our GP, when he came to stitch up my wife. I should have thought it was common sense.'

More no-listening. She sat on the corner of Steve's bed next to him with her hand on his shoulder, still looking at him closely, asking him now a string of quite friendly questions about what he wanted to do and where he wanted to be, soon agreeing that he should stay as he was for the moment and then get into bed if he felt like it. I was just starting to think that she might be some good when she turned towards me and said, 'What have you been doing to your son?'

I stopped breathing. The sister sent me a glance of sympathy with a touch of despair. The white-haired loony did nothing but the toothless one, either catching the feel of things or driven by a sudden extra bit of delusion, backed into a corner and crouched there with his arms held out in front of him like a wrestler's. When the sister went over and spoke gently to him he dropped his arms to his sides and started blinking and shaking his head very fast.

After a while I gave up watching this and said to Collings, 'Can we go somewhere and have a talk?'

'Here will do, for anything you have to say to me, Stanley.' Her tone, somewhere in the anger-resentment bracket, did an unusually good matching job with her expression. At the same time during what followed she kept switching them both off and paying attention to Steve, now and then muttering to him too quietly for me to hear.

'Well,' I said, 'what do you mean, what have I done to him?'

'It's obvious enough I should have thought. He goes through an acute phase, he starts responding to treatment, he's gradually pulling out and coming to terms with himself and getting in touch with his emotions, doing so well that I put him back with family, which in practice means you, and he promptly turns round and retreats behind his defences again.'

'Oh, that's what happened, is it? I thought you took him off his drugs and he promptly tried to join the Arab secret service, climbed a tree to insulate himself from blokes who were reading his mind with radio waves and went for his stepmother with a knife.'

While I was saying this she sent Sister Wheatley out of the room to fetch or do something or other and then took a bit of notice of me. 'If he did. It's just the sort of tale somebody might dream up if they wanted to get him taken off their hands and back into hospital.'

'You think I,' I said, and stopped, taking good care not to move my head suddenly in case it fell off. 'But if he didn't . . . ' I stopped again.

This I thought she missed altogether for what it was worth. 'He's obviously suffered a major relapse and requires rehospitalization. All those weeks of work gone for nothing,' she said, glaring indignantly at me.

'You're a scream, you are, Collings, and no mistake.' I realized I must have sounded fairly angry. 'You decided Steve was ready to spend some of his time at home. Wrong. You decided he was ready to come off drugs. Wrong again. Two whacking errors of judgement that might have got somebody killed. And you put it all down to me. Incidentally till a moment ago you must have thought I was a quite fit person to be in charge of him, mustn't you? Another floater.'

'What's the matter with you? Been having trouble with Nowell again?'

'Oh for Christ's sake,' I said, and the white-haired loony gasped and winced and the one with no teeth raised his arms as before. 'You can't stay ten years old for ever,' – the best I could do at short notice.

'Don't you talk like that to me, my lad.' She stared at me with her eyes half-shut and her eyebrows lifted in the mysterious expression I had seen in the Crown and Sceptre that time, only now there was no mystery any more.

Sheer rage was there but also menace, a stated purpose to level the score. 'One more crack out of you and I'll discharge him and then you'll fucking know all about it. Is that clear?'

All my own anger died away. I just felt a dull horror that a doctor, a woman, anybody could turn a madman loose to avenge a passing slight. No, I felt incredulity too – surely not, no one would, she was merely furious for the moment. But this brought no comfort.

The Sister came back into the room having fetched a file or part of one, presumably Steve's part. Collings started checking through it. I said goodbye to Steve in the hope that he might at least raise his head, but he gave no sign of having heard, so I went.

While I was making my way through the boarding-house part of the ground floor I heard my name called. As more than half expected it was Sister Wheatley. I turned back.

'I just wanted to say, Mr Duke, I'll keep an eye on Steve for you. Can I have your telephone number?' She wrote it efficiently down on a small pad from her top pocket. 'If anything, well, untoward happens I'll let you know. It won't because she can't afford it to, not anything awful, but I thought perhaps you might like to have something you felt you could rely on. She's all right really, just a bit funny sometimes.'

'That's very kind of you, Sister. Thank you,' I said, and, and thought to myself you got good and bad in every crowd. You know, like Germans.

Outside there was a lot of sunshine, more than usual for the time of year, as bright as early evening in summer.

Immediately everyone and everything I had been thinking about up to that moment fell away and I was stuck with just myself and having no wife. It stayed with me throughout the drive to the office, the ride in the lift and the short walk to the private phone, and barely started to shift when Lindsey Lucas answered her extension, though it moved a bit further off when she agreed to meet me in the Crown and Sceptre after work. When that was over I spent a minute or so paying close attention to the wall, which had a great many unspecified people's numbers ball-pointed and otherwise written on it. Then I rang Nash's New Harley Street place and after an interval got some other male who told me to ring him, Nash, at home that evening. I said I would, fine, but the bloke hung about.

'Is it, er, very urgent?'

'I couldn't say *very*, no. But I would rather like to see him as soon as convenient.'

'Oh. Have you rung him before at that number? Recently?'

'No, never. Why?'

'I should, I should leave it till after seven if I were you. To make sure of getting him, you know.'

'Oh, I see,' I said. I wondered if I had struck Nash's grandfather, or at least somebody of that age-group. Then I thought whoever it was had sounded rather as though he would have liked to warn me about something but had not known how. Then I put the question aside. In my own office I sat for a time trying to work up the energy to tackle the whole immense matter of Stentor PA Systems' half-page. I had not got even as far as being able to start to think when my phone rang and I clutched at it.

'Stanley Duke? Good morning, Penangan High Commission calling. I have the Commercial Attaché for you.'

After a pause and a click a voice I knew said, 'Am I having Mr Joke?'

'Yes, speaking. Good morning, Mr One, I mean Mr Attaché. What can I do for you?'

'Mr Joke, I'm wanting to make some arrangements with you for four pages special report in your newspaper. It must be soon because our Minister of Trade will come to London next month for three days. Please telephone my secretary shortly to arrange lunch.'

'Is this definite, Mr Attaché? The last time we discussed the project it was still at the planning or provisional stage.' I remembered that it was only simple sentences that might throw Mr One – anything at all complicated he sailed through.

'Oh yes, definite. My government has completed its explorations.'

'That's fine – highly satisfactory. Tell me, sir, shall I be working with you direct or with that observer I spoke to recently?' Pretty crafty, I thought.

'Observer? What observer?'

'At the High Commission. That was what you – that was his official designation.'

'Observer,' said Mr One, lingering over the syllables. Eventually, '*Haw*,' he howled at some length, carried away by wonder at his own feat of memory. Like Mandy. 'He has been subducted.'

So now I knew. The lunch itself would be eatable and drinkable and there would be the fun of telling . . . Oh well, I had had a minute off.

When I had put the phone back Morgan was there. 'Stanley, you know that new girl, the one with the cage?'

'With the what? Is that the same as the one with the rope?'

'That's right. Going on like the hammers of hell she's been, about sexual harassment.'

'Really? Lucky to get any you'd think, with that comb. The limping porter again, I suppose.'

'No, it's the bloody tea-lady. Asks her if she had a good you-know-what last night and says she bets her boyfriend's got a nice big how's-your-father. In a nasty way, she says, the girl.'

I groaned. 'M'm, it's sexual in a sense, of course it is, and I can see how it might be harassing for her, but it doesn't quite add up to what the phrase is supposed to mean, does it? Not that there's the slightest point in telling her so, I realize that. When were you talking to her?'

'Now, just while you were on the phone.'

'Oh, yeah, that was the King of Penang wanting four pages. Firm.'

'Great. Come and have a word with her, would you, Stanley? She's in a hell of a tizzy.'

I looked round for an escape route and there was Harry Coote brilliantly standing in the doorway. I had not set eyes on him since what he quite likely thought of as the night of the taxi. 'Got a minute?' he said.

Well, I would have had a minute and more for Yasser Arafat at that stage rather than a word with a female in a hell of a tizzy, in fact one in almost any foreseeable condition. I told Morgan I would have the word later and he covered up his disappointment like a man, meaning none of it showed.

Since my last visit somebody had replaced Harry's fish-tank with a piece of sculpture in a dark blue veined material. The subject was probably a horse, or perhaps a cow, but it was impossible to be sure because the artist had died half-way through the job, or perhaps got fed up and left it. There was a new potted plant too with hairy leaves.

Harry sat down at his desk, which was completely bare but for a glass ashtray the size of a dustbin-lid, and took out his cheroots. I noticed that the packet design had a depressing Third-World look to it. 'Any news?' he asked.

'Well, the Penangans are taking those four pages.'

'Really.' He showed at least as much enthusiasm at hearing this as Morgan had done. 'How long have you been in the job now?'

'About eighteen months longer than you've been in yours. That's . . .'

'Ever thought of making a change?'

'Not seriously. Seeing as you ask.'

'That young fellow, now, what's he called, your number two, nice young fellow, Morgan something, Morgan, Morgan, Morgan *Wyndham*, Wyndham, tell me, Stan, in your view, is he, would he be, er, assuming he was interested of course, but do you think he'd be capable of running the show there for a time?'

'Well there again I haven't done much in the way of thinking, Harry, to be quite honest. Off the top of my head I reckon that's about what he'd be, capable. He doesn't get ideas much. Why?'

'Well, as I've told you before I have my doubts whether advertising manager has ever been the ideal outlet for your particular kind of expertise.'

'Have you now?' I asked him when it seemed he had had his last word on the subject. To my mind the conversation needed to get much funnier fast. 'You wouldn't be trying to tell me something, Harry, would you?'

'Yes,' he said quite briskly. 'Yes, I would, I am. Unofficially, I'm telling you unofficially that as from the end of the month your services in your present post will no longer be required.'

'Oh, yeah,' I said, wondering if the house in Hampstead was burning down as I sat there, and then saw he was looking at me with an awful sort of World War II film admiral's smile.

'But your services as motoring correspondent of this newspaper are very much in demand, my dear Stanley. Unofficially, the Board have been dissatisfied with the present arrangement for some time. Then, well, I just happened to run into your ex's husband, old Bert Hutchinson, I think I told you I see him in the Ladbroke Arms from time to time, and he said, well, he said he'd had a long talk with you recently and he said he'd never come across anybody who knows as much about cars as you do.' Did he? What had I said? When? 'And *cares* about them, he made a big point of that. And that's . . . essential,' said Harry with a lot of sincerity. 'And I know you've always wanted to be a writer.' How could he know that? What could possibly have made me tell him? Where? 'So . . . I went away, and I had a small think, and I dropped a word, and you'll be hearing . . . soon. I hope you're pleased, Stan.'

'Oh yes.' I was, or I would be one day. 'Thank you very much,' I went on, trying to sound as though I believed he had done it all himself.

'Forget it, lad. I just passed on a thought, that's all. Yes, nice to do that little thing on my way out. I'm er, I'm changing jobs myself. Going to edit a new English-language newspaper in South Africa. Quite a, you know, what would you say, a challenge.'

'You bet.'

'I thought it was time to make a shift. I thought if I don't do it now I'm never going to.'

'That's the spirit.'

As soon as I had spoken a horrible silence started. I could hardly spring up and be gone so soon after hearing these two fair-sized bits of news, at least I felt I hardly could, but at the same time I could think of nothing to say. Neither could Harry, it seemed, or rather, much worse than that, I saw he could think of something all right, but was far from sure whether he could or should or wanted to say it. The moment had come for him to ask me to marry him. His mouth opened. I slid my right foot round till it was alongside the front leg of my chair, heel lifted ready to give me a good take-off on my dash for the door.

'I'm going to tell you something I've never told anybody else,' he began. He had his hands clasped in front of him on the desk. 'You'll have noticed I not only have no wife, I also have no lady friend of any sort and as far as you know never have had. That's right. Some people of course have worked out that that must mean I'm, you know, queer.' He considerately went straight on at this point to save me having to start pretending I had never been one of those people. 'Well, I suppose I might be, deep down. All I can say to that is, it would have to be bloody deep down, Jack. No, as regards the *direction* of my sexual urges, you might call it boringly normal. But when we come to their *intensity*, then it's a different picture.'

He ground out his cheroot in slow motion while we both in different ways thought about the picture. 'Sub,' he said abruptly. 'Definitely sub. About once a month to six weeks. Speeds up a bit in the winter, I've noticed, funnily enough. Anyway, no problem, I get on the blower, by the time I'm along there she's ready and waiting, back indoors within the hour. Never let them come to me. Last time that happened she wanted to *stay the night* and I had a devil of a job shifting her. I've been going to the same one for over ten years now. No point in chopping and changing. They're all built the same.'

While he told me this much Harry had mostly looked away from me but had kept flicking his eyes to my face. Now, with the hard part presumably done, he relaxed a bit, lit another cheroot and gave me more of a proper glance, and when he went on he took his time.

'I don't suppose it's ever occurred to you, Stanley, to work out what it costs you to be married, even with the wife working. Well, it wouldn't, I dare say, your type of bloke. It occurred to me, though, very early in the game. You obviously get considerably more out of it, out of marriage, that is, than I would in all sorts of ways. But for someone like me it's simply not on.'

He spoke in an impressive, statesmanlike way, thumping the desk with his fist. 'As a commercial transaction it's just *not on*. Your money,' he said, managing to make it sound really grand, up there on a level with your country and your old mother, 'draining away twenty-four hours a day, seven days a week on goods and services that are . . . *non-requisite* and . . . *non-pleasurable*. Like Christmas all the year round. In 1969 men in Great Britain lost control on average of sixty-two per cent of their disposable income on getting married, according to my calculations. And it won't have gone down since, will it? Not with all this liberation. That's a laugh, that is.' He laughed. 'Liberation from what, pray? But we'd better not start on that. Just remember that wives in developed countries are in effect many times more highly paid for their contribution than any other group, certainly any other unskilled workers. And all this is assuming an average sex life. Whereas in my case . . .'

'What about companionship?' I asked, feeling somebody should.

He seemed puzzled. 'Having another person round the house, you mean?'

'Well, a bit more than that. To talk to, share things with kind of style.'

'M'm. I should imagine that would go along with a normal sex drive. Obviously does, in fact. I'm not trying to lay down a general law. The arrangement suits most people. I mean most men. Needless to say it suits most women. Well . . .'

He looked at his watch and we both stood up. But he had not quite finished. 'In a way, you know, I don't really mind if here and there I get suspected of being a faggot. It's nothing so dreadful these days. Certainly far less objectionable to me than giving someone else my money to spend for the rest of my life. But the result is, of being suspected of it is it's harder to make friends, men friends that is of course. For instance I'd have liked to get to know you better, Stan, but it wasn't to be. And then when a man on his own has passed his first youth there's a lot he doesn't get invited to. Eh, the world's made for the marrieds. It's taken a mortal time for all that to sink in in my case. I intend to do something about it when I get to Cape Town. I can't do anything about being on my own, at least I won't, but I can have had a wife in England now rather long dead. Something never discussed. See you before I go.'

All the way back to my office I succeeded in not

collapsing with woe at the thought of the friendship that never was. Once or twice during Harry's recital I had wondered whether his sexual policy might be based on a deep, perhaps unconscious hatred or horror of women, but I concluded now that it was nothing more than hatred and horror of exposing his wallet to the light. In the eyes of most men this was surely a more powerful disincentive to chumming up with him than any inklings of faggotism. He had incidentally not explained what he had against the common practice of other non-marriers, picking girls up at parties and putting them down on the morrow – cheaper, you might have thought, than a Harry-type solution. Ah, but only in theory. You never knew what you might be letting yourself in for in the way of providing a hot bath or a cooked breakfast, lending cab fare with nothing in writing about getting it back, etc. Still, I had to thank him for neither saying what a shame he had always thought it was that Nowell and I had failed to make a go of things nor asking meaningly if things were all right at home. But then perhaps he had never felt much personal commitment to either concern.

Lindsey was looking very trim when she turned up in the pub just after six, even healthier than usual and sort of better defined, as though I were seeing her closer to. Her high-collared metal-buttoned jacket and tan boots gave an outdoorsy effect. From the start she paid close attention to everything I said and quite soon she was paying it to my story of what had happened up to and including Susan's exit. She, Lindsey, made some faces and a few noises at high or low points but she came out with none of those dispensable prompts I had known females to hand out so as to stay in shot while someone else tried to talk. I carried on for about ten minutes instead of the couple of weeks I could easily have filled. When it was over she went to the bar for more drinks, getting them just in time before the place filled up in a wink like a lift on the underground.

'Well I never did,' she said. 'Do you think she actually went and stabbed herself like that?'

'No, I . . . No. A clever, educated woman like Susan, with a responsible job, always in such marvellous control of herself? Surely not. After all I've been living with her for four years now. The thing's too messy, too hasty. Rubbishy. Silly. No. Though I suppose I must have – '

'She'd have been doing it on the spur of the moment right enough. And when somebody like that loses control they lose it good and proper. Oh, she's capable of it, believe me.'

'So you say.'

'So would others say if you ever got a chance to ask them. Listen, in those four years have you ever met any of her friends from before?'

'Well, there's her boss, old Robbie Whatname Jamieson, and his wife, and a fellow called . . . No, not a lot, not really.'

'She does that, she cuts off completely and moves on. Do you know, she's never been near any of the people we used to know at Somerville in the Sixties? What you've got to grasp, Stanley, what you've got to take in is she's mad. Off her educated head. It was educated in an interesting way, which I don't imagine you know about either.'

The fruit-machine started up. Apparently without meaning it or even noticing, someone gave me a boof in the small of the back that nearly sent me off my stool.

Someone else came with his pint and stood so close that his bent elbow hid Lindsey's face. She shifted and looked at me through her glasses, which were very clean and had crimson frames that day.

'Would you like to come home, Stan?'

'Oh, I'd love to.'

When we had been at home, in her stately garden flat off Fulham Road, for some little time, she said, 'You're not really Jewish at all, are you darling?'

'No. My grandfather came from East Anglia. Well, I suppose he could have come from Tel Aviv before that but he didn't. I know I look it a bit.'

'All right, but what about this then?'

'Lindsey, where have you been? Oh, of course, I was forgetting. Just let me tell you that over *here* that's been done to practically everybody from way back. Even lower-class turds. It's supposed to help you to pee or something.'

'Look, I know it's a dodgy topic, but you are lower-class, aren't you darling? Just between ourselves, naturally.'

'I was before I came up in the world, true, but lower-middle-class, not working-class. Very important distinction. My old dad got really wild if you said he was working-class. Worse than calling him a Jew.'

'You do go on about it a bit, don't you?'

'I'd drop it like a shot if people would let me. And you asked. And which bit of the mick working class do you come from, Lucas?'

'That's much worse than calling your father a Jew. Micks are Catholics, bog Irish, and I'm right bang in the middle of the middle class – I'll have you know my father's a big wheel in the Manpower Services Commission, and everybody there talks with this hick accent except the real nobs who've been to school in England. *And* the family home's in Lisburn, which is the Godalming of the Six Counties. A very nice place, Northern Ireland. Lovely and quiet. Oh, if you're a bloody fool and know just where to go you can get your head blown off all right, but it's quiet everywhere else. No race problem. Peaceful.'

She stopped speaking on the last word. I thought of suggesting that it was rather quaint to say a place had no race problem when it was all Irish there, but then thought not. In a minute or two I was deep into one of the nicest silences I could remember for a long time. It was not quite total – not much traffic came down this way, but I heard a couple of taxis, muffled though by the old thick windows and the heavy curtains, scattered footsteps passed, and now and then I caught Lindsey's breathing, so slow I thought she must be asleep. The things in the rest of my life were still there, only for the time being there was nothing they could do. Very little light came into the room, just enough to make out the dark patch that was her head and the white of her shoulder. Eventually I sighed and shifted. She was awake after all and got me wrong, though not seriously.

'Do you want a drink?' she asked without moving.

'Not yet, thank you. Darling.'

Later on I did have a drink, a Scotch and water actually, and called the number I had been given for Nash. It answered so quickly that someone must have either happened to be dusting the telephone at the time or been sitting waiting for it to ring.

'Yes?' A harsh, uninformative voice.

'May I speak to Dr Nash, please?'

'Who are you?' A woman, not very young, posh, like Alethea as much as anyone.

'Duke's the name. I was hoping to – '

'Who are you?' Drunk.

'My son is one of Dr Nash's – '

'Get off this line and stay off it.' Like a send-up of a ham actor being threatening. Also mad. 'He's not coming . . . *got it*? He's staying right here, okay? And that is straight from the horse's mouth, brother. You can tell your *floosies* that Dr Nash regrets he will be unable to attend the . . . ffffunction.'

I went on standing there by the oriental-style earthenware umbrella jar in Lindsey's hall listening to this and feeling a certain amount of a charlie, none the less quite incapable of coming up with something to say. Then after another word or two from the drunken upper-crust madwoman there was a sudden complete silence at the far end, the sort you get when somebody puts his hand over the mouthpiece. Then Nash came on.

'Hallo, Alfred Nash here, who is calling?'

His composure was so ironclad that for more than an instant I thought I must have dreamt up the contents of the last half-minute. Of course, being that much older he must be more used to them, though perhaps . . . I just beat him to asking again by telling him who I was, then went on to fill him in about Steve, who I said had attacked his stepmother. 'I wish you'd go and see him there, doctor,' I said finally. 'I'm worried about him. The woman is a dangerous psychopath, sorry, I mean, you know, a hysterical neurotic.'

Only a touch more sharply he said, 'What, what woman is that?'

'Er, Dr – '

'Yes yes, Dr Collings, m'm. M'm. As it happens I can visit your son tomorrow morning.'

'I was going over then myself. Shall I meet you there?'

'Would you forgive me a moment?' More dead silence, for a bit longer this time. When he emerged again there was a sort of echo of a yell in the background. 'No, I think I should advise you to stay away, Mr Duke,' he said consideringly. 'I'll see you at New Harley Street at twelve, if that's all right.'

'I'll be there. This is very kind of you.'

'Well. The alternative was a workshop on social psychiatry.'

He hung up with headlong speed, so much so that he chopped off half the last syllable. I helped myself to another drink and took a refill in to Lindsey, who was sitting up in bed, though not very far. She looked about two without her glasses.

'Cheers,' she said. 'Every success.'

'Thanks. With what?'

'Your new job. Car critic.'

'Oh that.' I had honestly not thought of it above once since telling her on the way here. 'I hope I take over in time for the Motor Show. Of course I was going anyway but only as a bloke, as it were.'

She could just about have managed without this information, I reckoned, and the same was true of one or two of the things I went on to tell her, but I was set on keeping control of the conversation because of a superstitious feeling that it would be a good-luck sign if Susan stayed unmentioned till we were out of the flat and, as arranged earlier, in the quite good Greek restaurant a couple of streets away. As it turned out I won bonus points for a further hold-off up to when we had ordered. Then I could stand it no longer.

'You were saying something about the way she was educated. Susan.'

'None other. Yes, she didn't go to school, or only for a term, then her parents had to take her away and get her tutored at home. She was terribly homesick and was subjected to the most frightful bullying.' Lindsey did a better job on Susan's accent than I would have expected, but she was still not as good as Mrs Shillibeer. 'You hadn't heard that, I take it.'

'No. How did you hear about it? Isn't that funny, she never said anything to me about that part of her life and I never thought to ask her.'

'She told me is how I heard about it. Well, by the time you came along it must have dawned on her that those facts are a pretty unprepossessing lot.'

'What are you talking about? She couldn't help them.'

'Only if you take them at their face value. You think of what happens at school, at any school. There are two things everyone gets plenty of, enough and to spare, especially at first – opposition and competition. Susan hates those. She won't have them. Who does she think she is or he think he is, that was her watchword at Oxford. When the answer would be like the Principal of the college or the Professor of English Language and Literature, you know, bloody understrappers of that kidney, with no right to make Susan Daly do what she didn't want to do or prevent her from doing what she wanted to do. And then, she was bright as hell and that tutor must have been damn good, but when the final exams came along she had a breakdown. Couldn't sit. Well, you can never know with a thing like that, but my feeling was at the time, she might not have got a First, you see, and Kate Oliver who we were both friendly with was going to get one, and did.

She wasn't speaking to Kate anyway by then because Kate had told a lot of lies about her to her boyfriend and taken him off her. Maybe. How it looked to me was he met Kate through her and fancied Kate better. I wouldn't have said thank you for him myself. He was reading engineering.'

'Oh, yeah. Er, did you ever meet her first husband? Book illustrator, wasn't he?'

'Mainly. I never met him but I heard a bit about him. Illustrating books was what he liked doing best, well you know what I mean. What he liked doing next best was looking at books that had illustrations by other people and reading books about them. He liked doing anything like that much better than going to parties that had writers and artists and people like that at them.'

'Well, I must say I can see his . . . Good God.'

'What's up?'

'Nothing, I've just remembered something somebody told me about Nowell. Any more on this fellow?'

'Apparently, I've forgotten who I had this from but he didn't go about the business of illustrating books in an intelligent way. He wanted to do good illustrations in serious books, proper books. Not trendy illustrations in trendy books that made a lot of money.'

'I don't believe it,' I said, not telling nothing but the truth.

'Suit yourself, Stanley, it's only what I heard.'

With disastrous timing the waiter brought the humous and the taramasalata and the rest of it at this point, failing miserably to encroach on an intimate moment or kill a punch line. I put my hand out to my glass and then left it. Easy on the ouzo tonight, and not just that either.

Lindsey caught my movement. 'You're not drinking. Not by your standards.'

'No, sod it. Daren't. Getting into practice. Motoring correspondent loses licence? It's going to change my bleeding life. Turn driving into just another thing I do, like playing squash or writing letters to the motoring press. Don't know how I'll adjust to it.'

After a pause she said quietly, 'Do you want to talk about your son?'

'No,' I said. 'No, I don't want to talk about him.'

'Worse than Susan, isn't it?'

I nodded.

'I know, I nearly lost my younger one six years ago. Hit and run. She was . . . Sorry.'

'Go back to those bleeding schooldays of Susan's,' I said. 'And what were they exactly, those unprepossessing facts?'

'She had to be taken away from school – had to be? – because, one, she was homesick. Translation – she very much wanted to be back in a place where she could do what she wanted to do all the time. Two, the bullying. Translation – some of the other little girls got rather cheesed off with the way she kept trying to do what she wanted to do all the time, including queening it over the rest of them, and showed her a bit of opposition. I used to wonder how much. Telling her to pipe down, I dare say. Perhaps getting together and jeering at her and even pulling her hair. Fiendish things like that.

'Her parents came up to Oxford once, at least I saw them once. The old lady was very straightforward about looking at me as if I was talking Swahili whenever I opened my mouth, which wasn't often after the first minute as you might imagine. And looking at the others for help too. You know, for Christ's sake don't leave me alone with this savage.'

'Yes, actually I do know.'

'But the old gentleman was the one. Would you believe it, you probably wouldn't believe it but he said to me when she'd gone off for a pee or something, he said, honest he said, "What do you think of my little gel? Rather splendid, isn't she?" That's what he said. I told you you wouldn't believe it.'

'Nor I do. Else he was trying to be funny.'

'He was not trying to be funny, Stanley. He was, how shall I put it, he was the archetype of the ridiculously indulgent father who worships the ground his little gel walks on and, you know, fancies her quite a bit. Oh yes. Seriously. I don't mean of course anything happened, nowhere near, but it was there, there was something there. Obviously it's all years ago now.'

'Look, love, this is fascinating, and I believe every word of it, but you started off by saying you thought she was quite capable of er, putting on a show like the one with the knife, and that's what I really want to hear about. Is there any more to come? I mean what you've told me so far . . .'

'What about it?' asked Lindsey when I failed to go on.

'I was going to say just, the whole thing sounds no worse than the dossier of any other deranged bleeding completely wrapped up in herself female, and then I remembered I always thought she was better than that. I thought she was, you know, reasonable and listened to what you said to her and you could disagree with her.'

'You could until it started to matter. You gave her a soft ride from what you've told me in the past, and then quite suddenly she finds she's coming second. And the lady simply is not cut out for coming second.

'Now Stanley dear, I hope you believe I'd never have breathed a word of this if things had been going on as before. But now they're all over the shop . . . I wasn't going to tell you, sweetheart, but there was this time a friend of Kate's gave a party in her digs, nothing grand, I was there, just drinks before hall, and old Susan thought she ought to have been invited, well maybe. Anyway, after about an hour she walked in carrying a bottle of champagne and looking, well, I'd read about people's faces looking like masks, but hers really did. Everybody said Hallo, rather awkward like, and she didn't say anything, but she hurled the bottle of champagne clean through the window of this sitting room place which was on the first floor, and the thing burst like a bloody bomb in the street, lucky it didn't hit anyone, and then she just went wild and smashed every glass and everything she could get her hands on until she was, you have to say over-powered, it took about four rugger-players to hold her down. Then she started crying and apologizing, and that went on a long time. Oh, there was no doubt about who'd come first that evening, not in popularity, no, but in attention-grabbing she was well in front.

'Afterwards she said she didn't know what had got into her. I thought about it a fair amount. That bottle of champagne now, a fucking expensive missile if that's all you'd ever wanted it for. A half-brick would have done just as well. I reckoned what she'd done, she'd bought the champagne and was going to come and hand it over as a gift to the hostess, a gift with a kind of a string to it because it would put paid to any crap about not being invited. A performance that would have made a bit of a stir for a short while, nothing like what she did do. She changed her mind at the last minute, perhaps as late as when she came into the room and saw all the buggers laughing and chattering and boozing happily away without her. Acting on the spur of the moment. Like I bet she did with that knife last night.' Lindsey had turned quite grim, staring at me through the big lenses. 'As for being mad, you should have seen her face that time. She was un-recognizable, well I recognized her but I wouldn't have if, what, if I'd passed her in the street. Off her head. Temporarily. Or temporarily letting it show.'

From being well on the way to something like certainty that Susan had been telling the truth about the knife I was now back to not knowing what I believed or felt about any of that. Or anything else I could turn my mind to. Trying to think was like picking through a rubbish-dump looking for nothing in particular. Eventually I said, 'If this hadn't come up I might never have found out about her,' only because I had been able to see how to get to the end of the sentence.

'Something else would have, it was bound to. People like that, it's as if they have to make something like that happen sooner or later. Their natures need it. Like a drunk wanting a fight. They're more bothered about getting one than where it comes from.'

'Why did she marry me?'

For once Lindsey was stumped for a quick answer, or more likely turned down the one she first thought of. 'Well,' she said, 'you're successful, but in a different line so you wouldn't be competing with her, you gave her a lot of rope and what the fuck can I say, Stanley dear, you're a nice enough fellow and quite an attractive fellow and I should imagine she was as fond of you as she could be of anybody. Still is, I dare say, or could be again.'

With the last few words the waiter brought the mous-saka and the stifadou and the rest of the rubbish, which was not much but the worst he could manage in the circumstances. Susan was shut out of the conversation after that but she hung about in my head, not the look of her but the feel of her presence, the kind of thing I got when I came into the house and knew she was there even though there was nothing to see or hear. Oh well, it would be all right when we were back in the flat, I thought to myself, and Lindsey seemed to have the same idea, turning down sweet and coffee and looking at her watch. But then when we were back drinking the coffee she had made she put me right on more than one point. Actually the way she measured me with her eye told me most of it before she opened her mouth.

'I'm sorry, Stanley, but – '

'Barry due back, is he?' I had seen signs of male occupation, though long rather than short term, suits but no shirts, boots, slippers and plimsolls but only one pair of shoes. 'Or somebody?'

'No, nobody. Just, I have these interviews fixed in Glasgow tomorrow and I'm getting the sleeper up there tonight, and I have to put my gear together first. So if you – '

'Fly up in the morning,' I said, knowing it was hopeless. 'I'll drive you to the airport.'

'No, sweetheart, I can't, I'd like to but everything's arranged.'

'But as long as I . . . No of course, I see.'

She refused my offer of a lift to the station in half an hour from now, as it would have been. Whether to put her gear together or not she clearly wanted some time to herself before she took off. Quite understandable. On the way to the front door I realized I had got as far as not being sure what names to give our second child if it was a girl. Ha ha, very funny.

'Sorry, darling,' she said. 'This was all fixed up a couple of weeks ago and you only rang this morning.'

'I know. It's all right. See you when you get back.'

'I don't like thinking of you going back to that empty house.'

'I'm not mad about it myself.'

At the Paki supermarket in Hampstead I bought a jar of crunchy peanut butter, a pot of savoury spread, a large jar of pickled onions, a jar of sweet pickle, a small sliced white loaf, a packet of Cheddar, a packet of Brazil nut kernels, a box of liqueur chocolates and a box of chocolate truffles. The other things I needed, butter and whisky, were in stock at home. I unpacked the stuff on the kitchen table, drank some whisky and thought about launderettes, Chinese takeaways and kindred matters for some minutes. Then I rang Cliff, late as it was, and told him the score. By now I had got it down to about five sentences.

He seemed more shaken than I had expected him to be. After a silence he said, 'So you're on your own there.'

'Yes.'

'Has she gone for good, do you think?'

'I don't know.'

'Well, we can't discuss it now,' he said rather peevishly, and there was another short pause. Then, 'Come to dinner tomorrow, I mean supper. Just the three of us.' When I had accepted he said, 'So I'll see you in the Admiral Byron about seven, where it'll just be the two of us. Stan, I'm sorry.'

Nash said, 'I think we can be reasonably confident that he'll now be more or less suitably looked after and will be given suitable treatment, at any rate for a time. The effect

303

of that assault . . . which you described to me . . .' he went into his spaced-out mode, 'one effect . . . has been to put the fear of God into Dr Collings. Even she rather balks at the idea of an unmedicated and . . . presumptively violent patient of hers on the loose. You can discount her threat of discharging your boy. Sheer anger. She spoke out of sheer anger at her . . . apparent professional failure. As you surmised.'

'I'm still not happy about leaving my son in her charge,' I said.

'Nobody could be *happy* at the thought of someone in that position with the ideas that she professes to hold. But while in the intervals of talking modish twaddle, or even démodé twaddle, she administers reasonably appropriate chemotherapy . . . The boy would find much the same thing in most other places. A different line in twaddle, perhaps.'

'I see. Dr Nash, I should tell you that there is a possibility that my wife's wound was self-inflicted.'

He looked as though I had told him that somebody was dead, lowering his eyes, sighing deeply and sitting in silence for a time. Eventually he said, 'With the aim of bringing about the result I've just described to you? To get shot of the lad, was that the idea?'

'Could be. But I think more likely for my benefit, to draw attention away from him and on to herself.'

He had started doing little rapid nods before I was halfway through. 'If you come to any conclusion on the matter, however tentative, I hope you'll let me know. Talk to Dr Wainwright about it.'

'I will. When she thought I doubted her story she walked out. Left me.' It came out without much in the way of intention.

This news he took more or less in his stride, as something almost to be expected, but he said seriously enough, 'You have my profound sympathy in all senses of the word.'

'Doctor, if we assume my son did attack my wife,' – now there was a ridiculous phrase if ever there was one – 'does that make his prospects of recovery a lot worse? I'm afraid that's not very well put.'

'I follow you perfectly. No. In effect, in itself no. In the sense that very violent cases may recover and harmless peaceable ones become and remain isolated. But as I said I would welcome information on the point.'

I waited for a bit in the hope that he would offer me sherry for something to say, but he held his peace. I said hesitantly, 'Could we go back to Dr Collings for a moment? When we talked about her before, I thought you were saying, of course it was difficult in front of my wife, but I thought you were saying that she was getting at me, sorry, that Dr Collings was getting at me out of sheer malice, and I *thought* you meant that she was simply trying to . . .'

'Fuck you up because you were a man,' said Nash, disconcerting me to some extent. 'Yes, Mr Duke, that was what I meant. As you say, I was a little inhibited by your wife's presence.

'But surely, Dr Nash, that's not enough of a motive on its own to make somebody, you know, in a professional matter like that, with these very important things at stake . . .'

'Not enough of a motive?' His voice had gone high. 'Fucking up a man? Not enough of a motive? What are you talking about? Good God, you've had wives, haven't you? And not impossibly had some acquaintance with

305

other women as well? You can't be new to feeling the edge of the most powerful weapon in their armoury. You must have suffered before from the effect of their having noticed, at least the brighter ones among them having noticed, that men are different, men quite often wonder whether they're doing the right thing and worry about it, men have been known to blame themselves for behaving badly, men not only feel they've made mistakes but on occasion will actually admit having done so, and say they're sorry, and ask to be forgiven, and promise not to do it again, and mean it. Think of that! Mean it. All beyond female comprehension. Which incidentally is why they're not novelists and must never be priests. Not enough of a motive? They don't have motives as you and I understand them. They have the means and the opportunity, that is enough.'

At the start of this he had stared at me in what looked like stark fear, wondering whether I might not be an android or have been taken over by an alien entity. After that he calmed down, though not completely by any means, and now went back most of the way to the stark-fear mode when he said, 'For God's sake tell me you know what I'm talking about.'

'Oh, of course I do. But the way I see it, they have motives of a sort. It's the sort that's frightening. I think Collings let Steve out of hospital and took him off drugs to punish me for ticking her off for – '

'Oh, there'll have been some trigger, no doubt,' he said, making a sideways neck-chop motion. 'In sufferers from rabies a touch on the arm or showing a bright light is sufficient to provoke a violent suffocative paroxysm. No doubt you did annoy or displease the woman in some way. What of it?'

'Well, I think that makes her unfit to be in charge of –'

'Forget it, my dear fellow. If things went that far, can you imagine yourself telling a tribunal that in your opinion a certain qualified doctor and psychiatrist is unfit to be in charge of a certain case because in your opinion she has been swayed by personal motives? A tribunal that included at least one woman? Take your time.'

'I don't need any. No.'

'So be it. Let's leave Dr Collings, Mr Duke. I'll, I'll see to her, or keep her in order. My turn to go back. On our first meeting, at your house, do you remember my asking you if you thought all women were mad?'

'Very clearly,' I said. 'And I told you I thought a lot of them were. Well, what's happened in the meantime hasn't exactly forced me to change my mind.'

'I find that very natural. Would you say, would you go as far as to say that the real mad people are not the ones in mental hospitals, like your son, but . . . women, certain women?'

'It's tempting. Or rather – '

'It is tempting. Half of it, anyway.' Yes, he was calm, and yet not relaxed, holding himself down or in, mentally biding his time to leap out at you. 'It seems you hold to your view on certain selected women. M'm. That's young Wainwright's view, of course, or on the way to it. He thinks they're all mad, or says he does. Of course one must bear in mind that in the ordinary way a general practitioner has very little contact with insane people. Neurotic people, on the other hand . . .'

'For God's sake, Dr Nash, does somebody have to be frothing at the mouth or going for you with an axe or chattering about reincarnated Old Testament prophets before you'll pass them as mad? Can't they be mad part-time, a bit mad? Like you can have a grumbling appendix without actually . . .'

Nash was not listening. His chest slowly filled with air. This was going to be the big one. 'Would . . . that . . . they . . . *were* . . . mmmmad,' he grated out in five loud sliced-off screeches, displaying his off-white teeth and looking far from sane himself. 'If only . . . they *were* . . . off their *heads*. Then we could treat-'em, lock-'em-up, bung-'em-in-a-straitjacket, cut-'em-off-from-society. But they're not. They're not.'

He sprang up, came round his desk and advanced on me. I wondered briefly if he took me for a transvestite, a male impersonator, but he was only on the first leg of a series of pacings to and fro. 'Mad people,' he went on in a tone not much less strung-up than before, 'can't run their lives, they're incapable of dealing with reality. How many women are like that? Mad people are hopelessly muddled with their thoughts, their feelings, their behaviour, their talk at variance with one another and all over the place. Does that sound like a description of a woman? Mad people are confused, adrift, troubled, even frightened. What woman is? – really is, I mean.

'No,' he said, starting another crescendo. 'No. They're not mad. They're all too monstrously, sickeningly, *terrifyingly* sane. That's the *whole trouble*. That's the whole trouble,' he repeated in his normal voice, blinking and moving his head about like a fellow coming round after a blackout. 'Well, Mr Duke, I hope your marital difficulties sort themselves out. Because after all one has to *be* married. That's where they've . . . Now I know you're a busy man and I too have things to do. We will be in touch.'

At the door he said, 'Your boy has a good chance.'

*

I was as busy as I could manage to be for the rest of the day. I kept trying to throw off the thought of Steve, then when trying to think about Susan instead kept breaking down. I switched to trying to work out why I had the feeling that he would never be back. Perhaps it came from something Nash had said that morning. But he had said very little on the matter and nothing new. Perhaps there had been something in his manner, something more un-hopeful than his words. Perhaps, more likely, it went back to the previous morning and the tiny glimpse I had had of Steve as he used to be, an instant and complete reminder of the person I had already started to forget. No doubt what could happen once for a second could in theory happen again for longer, and I did my best to believe it without getting very far. In the end I had no real idea at all why that Steve seemed gone for good and the one I saw every day, the miserable, quaking, humourless nitwit who was also my son, looked like being a fixture. As for him, it would be better if he were dead, provided that could be arranged without him having to die.

Some of this went through my head while I sat drinking Scotch and waiting for Cliff. As I had found on previous visits with him, the Admiral Byron was frequented by Scottish labourers, probably building workers, given to shouting unreassuringly to one another. However, it seemed he had never seen an actual fight in here, perhaps because of something one of the Scotsmen had gone out of his way to explain to us, that anybody who looked like starting one was given a right good hiding and thrown out. The staff changed frequently and only the landlord ever knew what the place served or where it was kept, apart from the stuff on tap. Nobody would have called it cosy – it was vast, hangar-like, the result of the knocking-into-one of several smaller bars or even, to judge by the differences of structure and style from one end to the other, a couple of separate pubs. But it had no juke-box or fruit-machine and at the moment, before the Scotsmen, it was quiet.

Cliff came bustling in a little later than he had said, complaining as usual, quite cheerfully as usual, this time mostly about the one-way traffic system and the hospital staffs' trade union with a bit about a urologist thrown in. Then quite soon he looked at me and nodded his head several times and sighed.

'There's a splendid fellow called Sydney Smith,' he said. 'I don't mean, you know, that fucking old fool.'

'What fucking old fool?'

He gave a growl of disgust. 'Of course, I keep forgetting you haven't looked at a book since you left school and precious few before. There was a posturing old ponce of a clergyman in Jane Austen's time, oh Christ, never mind, anyway he was called Sydney Smith and a lot of people, people like, well I was going to say Susan, er, think he was a bloody scream. But as I say I don't mean him. Jesus. *Anyway*, my Sydney Smith wrote the standard work on forensic medicine, which I suppose I'm going to have to –'

'No, I can do that,' I said. 'Legal medicine. Medicine as regards the law.'

'Man's a genius. Well, in this work there is naturally a chapter on self-inflicted wounds.'

'Oh.'

'Yes, oh. How a genuine wound inflicted on a person trying to protect himself or herself against an assailant with a knife is usually on or in the hand, sometimes the wrist, the inside of the wrist. That's point one. The characteristics of a self-inflicted wound are, made in a safe part of the body unless of course we're talking about throat-cutting et cetera, so not for example the inside of the wrist where there are dodgy things like veins but for example the forearm, the top or outside of the forearm.' He made gestures in case I had never bothered to find out what a forearm was. 'Where Susan, er, was wounded.

'Next thing, the cut will not penetrate what we medical johnnies call the true skin, that's your corium, a quarter of an inch or so deep in places like that. As with Susan's wound. Then, the cut follows the curvature of the body if that part is curved, like the forearm. You can see how that wouldn't happen with a real stab. I'd have liked to take a better look but it's a pound to a pinch of shit that Susan's wound did that. And the last thing but perhaps the most telling, I've never quite understood why, but they all seem to have a dry run or two first, little tentative nicks alongside the main wound, even the cut-throat brigade – I've seen it. Anyway, there were a couple of those on Susan's arm. And there we are. I'd take my chance with a jury on it.

'Bloody silly of her, wouldn't you say, apart from anything else? You'd think an intelligent girl like that would realize it was on the cards there'd be some sort of give-away. She must have got the idea one moment and done it the next, on impulse. Mad as a hatter, like the lot of them. Must have seemed like a heaven-sent opportunity when poor old Steve came wandering in. What a marvellous bloody irony, eh, that it took that to get Collings and her gang to start looking after him properly at Kev's. I talked to some Paki there.'

'Yeah. Nash went over.'

When Cliff saw I had nothing more to offer about Nash

he said, 'Disasters are just crappy things that happen, you know, Stan. It's a waste of time to try to explain them or make sense of them.'

'Which one are you talking about?'

'Steve, of course. I'm afraid I don't regard the other one, her walking out that is, as all that much of a disaster.' When I made no reply to that he said, 'Another irony, if we're collecting the buggers, is that she attains her object and successfully got Steve out of her hair and now she's not around to enjoy it. What?'

'Oh, I don't think that was her object. I think she was scene-stealing.' It was clear that he understood me immediately. 'At least that was what I thought at the time. I'm not so sure that I'm so sure now. It's hard to feel it makes much difference. I'll tell Nash about her arm and the rest of it.'

'I'll tell him, I want a word with him anyway. Let's have it again now. She walked out on you because she thought you thought she'd stabbed herself and said Steve did it, right?'

'Next time, take more care. She walked out *after saying* she knew I thought that. After saying a great deal more besides. She was . . . mad with rage that I'd seen through or I might have seen through an extremely dodgy operation she may already have been regretting – as unwise, naturally, not bad form or anything silly like that. If seen through, eh? it would show her up as some kind of monster. At the same time she was calculating that anything short of mad rage would be as bad as a half-hearted denial – but there of course she was going by what her own reaction would have been and didn't realize that a wholehearted denial would have cut much more ice with me, or you or any other man. But then again she was mad with rage. I must have annoyed her quite a bit in the past and she'd bottled it up and it all came out at once. She was frightened too – you showed you suspected her. What was that for, by the way?'

'For just that, to frighten her, frighten her off. I didn't know what she might have got up to next. I meant to signal to her but not to you, but I was so bloody cross myself that I muffed it, clearly. Terrible how they drag us down to their level, isn't it? Crikey, you do know her well, Stan. Pity you didn't before, but then you never do, one doesn't I mean. Did you work all that out in just those couple of minutes just now?'

'No, I was on it all the time I was going round telling myself that of course the whole thing was perfectly genuine. Men's minds are funny things too, you know. Oh, the rest of it was, the walking-out was an escalation of the bawling-out. Plus it would have been a wee bit awkward for her to stay in the same house after some of the things she'd said.'

'She'll come walking back in again, won't she?' said Cliff a moment or two later.

'No. Live with a man who thinks or knows she did a thing like that?'

'She'll pretend you don't think or know it. So will you. It never happened. Easy as winking.'

'Some of what she said . . .'

'That's your problem. She was upset, wasn't she, after being attacked with a knife? Who wouldn't be?'

'She won't be back.'

I went and got more drinks. The place was filling up, though mostly down the far end in the part that looked like an old-fashioned railway waiting room. When I gave my order the little slut with her hair green and half an inch long all over cut me off by saying 'Sorry?' almost as soon as I opened my mouth. When I was a kid you hung on a bit if you missed the first few words and hoped to pick up the drift later. Anyway, I had more luck with my second go and at least she knew where the Famous Grouse was.

Cliff was looking thoughtful. 'According to some bloke on the telly the other night,' he said, 'twenty-five per cent of violent crime in England and Wales is husbands assaulting wives. Amazing figure that, don't you think? You'd expect it to be more like eighty per cent. Just goes to show what an easy-going lot English husbands are, only one in four of them bashing his wife. No, it doesn't mean that, does it? But it's funny about wife-battering. Nobody ever even asks what the wife had been doing or saying. She's never anything but an ordinary God-fearing woman who happens to have a battering husband. Same as race prejudice. Here are a lot of fellows who belong to a race minding their own business and being as good as gold and not letting butter melt in their mouths, and bugger me if a gang of prejudiced chaps don't rush up and start discriminating against them. Frightfully unfair.'

'The root of all the trouble,' I said, 'is we want to fuck them, the pretty ones, women I mean. Just try and imagine it happening to you, everyone wanting to fuck you wherever you go. And of course being ready to pay for you if your father's stopped doing that. You'd have to be pretty tough to stand up to it, wouldn't you? In fact women only want one thing, for men to want to fuck them. If they do, it means they can fuck them up. Am I drunk? What I was trying to say, if you want to fuck a woman she can fuck you up. And if you don't want to she fucks you up anyway for not wanting to.'

'I read somewhere about a Hollywood film star,' said Cliff. 'I forget which one, years ago anyway, she was getting on a bit, used to go to a lot of parties, it might have been Madeleine Carroll, one night she went to one and nobody made a pass at her, so she went home and took an overdose. That was coming out into the open a bit, I agree.'

'Actually they used to feel they needed something in the way of provocation,' I said, 'but now they seem to feel they can get on with the job of fucking you up any time they feel like it. That's what Women's Lib is for.'

'It's getting worse,' said Cliff, 'now they're competing on equal terms in so many places and find they still finish behind men. They can't even produce a few decent fucking *jugglers*. Like the race thing again.'

'They say people go on getting married to the same person time after time,' I said. 'Well men certainly do. There isn't another other sex.'

'It's no use saying anything to a woman,' said Cliff ultimately, and drained his glass.

I waited, but there was no follow-up. 'When what?'
'What?'
'It's no use saying anything to a woman when what? Or unless what?'
'When nothing. Ever.'

We had a couple more drinks and were quite merry by the time we got to the Wainwrights' house in Holland Park, and were quite unmerry again two minutes later. Sandra was cross about something. I could not have said what was different from usual in her manner or tone or expression or anywhere else, not really, not in detail, and yet I could tell. I could have told at a hundred metres. Of course I could. Any man could. Any man was meant to.

I had sometimes wondered if they thought we thought they were really trying to keep their feelings to themselves at times like these, but if you knew *that* you could destroy the world.

I got half a minute of it to myself at the start because Cliff had broken off for a pee in the hall cloakroom. Sandra embraced me with all the warmth of a recent rape victim.

'Cliff tells me Susan's walked out on you,' she said. 'That must be upsetting for you.'

'Yes it is rather.' I wondered how she would talk and look if she were telling me instead that Susan was to be congratulated and whatever upset I got from this or anything else would do me a power of good.

'I suppose it's six of one and half a dozen of the other,' she said, meaning such was the impudent travesty I was preparing to palm off on the public. 'It usually seems to be.'

'Probably.'

'I expect you want a drink.' To go with the fourteen I clearly had inside me.

'Well . . .'

Cliff came in. While Sandra asked him if the pub had been fun and he told her it had been, thanks, I watched him notice, wonder what he had done, think of something, think surely not for Christ's sake, and resign himself. He widened his eyes at me but said nothing. I said nothing. In fact all three of us said nothing, pretty near literally, until Sandra went out to the kitchen. When he was sure she was clear he opened his mouth to start, but the phone rang first.

He went across the room and answered it. 'Yes,' he said, and held the handset out to me with a completely blank and completely informative face.

'Oh Stanley, thank God you're there,' said Susan's voice, strained but calm. 'I was going to give up if you weren't. Can you ever forgive me?'

'What for?' I said.

'Well, those terrible things I said to you.'

'Oh, those.'

While she hurried on about having been so desperately frightened and upset and one thing and another I turned towards Cliff, who did the brief lift of the chin South London people use to mean Told you so or Here we go again or Wouldn't you bleeding know. People elsewhere too, I dare say. Perhaps all over the world.